COLD
eye

COLD e y e

—

GILES BLUNT

ARBOR HOUSE
WILLIAM MORROW
New York

Library of Congress Cataloging-in-Publication Data

Blunt, Giles.
  Cold eye.

  I. Title.
PS3552.L887C6   1989   813'.54   88-34402
ISBN 1-55710-047-0

Printed in the United States of America

First Edition

1   2   3   4   5   6   7   8   9   10

BOOK DESIGN BY WILLIAM McCARTHY

Cast a cold eye
On life, on death
Horseman pass by.

—W. B. YEATS,
Under Ben Bulben

ONE

LOOKING down at the courtyard from this high, oblique, godlike angle, you didn't see the man and woman right away. You were caught up in the elegant architecture, the bone-white arches and pale, thin columns, lit from below by hidden lights, and from above by a scimitar moon. Neat little trees stood in ivory boxes lined up before the longest building, their leaves charcoal gray at this hour. So cool, this courtyard, it might be a computer's idea of peace and tranquility. Plain wooden benches were spaced evenly around the rectangular pool, where the blade of moon rippled. A Henry Moore figure reclining in the water was the softest thing in sight, until at last you saw the woman, and the man.

They engaged each other on one of those plain, flat benches. A knife glittered in the man's hand, as he brought it down toward the woman's breast. Even from this angle, you could see he'd only just pulled it out of her chest, and now he was going to put it in again. Her matchstick arms were no defense; her scream would not last long. What fury, what injury or sickness had locked them in murder and each other's arms? The bone-white arches and the mirrored moon gave no clue.

Like a kite plunging to earth at the jerk of a string, Hood suddenly tumbled from his vision at the sound of Susan's voice. Man, woman, and murder were gone, and the Sunday *New York Times* swam back into view, along with the kitchen table, his second cup of coffee, and Susan herself.

"Were you thinking about work?" She had just stepped out of the shower, and untwirled a towel from her hair. It fell in thick damp ropes to her shoulders. "I ran down to Battery Park today," she said. "It was freezing."

But Hood had returned his attentions to the *Times*, an article about contemporary sculpture. Morris Weintraub had exploded another of his constructions, to great effect, in the middle of Columbus Circle.

"I must be the only person in the world who gains weight with exercise."

Hood was skimming the rest of the article to see if it mentioned anyone else he knew. He felt like indulging himself in a lazy morning—he usually took Sundays off.

"They want me at St. Andrew's tonight."

This time Hood looked up.

"It's a special service. The Bishop's going to be there. It starts at seven, so I should be back by nine or nine-thirty."

Hood looked at her reflection in the large mirror across the room. "I don't know why you keep that job."

"We need the money!" She stopped toweling her hair and pulled at a wet strand that clung to her cheek. "It's fifty extra dollars a week—and they have a wonderful organ."

"It's not even your instrument."

"Playing Bach is always good practice." She began applying eyeliner—an unnecessary decoration, in Hood's opinion. He had tried many times to paint her portrait, but he could catch nothing of her character. Her huge brown eyes came off looking naïve, which she was not; the skepticism of her natural expression, and the frequent amusement, escaped his hand completely. After six years of marriage, he could not see her clearly. "Ugh," she said. "I look like a rag doll."

She was saved from further self-criticism when the telephone rang. She answered it, then held the receiver out to Hood. "It's Leo—he wants to speak to *Der Meister*."

"Yes, Nicholas—this is Leo here." The German accent would have identified him a block away.

"You're in a pay phone," Hood said. "Does that mean you're working on a Sunday?" There was no phone in their studio.

"*Ja*. And the work goes well for a change. Could you take my life class at four o'clock? Is it possible?"

"Yech."

"What does it mean, 'yech'?"

"It means 'Only if I absolutely have to.'"

"You get to keep the money—it goes without saying."

"It certainly does. But if I take your class, you're not allowed to play any country and western music when I'm in the studio."

"*Ja*, it's okay. I have to get back working now."

"See you later, then."

"Thanks, Nicholas."

Hood put the phone down. Susan was sitting at her harpsichord, sorting a stack of bills—which made him nervous. "Leo wants me to take his class this afternoon."

"Great. You'll be ogling some gorgeous nymph."

"Not me. The students. I guess I'll go into the studio, too—Leo made me feel guilty."

She held up a bill. "Sixty-five dollars for the phone? Where did you call?"

"Sherri called me when she was over in London. I had to call her back."

"Why didn't you call collect?"

"I guess I didn't think of it."

"How would you pay it, if I wasn't here?"

"I probably wouldn't. I'd let them cut the phone off."

"You would, too."

Hood was irritated that she was in the right. He hadn't sold a painting for eight months; that one had gone for very little. They lived on the income from Susan's music, and she almost never complained about money.

They rode down together in a huge freight elevator—a last vestige of their building's previous incarnation as an aluminum siding warehouse. Susan pulled her woolen cap down to her eyebrows, so that her eyes looked as huge as a nocturnal animal's.

"I'm sorry I was so bitchy," she said. "I just realized it's your birthday in about a week."

"Terrific."

"What will you be? Thirty-two?"

"Thirty-five." It was like her to forget his age; Hood was excessively aware of it.

"Imagine. And we were just children in our twenties when we met."

"Yes, it's wonderful to have achieved such success in such a short time."

"You will," she said, as if there were not the slightest doubt.

Outside, it was cold with the last of February, a frigid sunlight spilling down from the south. Hood liked New York's winter light; it brought out surface textures, accented architectural details. In summer, this late in the morning, the light would have been totally flat. He pulled his scarf tighter.

They walked along Broome Street to West Broadway, famous for its prestigious galleries. The street was empty now, but later it would fill up with tourists. Hood often wished he lived in a less interesting neighborhood.

Susan was telling him something, a concert coming up, but Hood was thinking of his painting. He could see where he had left off, down to the brushstroke. There was some question in his mind about the color of blood.

"It'll be three hours altogether, and I should make about four hundred dollars."

"When is this?"

"I just told you—tomorrow night. It's a good thing I'm not sensitive."

"Yes."

They stopped at the corner of Sixth Avenue. Susan had to turn uptown toward St. Andrew's. She pressed the cold tip of her nose against his cheek as she kissed him. "Work well," she said, and turned away.

Hood crossed the avenue to Watts Street, where the wind whipped up from the Hudson and chilled him to the marrow. He ran the last block to Debrosses Street and the rotting old pier building where he kept a studio with Leo Forstadt.

The wind howled through the unoccupied ground floor, which stank of urine. A loose door flapped open and shut on rusty hinges. Hood ran up a flight of iron steps, annoyed to hear Tammy Wynette wailing from above.

When he was inside, he put a battered kettle on the hot plate and held his hands to the heat. Leo was working by the window on his side of the studio, dabbing at a painting that looked mostly brown. Fond of the earth colors, Leo. Hood made them each a cup of instant coffee, setting a mug by Leo's chair without disturbing him. His friend was working on a portrait, the head of a girl, brown hair, brown dress, the background not yet indicated.

Hood kept his coat on, despite the space heater beside his chair. The wide windows looking over the disused docks of the Hudson cost them all their heat. Years ago, he had been thrilled to work in discomfort, but now he found nothing romantic in a falling-down warehouse, nothing inspiring in the decay. He would have given anything for a decent studio, but in Manhattan they were above the means of all but the rich and famous.

Hood's side of the studio was cut off from Leo's by a high-tech office divider made of sound-absorbing material. It looked absurdly out of place amid the rotting wood, and it didn't protect Hood from the tears of Dolly Parton and Patsy Cline.

He pulled the cover from his easel and looked at Friday's work. It was a monochrome reminiscent of Delvaux in shading and precision, but unlike Delvaux's dreamlike courtyards, this was a real place. He had chosen the square behind Avery Fisher Hall at Lincoln Center—a southern view, from high up.

Hood was pleased with the coolness of the scene, and with the accuracy of the details—the pool, the Moore, the trees and benches. But the murder wasn't quite right.

He had set the two figures off-center, so that the viewer would not catch them immediately. The man was forcing the woman backward over the bench; her hands tore frantically at his rigid arm that pushed her back. Her face was distorted by terror and pain; she could feel her life being ripped away. Hood had already drawn the tear in her dress, the first wound. The knife in the man's upraised hand was waiting for him to add blood.

The man's face was wrong. There was anger, fury—indeed the man's face was a vortex of rage—but it didn't look real.

Hood turned from this flaw to the female victim. He wanted the viewer to cry out for this girl, this figment of his imagination, to want to reach in and save her—a feat that was entirely within his own power. But his subject was murder, and so she would die.

Leo's chair scraped, and then he came around the partition, coffee in hand. He peered over Hood's shoulder. "Such violence in one so young and innocent."

"I know."

"There's a problem with the man, so." Leo pointed to the man's face.

"It looks like something out of a comic book, doesn't it?"

"Ja."

The last chords of a Merle Haggard ballad faded on the cassette machine, and Hood jumped up to change the tape.

"It's pretty good, I suppose—if one *must* paint a murder." Leo stroked his mustache with the point of his brush and stared down at the floor—a posture habitual with him. He looked more like a German bus conductor than an artist, and his accent was pure beer-hall, each word fully chewed.

Hood slipped a tape of Tangerine Dream into the machine, and ignored Leo's grimace. "At least it's new," he said.

"*Ja.*" Leo shuffled back to his own easel. "Like all good things."

Hood set about removing the figures from his canvas. He hated to work things over, almost never did, but at this stage the murder was largely a matter of pencil.

"Oh! I've nearly forgotten!" The beer-hall accent came over the partition. "Valerie called me at home to say she would be late."

"Fine. What are you talking about, Leo?"

"Valerie Vale—she's today's model. You met her last month. I was showing her your work when you came in."

"Oh, her!" Hood recalled a small girl with short black hair and the body of a gymnast. She had showered him with praise, which was not unpleasant, but she seemed to know nothing about art. She had raved about the "energy" of his work, rather than its precision, which he knew to be its chief merit. He had seen her around the local bars with Sam Weigel, a drunk she had tried to reform without success.

Hood and Leo worked on through the afternoon without further conversation, until Hood got up to change the cassette tape. He found a piece of paper someone had slipped under the door. An invitation. "We're invited to a party at Morris Weintraub's Tuesday night. He was in the news again today." Leo didn't hear him. Hood stuffed the invitation into his pocket, and put on a tape of Philip Glass.

"Take it off! I can't stand this garbage!"

"It's not garbage."

"Repetitive nonsense. How can one work?"

"I listened to Crystal Gayle for a bloody week!"

"Please, Nicholas!"

Hood didn't want to waste time arguing. He controlled his anger, and turned on the radio. They settled back to work to Pachelbel's ubiquitous Canon in D.

Hood realigned his murder. The woman he bent back so far that her face appeared upside down. Her attacker descended like the fury of hell, the dagger had entered her once, was poised to thrust again. Should the blood be black? Or red—the one spot of color in a field of gray. Blocked by this question, Hood's mind wandered in and out of his painting. He remembered a real murder at the opera house; someone had stabbed a clarinetist on the roof. Her husband was a painter. If Susan were murdered, he would—But it was bad luck to even think of such things.

The radio was giving a news summary. A Connecticut man who had raped and murdered several women had been granted a stay of execution. If it were ever carried out, his would be the first execution in the state in more than twenty-five years; and the first by lethal injection. An electric chair would make a more interesting painting, Hood thought.

He attempted to clear his head by performing the simple chore of cutting canvas. He unscrewed the handle of his razor knife, took out one of the new blades, and screwed the two halves back together. When he had measured out a length of canvas, he started to cut and immediately hurled the knife against the wall. "DAMN IT!" Blood flowed into the palm of his hand, a scarlet pennant of mortality.

Leo came around the partition. "What's the matter?"

"I didn't close the knife properly."

"Let me see."

"It's all right. Go back to work."

"Don't be stupid. Let me see." Leo took his hand and gazed at it, then tore off a length of paper towel. "Squeeze."

Hood crumpled it in his fist, and Leo bent his arm up at the elbow. "Keep it raised like that."

"Yes, Mother."

Leo dug out a small first-aid kit, and was soon putting Hood back together with gauze and disinfectant, calm as a nurse.

The radio had shifted its short attention span to an interview with a concert pianist, in town to play at Carnegie Hall. He was accepting the announcer's compliments with practiced modesty.

"Susan is just as good as those guys. Nobody ever asks her for an interview."

Leo was winding gauze over his cut. "Susan is maybe not so ambitious. A person doesn't play the harpsichord for fame and fortune."

"She's ambitious. She just doesn't go around telling people how wonderful she is, that's all."

"Well, I don't know the music business." He snipped off the end of the gauze, and taped it. "All better."

The injury had dampened Hood's spirits, and he sat on at the table in silence, while Leo went back to work. He looked over at his paunchy friend who concentrated fiercely, chewing his mustache. Leo was forty-five, and still lived like a student. He never had any money beyond what was in his pocket, and not a scrap of recognition. Yet he never complained. Hood was filled with fear at the prospect of hitting forty without having a great success—even if he still had six years to go.

He got up and put the cover over his painting. His cut hand had depressed him, but at least he knew how to proceed: not red blood—he would keep things cool, paint it black.

Out on the street, it was even colder than before. Hood was about to hail a cab when he remembered he had only seven dollars in his pocket. He had to wait a long time in the subway station, cursing his lack of money.

When he got out at Fourteenth Street, he saw Sherri Novack and Peter Laszlo coming the other way. She was his art dealer, proprietor of the Novack Gallery on West Broadway, and she was built like a small refrigerator. Laszlo was her star painter, six feet five, and moving beside her now like a stork. Juxtaposed like this, they resembled a political cartoon.

"Hiya, doll," she said, "You know Mistah Laszlo?" In the Waspy world of contemporary art, only a bulldog determination could have maintained such a Brooklyn accent all the way to success. It was one of the reasons Hood stayed with her.

He was about to acknowledge Laszlo by his first name, but the other bent forward and peered at him as if he were a mathematical problem, then shook his birdlike head. Hood wanted to punch the great beak, but recognized it as a poor career move.

Sherri introduced them.

"I'm just going over to the New School," he said, though no one had asked. "Taking Leo's life class."

"What's a Leo?"

"My studio partner. I showed you one of his things—you should take him on."

"Can't represent the world, doll—bad for my hot. Why you teachin' in the first place?"

"Money!"

"Thought you had a rich wife."

"Generous. Not rich." He didn't want to ask about the show, but couldn't stop himself. "How's the show coming?"

"Took the whole day to hang one pikcha. I got seven paintahs to hang before Wednesday. This rate, we'll all be dead."

"Save some wall for me."

Sherri tugged on Laszlo's sleeve. He was squinting up at the sky, a wingless creature contemplating flight. "C'mon, Tinker-bell." Sherri took his bony arm in hers and guided him across the street.

Five minutes later, Hood was in an overheated classroom under the buzz and glare of fluorescent lights. The students ranged in age from twenties to early fifties, men and women. Most sat silently, staring at their easels, or reading. Several older pupils chatted with one another, but they stopped when Hood came in.

He cleared his throat. "My name is Nicholas Hood. Leo asked me to take the class for him today. Our model is going to be a little late, so just open your sketchbooks, and I'll take a look at what you've done."

He went from student to student, examining their work. All were able to draw a competent figure—a necessary, but common, gift. Hood detected few signs of imagination, but you couldn't judge, really, without seeing a body of work.

He came to a hunched young man who looked about twenty. He had drawn last week's figure in one unbroken line. It had character, and rhythm, and was a slavish imitation of Picasso. Hood asked to see some others. Wordlessly, without looking up, the youth pulled out two more drawings—each with the same strength of line, each a minor Picasso.

"How many people have told you that you draw like Picasso?"

The bony shoulders were lifted and dropped in a shrug. "A couple."

"Well, they're right. You should get rid of all your Picasso books, Picasso posters—tear them up, give them away. The man will bury you."

The boy grumbled something unintelligible.

Hood sighed. He had always hated teaching; it was pointless to try to help anyone. Thank God Susan had relieved him of this burden. His remarks to the rest of the students were completely harmless, and he was glad when Valerie Vale finally came in, pink-faced from the cold.

"Is this the wrong room?"

Hood explained why he was there, and Valerie disappeared behind a wooden screen to change. She emerged a moment later wearing a silk robe with a dragon on it. She set an exercise pad on the large table at the front of the room, and removed her robe, handing it to Hood. "It's funny you should be here," she said. "I had a dream about you."

Hood ignored this. "Let's have you reclining on one elbow.

Good. Raise the right knee. Okay, now let's turn you this way."
Her skin was hot to the touch; she would have run all the way to
the school. "Okay. Right hand on right knee, yes, and a
three-quarter profile for depth." He took a step back. "Fine."

The class began to draw, and Hood went to the back of the
room. He looked out the window to avoid staring at Valerie's
body. It was nearly dark outside, and some children were
throwing snow at each other under a streetlight, demonic in the
way they stalked each other, then pounced. His eyes focused on
the pane of glass, where Valerie's nubile ghost was framed; he felt
a little breathless.

He went around again to each student, saying little. From
time to time he stole a glance at Valerie on the table—a study in
contrasts with her short black hair, dark blue eyes, pale translucent skin. She remained perfectly still, staring into space, and
except for the rise and fall of her breathing, she might have been
carved ivory. Hood wondered what she was thinking, if she *was*
thinking; she would not be a brainy girl. He noticed a very large
bruise above her elbow, turning yellow at the edges.

When the two hours were up, and the students were filing
out, Valerie remained on her table, stretching the stiffness from
her muscles. She bent forward and rested her head between her
outstretched knees with as little effort as a three-year-old.

"You think I should give up?"

Hood was startled by the young man who had come up
behind him. "You think I should quit, or what?"

"No. I don't."

"All I can do is copy. That's what you said."

Hood smiled. "Listen. When I was twenty-one, I couldn't see
anything without turning it into Delvaux. He's *still* a big
influence, but you have to leave your father sometime." He put
on his coat. "I wouldn't have said anything, if I didn't think you
had talent."

The young man snorted and looked down at his feet. Hood knew what he wanted: He wanted the world to kneel and kiss the feet of genius. One learned over time to hide it better.

Valerie came out from behind the wooden screen, all health and vitality. The boy fled, and her dark blue eyes went soft with concern. "Did I interrupt something?"

"No. All set?"

"Yeah, um . . . listen, Mr. Hood?"

"Nick. Please." She was not many years younger than he.

"Nick. I brought some of my stuff along to show Leo, but since he's not here, d'you think—"

"Another time, maybe. I couldn't recognize a Rembrandt, after all those drawings."

"Okay, sure." She tossed it off, as if it were nothing.

He couldn't imagine what her work would be like, but it wouldn't be good. He turned off the lights, and closed the classroom door behind them.

Valerie's voice echoed in the empty corridor. "When's your show coming up?"

"Soon."

"Who's all in it, besides you?"

"Several of the Novack people. Red Myers, Andy Stark . . . you know."

"Peter Laszlo?"

"Yeah."

"I think his work's brilliant."

Hood thought so, too, but he wasn't going to say anything good about Laszlo.

"You're brilliant, too, aren't you."

"I work hard."

"You're gonna make it really big, I bet—like really huge someday."

God, she sounded like a suburban teenager—and a dim one,

at that. He held the door open for her. A black man was standing in the alcove, out of the wind. A ridge of hair bristled along the top of his shaved head, and he wore gold earrings, the effect of which was not feminine. He thrust his jaw out at Valerie. "Fuck tookya so long!"

"Nothin'! I came right out!"

The black man eyed the two of them with blatant suspicion.

"This is Nick Hood," Valerie said. "He's teachin' class today." She indicated the black man. "Bill Lennox."

"How do you do," Hood said.

Lennox said nothing.

"Bill's an artist, too—he's got some stuff in a gallery over on Avenue C."

"Great. See you around." Hood hurried down the path to the sidewalk.

"See ya!" Valerie called after him.

When he'd gone halfway down the block, he looked back. Valerie and Lennox were wrapped around each other; the man's hand slid into the folds of her coat. Hood hoped never to see either of them again.

He found a note on the table when he got home. "Salmon in the oven. Love you, S." Beneath this an X and an O represented a hug and a kiss. When she was in particularly high spirits, Susan would leave two of each, and around Christmastime her notes looked like games of tick tack toe.

Hood removed the leftover soufflé from the oven, poured himself a glass of milk, and sat down to eat. The soufflé was heavy as meat loaf. Susan had many fine qualities, but the knack of cooking was not among them—a failing of which she was touchingly unaware. He sat at the table afterward, brooding, and picking his teeth.

She came home around nine, her lemur eyes huge beneath the woolen cap. "The service was lovely! Lots of candles and

incense, and the choir was fantastic! Fifty dollars, tax-free." She
put the money into a tin on the kitchen counter; it would go to
the bank later in the week. "Do you need any money?"

"No. Thank you." He would make the seven dollars last.

"How was the soufflé?"

"It was good."

"You didn't find it too heavy?" She looked over at him.
"What's wrong?"

"Nothing."

"Problems with work?"

"Leo's driving me up the wall with his fucking hillbilly
music, that's all. I'd do anything to get my own studio."

"One day, you'll have a beautiful studio."

After she had changed, and they were sitting on the couch,
he told her about bumping into Sherri Novack.

"How is Sherri?"

"All right."

"Is there something wrong with the show?"

"Not that I know of."

"What's wrong, then? Tell me."

"It's nothing. Really."

"*What's* nothing? God, it's like pulling teeth!"

"I've met Peter Laszlo several times—twice at the gallery,
once at the Guggenheim. I've been introduced to him at least
three times, and again today. Every time—every single time, he
pretends not to know me. He did it again today."

"It's just a way of saying 'I'm famous, and you're not.' Don't
let it get you down, sweetheart."

"I hate it! It's been gnawing at me ever since! I should've hit
the bastard—at least then he'd remember my name."

"You've got more important things to think about." She took
his face in her hands and kissed his forehead. "One day, my love,
they'll all come to you."

"Oh, sure."

"You'll see."

"You really believe that?"

"I wouldn't put up with you, otherwise." She noticed the bandage. "What did you do to your hand!"

"It's nothing. I was cutting canvas."

"Let me take a look at it."

To distract her, he pointed to the television. "There's a Fred Astaire on at ten o'clock."

Susan was delighted. She could always lose herself in an old musical, even if she'd seen it several times. She went into the kitchen to make popcorn, and later they sat together watching ridiculous people go through ridiculous contortions to make the plot turn out all right. Hood watched Fred Astaire gliding around his problems on the little glass screen, but he was thinking about Peter Laszlo.

TWO

BY the time Hood had showered Wednesday, Susan was already teaching her eight o'clock lesson. She sat at the harpsichord beside a reed-thin girl, correcting her fingering in the gentle voice she always used with her younger pupils. Hood ate a fast breakfast and hurried out without disturbing them.

At the studio, he said good morning to Leo and got quickly down to work. He finished the figures in his murder, added the blood (in black), and devoted the rest of the morning to correcting the light. Lincoln Center was lit by floodlights, so the man and woman could cast long shadows and yet be lit in a pale wash of reflected light. Hood was quite absorbed in the work, but part of his mind was dwelling on the famous Peter Laszlo. From outside, there came the occasional hoot from a passing tugboat.

"Did Valerie show you her drawings?"

"She wanted to. Is that why you wormed out of the class? You've seen her stuff?"

"Well . . . *ja*. I've seen some."

"And?"

"Well . . ." A long silence from Leo's side of the partition. "Perhaps it has a merit I cannot see."

Hood laughed. "What an indictment!"

"I'm not a critic, Nicholas."

"Every painter's a critic. Every painting is a critique of all the others."

"Please! You talk such nonsense all the time. More work, less talk."

"I *am* working!" Hood dipped his brush into black, but

hovered over the canvas, uncertain. "You think her work is terrible?"

"Look for yourself, if you're so interested." Leo chewed the words, extracting all the juice; the German accent was more pronounced when he was irritated. "With a body like hers she doesn't have to paint."

"I noticed. It's enough to make you believe in God."

"Not you, certainly."

Hood stepped back. Did the painting work? If one saw the murder too soon, the setting would be diminished. He wanted it to be a sudden shock, this murder in the cathedral of Art. "You know what I think, when I see Valerie Vale?"

"I know what everyone else thinks."

"I think: 'Murder victim.' Something about her. Isn't that strange?"

"You see everywhere murder victims—look at your subject matter."

"I don't see you as a victim. Or Susan. Or Sherri. Valerie's the only person I know who struck me that way. You should have seen the guy she was with! Big black guy with a Mohawk haircut and too many earrings. And before that, it was Sam Weigel—a drunk and a homosexual."

"Oh, ja, ja—so now she has to die."

"She has no sense of character! It's like a missing faculty! She treated this thug as if he was normal!"

"What is she supposed to do? The fellow is black. So?"

"I'm telling you he's dangerous! And she can't even see it! She had a nasty bruise on her arm, too."

"You have a cut hand. So Susan's a mad slasher?"

"Don't be obtuse, Leo. This guy is Bad News, and he was angry with her."

Leo said nothing.

"Someday she's going to get in a car with the wrong man and

she'll turn up in a ditch somewhere—flies buzzing around."
Hood was suddenly aware that he sounded like a crank, so he let
the matter drop. What was Leo's problem? All artists had their
chosen fields, their obsessions—Degas had his ballerinas,
Balthus his pubescent girls. With Nicholas Hood it happened to
be violence—a subject he had discovered at the age of nineteen,
when a letter from a friend had mentioned the murder of a
mutual acquaintance.

Hood had barely known the victim, had only been introduced to him at a state art exhibition. The letter said he had been
shot in the head in what was apparently a drug-related dispute.
Perhaps it was because he had been no older than Hood, or
maybe it was because the boy had been an artist, but Hood had
been haunted by the murder for weeks, and finally sought relief
from the pall it had cast over his life by painting it.

He had known no details of the actual event, and made no
effort to learn any. He had chosen to show the artist slumped and
bleeding at the foot of his easel, and without intending it, had
made a much more interesting study of the murderer. On his way
out the door, the hot gun still smoking in his hand, the killer has
hesitated out of sheer curiosity and glances backward for a look at
the canvas on which the dead boy had been working—a
sentimental landscape, not unlike Hood's own work up to that
time.

There were many technical defects in the painting, and it
showed in particular Hood's inexperience with the human figure.
Nobody had liked it, and the thing had never sold, but Hood had
known instantly that he had found his subject. He would go
through many different phases in the intervening years, and take
up many different enthusiasms, but these side trips and detours
always brought him sooner or later back to violence. The paint
had not yet dried on that early effort when an inner voice had
announced to him the discovery of his New World. Slaughter

was unclaimed territory. Hood had set out to conquer it—to define its boundaries and make it his sole domain. He would become its crown prince. If in the course of this adventure he occasionally sounded like a crank, so be it—what legend ever suffered from a touch of madness?

He started clearing up in the early afternoon. When he had cleaned his brushes and set his paints in order, he stepped around the partition. "You want to come with me to the gallery? Have a sneak preview?"

"Thanks, Nicholas. I'll see you there tonight. You're getting excited?"

"I've been in too many group shows for that."

"Wish I could say the same."

The afternoon was cold and damp. Heavy clouds moved sluggishly across the building tops; there was a feeling of impending snow.

He had to ring the front doorbell several times, before Marcia appeared behind the *Novack Gallery* lettering. She was a tall girl with glasses who worked at the gallery part time. "Hi, Nick—I'm not supposed to let anyone in."

"But it opens in a few hours!"

"They're still getting ready."

Hood knew they'd let Laszlo in. "Are you telling me I can't see my own—"

Sherri waddled into view behind Marcia. "It's okay, hon—let'im in."

"Thank you very much," Hood said, primly.

Sherri said, "Bully," and gave him a big smile.

The front gallery was dominated by a huge Laszlo. It showed a clearing in an emerald forest, where Giacomettilike figures were gathered in a mysterious ritual. Around the dark circle where they moved, the sunlight was rendered in bright gold, the leaves in brilliant greens. Except for the distortion of the figures, it might have been from a medieval manuscript. It was a haunting picture, before which Laszlo himself stood, ruffled and ungainly as a pelican. Hood thought the painting beautiful, but said nothing.

The next place of honor had been given to one of his own efforts. It was a street scene not unlike an Edward Hopper. The windows of the brownstones poured out warm yellow light. But on the sidewalk before them, one man held a gun, and another was blown backward, perhaps already dead. The coziness of the windows then took on another aspect: the woman combing her hair at one, a man glancing up from his newspaper in another— one could even make out the television inside, and a shelf of books. It spoke of separate lives, continuing separate ways, while another life was halted, not thirty yards away. The killer was contorted in a half-turn, about to flee, although on this placid, happy street there seemed no need to rush.

Hood walked through the remaining rooms. His work was displayed to advantage, but he was irritated to find a smaller picture tucked away in a back hall where no one would ever find it. He paid little attention to anyone else's work. He noted that the sculptures of Red Myers were spaced at random throughout the gallery, and Andy Stark's portraits had a whole back room to themselves. But he found portraits boring, and had no feeling at all for sculpture.

Sherri was in her office, terrorizing someone on the phone. "You drag your ass in here, Nigel! I don't care if you got yellow fevah! I got the goddam show in town and if you don't show up I am personally gonna haul you outa bed—if you should *be* in bed—and if you are lyin' to me, I will *nevah, nevah* let you forget it! I will send anonymous letters to your mothah! I will write your numbah on washroom walls!" She made a face and held the receiver away from her ear. "Nige, if you miss this show, I will make your life a living hell!" She gave a raucous laugh. "That'll be the day, sweethot!"

Hood said, "You're so good with people."

"That was not people; that was a critic."

"Nigel Thorne?"

"Nigel Thorne-in-my-ass. I made him promise to be here months ago. Months ago! Now he says he's sick! Huh! Tryin' that on me! Who does he think I am?" She looked at Hood sharply. "Whataya want?"

"I just wondered if you wanted to move Laszlo's forest scene."

"You got a hope! Get outa here! I got serious work to do."

On his way out, he saw Laszlo slumped in a chair, staring at the floor. He wondered if his refusal to say anything about the forest scene had upset him. He hoped so.

By a quarter to seven, Hood was waiting by the apartment door, holding Susan's coat. "For Christ's sake, Susan!"

She came out of the bedroom, head cocked to one side as she fastened an earring. "It's only ten to seven!"

"I should be there!"

"All right, all right."

"You show up for your concerts on time."

"Nicky, they're not coming to watch you paint." She slipped her arms into the coat. Even through his irritation, Hood could see she looked lovely in her black leotard top and skirt, her hair shining.

The gallery was still half-empty when they arrived. Leo was perched on a stool, looking pinched and uncomfortable in jacket and tie. He was eating from a plate piled high with hors d'oeuvres. Susan crossed the room and gave him a hug. Hood knew she was attracted by Leo's lost-little-bear appeal.

"Grab some food before the crowd is here—there's many good things." He had probably come early to take advantage of a free supper.

"Susan hasn't seen the show yet."

"Ach! Art is immortal; food is not. How is your harpsichord, Frau Hood?"

Susan chatted with Leo while Hood went to hang up their coats. He poured them each a glass of wine, and noticed that Sherri had spared no expense. The wine was good, and the glasses were real—not the plastic throwaways common at such affairs. Two slender young men offered him various delicacies from the buffet spread out before him, but Hood declined. More and more people were arriving.

Hood sipped his wine impatiently, waiting for Susan to tear herself away from Leo. A cold blast of air hit them when a particularly large group of people came in from the street. Hood didn't know any of them—Park Avenue matrons, corporate lawyers, cosmetic surgeons—why should he? There was a very small man, almost a dwarf, with a cane. Hood caught his breath when the man turned in his direction, for he was the ugliest human being he'd ever seen. His face was a mass of warts and pustules; the skin had split open in places, and then healed badly. The lips were fixed in a curled-back position, so that the slimy, crooked teeth were constantly exposed, and from out of the reddened eyes poured a look of pure malevolence.

Hood almost laughed. There was something ridiculous about anyone that ugly. He could see others in the front gallery pull back from the short man as they caught a glimpse of his face. To top it all off—the blistered visage, the hateful eyes—was a tidy crop of pretty blond hair, combed to one side like a schoolboy's. Hood couldn't take his eyes off him; he watched with anticipation as Marcia reached out to take the creature's coat, and noted the traces of fear she couldn't hide.

Hood grabbed her arm as she moved toward the coatrack. "Who's the blond guy with the cane?"

"I don't know!" She looked on the verge of panic.

Susan had wandered into the back gallery, and Hood found

her there approaching each of Andy Stark's portraits like a young nun making her stations of the cross. She would gaze at each intensely before reluctantly moving to the next. Hood went to stand beside her when she reached the best one.

It was a portrait of a homeless man, sitting on the stone steps of a church. There was a Gothic door behind him, and a sign that listed the hours of church services. Susan made a slight sound when she saw the face—an eloquent delineation of life lived at the poles of numbness and pain. "It's so sad!" She looked quite bereft.

Hood suddenly felt he was being watched. He turned to see the ugly man staring at them from the doorway. There was a kind of power in such ugliness, Hood thought, but the man turned on his heel and was gone, leaving nothing but his aura of ugliness, money, and time—his clothes, Hood noticed, were very expensive. And he thought he'd seen a gold top on the cane he could hear tapping away, around the corner.

Susan shivered. "I should've brought a sweater."

"I'll see if Sherri has one."

"No, don't bother. I want to see your work."

"I'll let you find it for yourself. Sherri wants me out front." He could see her gesticulating at him from the front of the gallery, calling out to him in her cabdriver's voice.

He left Susan and went to join Sherri near a table where five of the represented artists were seated. Red Myers was feeling his wine; he was pounding the table for emphasis, making the wineglasses jump. Hood sat down between him and Andy Stark, whose ears stuck out.

"Smile!" Marcia took several photographs of Sherri and her brood, blinding them all with her flash. Sherri went back to the rich people then, and when Red Myers tried to do the same, Marcia stopped him. "No, you don't. Sherri wants you right here where people can find you."

"Where's Laszlo?" Andy Stark had only just noticed the absence of their distinguished colleague.

Myers breathed wine fumes across Hood. "Mr. Laszlo doesn't deign to appear with his inferiors."

"Is he sick or something?"

"He looked all right this afternoon," Hood said.

"Kinda rude, isn't it? People go to all this trouble."

Myers pointed an accusatory finger. "You're from Missouri, aren't you?"

"St. Louis."

"Thought so." Myers sat back as if he had proved an important point.

The artists stayed at the table for the next forty-five minutes, accepting congratulations, answering questions, and signing catalogues. Sherri paid them no further attention. Hood saw her clutch one gentleman in excitement before hauling him off to point out the virtues of a watercolor. Some might be put off by her brash Brooklyn manner, Hood thought, but she made up with enthusiasm what she lacked in polish—and only a fool would mistake her excitement for naïveté.

The ladies in attendance proved partial to Stark's portraits. One by one, they presented him with effusive praise and repetitive questions. There was one such hovering over the table at this moment, in a cloud of expensive perfume. "How on earth did you get that bum to sit still for so long?"

"Well, if you notice, ma'am, those fellas don't tend to move around so much."

"Did you have to pay him?"

"No, I had to hit him several times, though."

"Oh, you!" The woman moved on to Hood, and looked him coolly up and down as if he were himself on exhibit. "You're the one that did all those murders!"

"The paintings," Hood said. "Not the murders."

"It's like watching the news! I can see that on television."

"In a world of violence, one should paint violence."

She shook her perfectly white head. "Art should cheer us up. That's my belief."

"Like a little pill, you mean." But the lady had no interest in the aesthetic philosophy of Nicholas Hood. She was already complimenting Red Myers on his sculptures.

Hood craned his neck to get a glimpse of Susan, who was standing in front of his most violent piece. The background was a wash of purple and black, as if the figures might be at the bottom of the sea. This one differed from his usual work in that the figures were close up, nearly bursting from the frame. They were fighting over a gun, which had just fired. Blood and brains exploded from the back of a head. Susan turned from this, a slight frown on her face.

A very thin man stepped into the space where she had been standing. Hood saw that it was Nigel Thorne, the *New York Times* critic. He moved on to Hood's next picture, and stood there for some time scratching his head. Hood felt a stirring of hope.

Susan came across the room, and Hood went to fetch their coats. When he came back, Leo had his arms draped around Susan's neck. He swiveled a glassy eye at Hood. "Nicholas, it's too bad for you—I'm going to marry Susan."

"You can't. She's taken."

"Her sister, then."

"I don't have one, Leo." Susan gently untangled his arms, and Leo stood there, swaying slightly, as they put their coats on. Hood excused himself to find Sherri.

She was talking to Nigel Thorne across a small Myers statue called "Fat Man on Skates." "How many people you know can cut stone like this? How many? I'll tellya how many, Nigel— none. I got the only one."

Hood interrupted to thank Sherri for the show.

She bowed in mock majesty. "You may come again."

"Good night."

"'Night, doll."

As he walked away, Hood heard Thorne ask if he were Nicholas Hood, and felt a thrill of pleasure. He was glad Peter Laszlo hadn't come.

Young couples with outrageous purple-and-orange hairstyles strolled arm in arm along West Broadway. They drifted past the bright windows like tropical fish. Susan was quiet as she and Hood made their way back to Broome Street. She didn't say a word until they were rattling up to their apartment in the old freight elevator. "Your work is really strong."

"I certainly hope so."

"It *is*. They're quite frightening, some of them. The man getting shot in the head." She was looking at the floor of the elevator, not at him.

"Not the kind of thing you want in the living room, I guess."

She'd gone quiet again. Thinking.

"You're not sure you like them. Is that it?"

"No, I just didn't realize you spent so much time thinking about violence. Murder. Doesn't it affect you?"

"It's not something I worry about." The elevator door opened, and they crossed the hall to their apartment.

When they were inside, Susan spoke in a brighter tone, as if realizing she might have upset him. "I liked the one of the neighborhood street. It looks so peaceful at first—it makes you wish there wasn't a murder in it."

"You think it's a mistake?"

"Oh, no! Please don't misunderstand! I think your paintings are wonderful! They're all really, really good! It just set me back a little, seeing how much time you spend dwelling on horrible things. It can't be pleasant for you."

"I don't think about it one way or the other. Mostly I think about what size brush to use, what shade of gray, that kind of stuff."

"Well, good. I don't want you thinking about daggers and bullets." She hugged him, and kissed his neck.

Hood said, "My work embarrasses you."

"Never. I was very, very proud of you tonight."

In bed later, she lay beside him, reading a mystery novel. Hood was halfway through a biography of Augustus John, but he was beginning to tire of the subject's flamboyant life. He put the book aside. "Herr Forstadt seems to be in love with you."

"Leo? He might have a little crush on me," she said, matter-of-factly. "He'd had a lot to drink, though."

"He wouldn't have said a word, sober."

"He's so sweet—it's a shame he's all alone. The nicest people seem to get so isolated. Then others get married and you don't know how anyone could live with them."

"Like me, you mean."

"You're just moody, not difficult . . . I'd die if I was on my own again."

"You'd get used to it."

"But I wouldn't!" She turned her huge brown eyes on him. "You're not leaving, are you?"

"Don't be silly."

Her eyes, round and vulnerable, lingered on him a moment longer before she settled back to her book. Hood knew he should feel lucky to have Susan, but it was like trying to feel happy because you're not sick. He took her completely for granted; it surprised him that she didn't do the same.

"What are you thinking?"

"Reviews. I was thinking that with a few good reviews I might actually sell something. Make some real money."

"The prices were so high! One of them was over thirty thousand dollars!"

"Well, Sherri keeps half."

"Nice way to make a living."

"She works pretty hard. It's not easy to fill a show with rich people. Dealing with me is the least of her concerns."

He turned off his light and rolled over, but remained far from sleep. His imagination was writing a glorious review: "the poet of violence . . . a bid for greatness . . . the master of urban *angst.*" That kind of thing would have them lining up around the block.

Three days went by. Hood fell out of his usual routine of going straight to work in the mornings. Instead, he would stop in at a Sixth Avenue coffee shop to read all the papers. He would spread them out on the Formica table and leaf through rapidly to the arts pages, only to be disappointed on finding no mention of the Novack show. He knew this was completely irrational, that the reviews would not appear until Sunday, but he couldn't stop himself.

These mornings, he would find Leo deep into his work on the "brown thing." Hood envied him his power of concentration. He himself was in no shape to start a major project, so he made a few sketches that went nowhere, and stretched out some canvasses.

He went to the gallery on Saturday to find Sherri out, and the place empty. Marcia was filing her nails. The gallery turned out to be less empty than he'd thought; it contained exactly one visitor, dressed in an old trench coat and very bright check trousers. The cuffs hung a little long over the kind of heavy black shoes that policemen wear. What was really striking, however, was his apparent fascination with Hood's street scene. He stood before it, rocking back and forth on his heel like a cop on the beat. As Hood went by, the fellow startled him by speaking. "Have you seen this thing here?"

Hood stopped.

"Quite a picture. Reminds me of Goya."

"Goya?" That was a new one.

"I'm probably way out in the left field—I'm new at this stuff—but if you look closely, it *feels* like a Goya. The one where the guys are lined up against a wall and shot."

"I don't see the resemblance."

The man passed a hand slowly over the crown of his head where hair used to be. "'Wasted life'—that's what it makes me think. 'Wasted life.' Injustice, also. You like it?" He turned hopeful green eyes to Hood, as if he had painted the picture himself.

"It's not my favorite."

"He's got talent, this fella. He's got a recognizable subject, which is murder. And he's got expressions. Look at those faces! You don't get many guys can catch expressions."

"Have you seen Andy Stark's work?"

"Doesn't interest me. Portraits et cetera. These Hood things tell a story—not a nice story—but it's about the real world, that's all I'm saying."

Hood murmured something noncommittal.

"There is one thing wrong, in my opinion."

"Oh?"

"A small thing, maybe—I could be way off base—but it seems to me if you're going to paint realistic pictures about a real subject, you should know more about it. This guy has obviously never been within miles of a real murder, and the result is you get a *sort of* realistic effect, but the details are all wrong. I must be boring the hell out of you."

"Not at all. Go on."

"This art is a new interest of mine. My wife tells me I tend to get overenthusiastic. It's true, too." He didn't seem to think it a fault. "Anyway. If you notice, here, the victim is being blown back by the force of the bullet."

"And?"

"Never happen! That is strictly a conceit of the motion picture industry. Think about it—basic laws of physics, namely inertia. The victim is an object more or less at rest: He's standing there—a massive object compared to the bullet which as you can see is a nine-millimeter, smaller than a cigarette butt." The man peered closely at the gun. "He did a good job on the weapon. But my point is, even if the thing was a magnum, it isn't going to blow the guy backwards, because it doesn't have the mass. You get shot, you fall down. Not back."

"The general public doesn't know that."

"They won't *know* it, but they'll *sense* it. They'll know it's a made-up thing, which is fine for a movie—but this artist is aiming for realism, and in that context I'd say it's a real fault. It keeps the picture just this side of a masterpiece."

"You've got to be a cop. But you don't sound like one, entirely."

"I *am* a cop. Nobody wants to sound like one. By that I take it you mean I don't sound like a graduate of grade six only."

Hood laughed.

"I have to get back to work—this is just my lunch break here. If you have a second, I'll show you something else." He led Hood around to the blacker painting, the two figures in close-up. "God, this is gory, this thing. You got all that junk blowing out of the guy's head. Effective. But I'll tell you something about head wounds: They bleed. And if you look here, there's not a trace of blood on the entrance wound. The guy's already falling, so in real life that little hole would be a geyser. Sickening, but true."

"That would ruin the composition."

"I understand that. But either you're being realistic or you aren't."

"Well, artistic truth and factual truth don't necessarily coincide. Thank God."

"Thank God is right." He took a step back from the picture. "This guy is great, though. Really great."

Hood looked at the compact figure. He carried a lot of intensity in a small package, like an overcharged battery. He looked at his watch. "Damn it—I got so wrapped up in this guy I forgot to eat lunch."

"Pleasure talking to you," Hood said.

"I have a terrible habit of buttonholing people. Sorry if I spoiled the pictures for you." He waved a ring-studded hand at Hood. "Gotta go," he said, and walked out into the sunlight.

Hood left a few moments later. On his way out, he noticed that Laszlo's forest scene had been sold—for more money than Hood had earned in a lifetime.

That Sunday, Hood went out to pick up *The New York Times*. He clutched it tightly in the elevator, forcing himself to wait until he was back in the apartment before opening the Arts and Leisure section.

Nigel Thorne began his review with a flourish:

> Anybody who cares about art and is at all familiar with today's New York scene must be approaching suicide. If you admire craftsmanship, you're better off seeing a movie than the inside of an art gallery. If keen observation is what you like, don't bother with a trip to Alphabet City; you'd be better advised to pick up a novel—there's no shortage of accurate detail in our contemporary fiction. And for sheer expression, the choreography of Twyla Tharpe dances rings around any painting since the forties.

Hood scanned the rest of the article for a glimpse of his name. But he didn't see his name. Red Myers, yes. Andy Stark, yes. And Laszlo. But not a sign of Nicholas Hood. He sat down to read more slowly.

> I am happy to report that the human figure is alive and well at the Novack Gallery on West Broadway. Sherri

Novack, the plain-spoken proprietor, has brought together some of the most exciting artists working today, in
a show called Contemporary Figures.

Thorne went on to trace a brief history of the human figure
through pop art (no good), and hyper-realism (so-so), coming
around at last to the work of Peter Laszlo: "simply the most
prodigious practitioner of pictorial art working today." He raved
about the forest scene, gave luxurious descriptions of several
others, and concluded that Laszlo was about to step into his
prime, "a prospect those of us who care about such things can
only anticipate with bated breath."

Logically, Hood's work should have been reviewed next. His
paintings made up the bulk of the exhibit, and to Hood's mind,
even if they weren't the best, they were undeniably the most
interesting. Nigel Thorne apparently thought otherwise, bound-
ing directly to Andy Stark.

I can't remember when I was so moved by a portrait as
I was by Stark's "Homeless Man." The depiction gives to
that unfortunate class of people a history, some beauty,
and a name. It is the kind of painting that haunts one for
days after a single viewing. If the rest of Stark's oeuvre has
less immediate impact, it is no less rich in staying power,
and while there may be something a little old-fashioned
about these portraits, that is not necessarily bad.

Stark is an artist who benefits by having his work
brought together in one room. Red Myers is not, and Ms.
Novack has wisely spaced his eloquent little sculptures,
one here, one there, throughout the gallery. Taken one at
a time, these figures carved out of materials diverse as
alabaster, pink marble, and oak give the viewer quite a
lift. Myers is a carver in the oldest tradition, and though

he sometimes leaves things a little heavy for my taste, they are for the most part satisfying. And when was the last time you saw a sculpture with a sense of humor? Try his "Fat Man on Skates."

All of these artists have talent. Kronin's watercolors are pretty, but not sentimental; Burke's painted photographs show a delicate hand; and Stamelman's New York scenes show a wealth of textural detail.

Contemporary Figures is easily the most interesting show to open in the past year, and it's gratifying to see that Sherri Novack's perseverance through what must have been some very lean years has paid off handsomely.

Hood stood up and let go of the paper, which slithered from the table to the floor. He felt as if he had been shot. He went into the bathroom and stood for a long time bent over the sink, splashing cold water on his face. He was weak with nausea, he wanted to throw up, but this nausea was located not in his stomach but in his heart—it turned his blood bitter, coursing through his veins to every cell of his body. Water ran into his eyes as he looked at himself in the mirror. He wanted to vomit over the image, spew blood all over it; his blood would be black as paint.

Susan called his name brightly as she came in from her run. Nick. An ugly name. He couldn't answer to that name.

"Nick?" She was closer now, just outside the bathroom door. He dried his face and opened the door. He would go . . . where? Not knowing where to go, he stood motionless in the doorway.

"What's wrong?" Susan's face, ruddy with exercise, opened in alarm. "You're completely white! Are you sick?"

Hood opened his mouth, but he was empty of words.

Susan took his arm. "You'd better lie down." She led him

into the bedroom, and he sat on the edge of the bed.

"I'm all right," he said, but his voice belonged to another person, in another room. He lay down on his back and covered his eyes with the crook of his arm.

"Please tell me what's wrong, hon."

That voice from another room said, "I'd better be alone for a while."

"Well, if that's what you want . . . I'll be right outside, if you need me." When she had gone out, Hood cried a little. It wasn't a dam breaking, just a few meager sobs. He was thirty-four years old, and quite beyond the relief of tears. They only increased his humiliation.

Susan brought him a cup of tea and sat beside him on the bed. "I read Thorne's review. I don't see why he couldn't at least have *mentioned* your paintings." She squeezed his shoulder. "It isn't fair, after you worked so hard. It's ridiculous."

"It doesn't matter."

"Of course it matters! That stupid bastard! Doesn't he fucking realize how good you are! Doesn't he have eyes! God knows what his qualifications are—probably a degree in chemistry or something."

"If he'd raved about me, I wouldn't care a damn about his qualifications." He put down his cup of tea, and rubbed his eyes. "I'm so tired of working in the dark. I'm thirty-four. I have a hundred and fifty dollars in the bank. I have to think twice about buying a tube of paint."

"Nigel Thorne. What a jerk. What a fucking jerk." Susan rarely cursed. Hood was touched to see her so fierce for his sake.

Later that night he called Leo. "Did you read today's *Times*?"

"I was going to, but then I got working and forgot. It's a new painting, Nick—quite nice I think it's going to be. I can show you the drawings, if you—"

"Don't you even care what they said?"

"The *Times*? If it affects you, I suppose."

"Hold on, I'll get it." Hood had to extract the Arts and Leisure section from the garbage, where Susan had shoved it with some force. He smoothed it out on the kitchen table, then read the review to Leo from beginning to end.

"That's all?"

"That's it."

"He doesn't mention your work?"

"Not a word."

"This is very stupid. Only a stupid person would do this."

"His remarks about Stark and Laszlo aren't stupid."

"It's *air*, Nicholas. *Air*. It's nothing. Why he ignores your work I can't imagine."

"Because he hated it! He knows a really *bad* review would interest people!"

"There's only one way to deal with such things. Put your head to the grinder. Forget reviews. Work is all there is."

"How do you keep going, Leo? You're much worse off than I am, and it doesn't get to you. I'm in a rage every minute of the day!"

"I'm just stupid, perhaps."

"No, you're not."

"Honestly, Nicholas, I don't want to think of it. If I sell, okay. If I get money, okay. But not to become the object of my life—I would get quickly very miserable. Once you start worrying about it, everything else goes, I think."

Hood didn't feel any better after talking to Leo. He knew the conversation should have put things back in perspective, but it was no good knowing what one *should* feel. He sat down heavily, beside Susan. On the TV screen, Lauren Bacall was lying to Humphrey Bogart. Susan held his hand, for a time, before she fell asleep beside him on the couch.

THREE

HOOD slept badly, and woke early, so for once he had the studio to himself, arriving well before Leo. He put the kettle on, turned on the space heaters, and set his freshly prepared canvas on the easel. This was usually a happy moment for him—he would be in a hurry to join the fray of composition, to claim the white field for himself. But today was different. In surveying that wide expanse of white canvas he sensed no victory, but only vast opportunities for failure.

To his dismay, Hood found that his idea had vanished; he could not recall his subject. He knew it was to be a murder against an architectural background—no surprise there—but where it was to take place, and who was to kill whom, he could not recall. Male against female? Two figures? Three? He had no idea.

The size of the canvas told him it was to be a large painting. And the tubes of paint laid out beside the easel told him he had planned to work primarily in black and red. But the image, the design, had deserted him.

He snatched up his sketchbook in a sudden panic. Perhaps he had made a drawing! But no. He found nothing there but ideas he had either rejected or completed. The Lincoln Center murder had so occupied his attention that he had failed to record the conception he'd had in mind. And it had been so clear! By the time Leo entered the studio, Hood was frantic. "I can't remember what I was going to paint!"

Leo was making himself an instant coffee, and paused with the kettle in midair. "Oh? *Ja?*"

"It's completely gone! As if someone lifted it right out of my head!"

"My *Gott*! Art thieves!" Leo finished making his coffee.

"It's not funny! There's not an idea in my head!"

"Calm down, Nicholas—there's probably somewhere a drawing."

"There isn't! I didn't make any!"

Leo shrugged. "There's always something to paint. I'm sure it's only temporary." He vanished into his corner of the studio, and Hood listened to him setting up for a day's work.

"Has this ever happened to you?"

"Not with anything I was ready to paint. Nothing serious."

"This was serious."

"It will come back, in that case." His tone indicated he wanted silence. Hood looked at his canvas and saw nothing. Sorrow welled in his heart, as if someone had died. He had not lost a painting, but an idea for a painting, and in a way that was worse—it had not yet been sullied by weak anatomy, strained perspective, or botched light. Hood mourned his unborn masterpiece.

He peered around the partition and watched Leo working, like a sick man envying the healthy. Leo's brush fluttered gently over the canvas, applying pale yellow to the dress of a middle-aged woman who stood before a very white, very modern stove. It could have been an advertisement for a cooking range, except that the woman's smile was so obviously fake. It was a sad picture.

Hood stalked outside into the cold and damp—it was the second week in March, and New York was still sullenly resisting the advances of spring. He headed north, skirting the edge of SoHo and the Village, walking fast enough to work up a sweat. Never had he felt so impotent; never had life seemed so futile; he had led a blameless life only to be thrown into a hell he had thought was reserved for the stupid. He kept walking angrily uptown and completely lost track of the time until he found himself near Columbia University in half darkness. He took the subway back down from 116th Street, and by the time he got home he felt sick and guilty—a whole day wasted, never to come again.

Susan stopped playing and looked up from the harpsichord, her brown eyes huge and happy. Hood went right by her to the bedroom, and closed the door.

It opened a moment later, and Susan entered. "What's wrong, love?"

"Nothing. I don't want to talk about it."

"Is there anything I can—"

"No!"

The brightness vanished from her eyes. "All right," she said, and left him.

Hood picked up a magazine and tried to read. Susan began to practice, in the other room. The harpsichord halted, stuttered, then chattered over the same brief passage again and again, until it sounded no more musical than a typewriter. Hood found it impossible to read a simple sentence. He left the apartment once more.

Hood didn't particularly like the Broome Street Café—it attracted a regular crowd of pseudo-artists—but it was just around the corner. He ordered a beer and stood at the end of the bar. Waitresses had to squeeze by him to fetch drinks, jostling him as they came and went. He drank the beer down and ordered another.

Sam Weigel came in, brushing snow from his coat. Hood didn't know him very well, although he had met him a few times. He remembered seeing him at parties with Valerie Vale. Weigel joined him at the bar. "How are things going?"

"Not very well."

"I was over at the Novack yesterday. You have some very impressive work on display."

"Glad someone likes it."

Weigel looked at him, catching the bitterness in his tone. "I get the feeling you're in a bad mood."

"You're right."

"Perrier, please. Squeeze of lime." Weigel smiled at the bartender. Old friends.

Hood said, "You're on the wagon?"

Weigel returned his gaze. He was one of those people who never spoke unless they looked you in the eye. "I haven't had a drink in six months," he said, and rapped three times on the bar.

"You shouldn't deny your demons. They'll come back to haunt you."

Weigel blinked. "I don't think you realize what a terrible thing that is to say to me."

"Sorry."

"Besides, I used alcohol to drown my demons, not to summon them. So, you needn't worry on that score. They're alive and well, and I hope to deal with them in a manner more creative than puking in the gutter."

Hood took a long drink from his beer. "I saw Valerie Vale the other day."

"How is Valerie?"

"She was with a black guy. Mohawk haircut."

"Oh, I know him! William Lennox! He's one of the graffiti fellows over in Alphabet City. Quite talented, from what I hear."

"He looks like a killer."

"Just a pose, I'm sure. We all have our little disguises."

"This guy is seriously disturbed."

"Really? Or are you just trying to alarm me?"

"Not at all. He looks like a paranoid."

"Oh, dear. Valerie is not strong on judgment, character-wise—as witness her taking up with me. It didn't faze her one bit that I'm gay. I think she's a kind of saint."

"Is she as stupid as she seems?"

Weigel put down his glass and motioned to the bartender. "Rick, I'm going to drink this at the other end of the bar."

"Sure thing, Sam." The bartender scooped up his glass and the little green bottle and hustled them away.

Hood ordered another beer. He didn't want one, but he didn't want Weigel to think he cared about his prissy little maneuver. He drank half of it, and left.

Susan didn't look up from her book when he came in. Hood sat at the kitchen table with a cheese sandwich and a glass of milk. He felt a bit better after he ate. He said, "My work has gone haywire on me."

"Oh."

"That's why I'm a little tense. So, you know . . ."

"All right."

Hood went over to the couch and sat beside her. She looked up from her book, but not at him, and said softly, "It devastates me when you're unhappy."

Morning brought no change; he was again defeated by blank canvas. To keep calm, he leafed through some art books he kept at the studio. There was a volume of famous masterpieces—a collection of fine reproductions Susan had given him, and smaller books representing individual artists.

In the afternoon he sketched a picture of Susan at the harpsichord. Even after several variations, he couldn't get her face right. He set the harpsichord on an ice floe in the Arctic Sea. The hours went by, and still he could recall nothing of the painting he had planned.

Another day gone.

He sat by the studio window the next day, not speaking to

Leo, and sketched scenes from his everyday life the way a photographer might resort to snapshots in a dry period. He considered drawing the Broome Street Café, which made him think of Sam Weigel, and then of Valerie Vale. From out of this, a strange picture emerged beneath his hand—Valerie, nude, in a clearing somewhere, surrounded by rolling clouds of fog. From out of the fog a pair of outstretched hands reached for her throat.

He decided to put some architecture on the canvas as a beginning, just to see what happened. He drew a single black line down the left-hand side of the canvas and stopped dead. It was the wrong line—a hopeless non sequitur. In a rage, Hood squeezed the tube of black all over the canvas until it was empty. He smeared it in wild circles with a filthy rag, then threw the canvas from his easel.

Leo came around the partition. "Nicholas—for God's sake!" Hood kicked at the black smear. Leo grabbed him. "Calm down!"

"What the fuck for! What is this agony for! So I can earn three thousand dollars a year! So I can live off my wife!"

"You've got to get this painting off your mind. Let's go for a beer."

"I had a beer last night. It doesn't help."

"You can't be working in a rage."

"I can't work at all! I have nothing to paint!"

"Nicholas. Please. You'll never help with all this tension. You get so wound up!"

"Wouldn't you? My whole life is nothing but a waste of time and paint!"

Susan was out, and there was nothing ready for supper when he got home. Very well, he'd starve. He sat on the couch and stared at the television, flipping channels from one senseless image to another. Then he lay down and fell into a kind of half sleep from which he awoke feeling stiff and grimy.

He undressed, and stood under the shower. The plumbing was even more unpredictable than usual, so that he alternately froze, then burned himself, which did nothing to ease his foul temper.

Susan came in at ten o'clock.

"Where the hell have you been!"

"At the concert. Which you forgot, obviously."

"What concert?"

"At St. Thomas! I told you about it days ago! Anyway, it went better than I expected." She put her things into the hall closet. "I take it you had a bad day."

"I'm having a bad life. I hate my life. You hear what I'm saying? I hate my life. I don't want to wake up in the morning. Not if this is all I'm going to have—a shitty apartment in a hideous city, a career dead in its tracks. I don't want failure. I don't want an inventory of unsold work."

"One day that work will be worth—"

"Nothing! It's worthless! You can't sell something nobody wants! All these years I've been blind! I thought I had talent—a talent other people would recognize!"

Susan opened her purse absently, and removed some money, which she placed in her tin on the kitchen counter. Hood pointed. "See! You have something to sell! You can make a living! People want to see you, hear you—I'm nothing! Nothing! If this is my life, I don't want it!"

"Oh, honey. We have a pretty good life . . ."

"No. *You* have a good life. I'm the butt of a joke! You at least make a living! How much did they pay you? How much have you got there?"

"Three hundred dollars—hardly riches. It's just lucky I do something I love to do and get paid for it. I don't do anything original, like you. It could be anybody playing Bach, or Vivaldi, or whoever—it's *them* I'm selling. Not me."

Hood looked out the window at the street below. It was snowing—heavy wet flakes that fell straight to earth. "You should have more ambition."

"What do you mean?"

"You should write music. You used to."

"Oh, God, Nick—I was never any good."

"If you *can* write music, you *should* write music."

"Well, I can't."

"You go around playing these tired old things that have been played to death for hundreds of years. My God, who needs to hear Vivaldi! You're a music museum! Don't you have the slightest ambition to be an artist?"

He turned to see if his words hit home. Her shoulders sagged, and she moved away from him to the bedroom. Susan was not at all prone to tears, but there was a part of Hood that liked to see her cry. It gave him a sense of power to send a charge, however negative, snarling across the synapse between their two minds.

The snow fell so heavily it muffled the sounds of the city. It clung to Hood's face and eyelashes, making it difficult to see. He didn't know where he was going—not far, since he'd forgotten his gloves. He jammed his hands into his pockets and felt a piece of paper. He pulled it out and peered at it. "You are invited . . ." The address was only three blocks away.

Morris Weintraub opened the door, wearing a miniscule bathing suit. "Nick, you hot dog! Come in!" He ushered Hood into his gigantic loft, which was jammed with artists, dealers, and a colorful assortment of civilians. Weintraub, all ribs and ropy muscles, was the only one dressed for the beach. They had to shout over blaring rock music. "What are you drinking?"

"Beer!"

"Walk this way!" Weintraub twisted himself into a Quasimodo posture, and lurched ahead of Hood toward the bathroom. The bathtub was crammed to the top with ice and wine and beer.

"Climb in." Weintraub suggested, and sashayed back to the roar in the front room.

"One beer," Hood thought, "then I'll go."

A very thin man separated himself from the crowd and came into the hallway, politely excusing himself as he brushed against Hood's sleeve. Hood noticed the expensive tweed, the old brown brogans. "You're Nigel Thorne."

Startled eyes, behind the flash of spectacles. "I—yes. That is my burden. You, er, look familiar, but—"

"Nicholas Hood." His hand went out like a salesman's, accompanied by what he hoped was a disarming grin. Thorne shook his hand with that politeness instinctive to the British, but he looked nervously over Hood's shoulders, evaluating chances of escape. Hood announced, "I'm a painter."

"Oh, yes! Well, of course, I knew that. Excuse me, I was just on my way to—"

"Don't worry. I won't assault you."

"I didn't suppose you would."

"Despite my subject matter, I am quite stable. I just wanted to ask why you chose not to mention my work in your review."

"Indeed. Well, there wasn't all that much space." Thorne had bushy eyebrows, which knit and unknit themselves over his glasses. "It was a long review, which required a certain amount of background information. Sort of laying things out, you know, and—I would've liked to say more."

"You don't have to spare my feelings. I'm thirty-four years old, and if I were going to worry about what people thought, it would've killed me long ago. I'm just interested in why you left me out, and no one else. It wasn't accidental."

Thorne's eyebrows went through a worried semaphore. "I don't generally go in for personal criticism—it's not really my function. If I had to deal with every artist on a personal level, it would inevitably cloud my judgment."

"You're drinking Morris Weintraub's wine."

"Morris is a friend; I don't review him."

"You'd be doing me a favor—giving me an insight into the critical process."

"I'm sure you don't paint for the critics."

"Everyone is a critic. Only one writes for the *Times*."

"Frankly, I wish the *Times* hadn't so much influence. It's the paper of course, and not myself, that wields the power. A child could replace me tomorrow, with as much effect."

Hood was annoyed to find in Thorne this gentle, unassuming manner where he had expected arrogance and insensitivity. "Look. I'm not going to make a scene. It would be very helpful to me, that's all—unless you've forgotten the paintings entirely."

"Oh, no, no—not at all. They're quite clear in my mind."

"So why didn't you say anything?"

"The short answer is, I didn't say anything, because I had nothing good to say." His gaze skittered over Hood's face, searching for signs of blood.

"Fine. Continue."

"Obviously, you've mastered your technique long ago. You have a sharp eye for perspective, your brushwork is nearly invisible, and you have a certain talent for setting mood."

"You could've said so in your review."

"Pretty faint praise, all in all."

Hood shrugged, carelessly.

"Let me also say that I have no problem with your subject matter. The depiction of murder is nearly as old as painting itself, and is an entirely appropriate theme. But it comes down to a matter of attitude. What you intend to convey, I neither know nor care. But there is a certain coolness expressed in your paintings."

"People seem to think so."

"Well, yes! It's there in your restriction of palette, on the smooth, untroubled surfaces, and with one exception, in your literal distance from the figures. The paintings are almost all large, the figures usually small."

"I'm trying to—"

Thorne's hand went up, forestalling interruption. "I cannot deal with intentions; I deal with effects. Your pictures convey a complete unconcern for the victims of murder. Not on the part of the bystanders, when you show them; not on the part of society in general, or of God—let me finish—but on *your* part. Maybe not you *personally*, but the artist in you, the man who sets this violence down in such pitiless detail—in him, I detect no feeling whatever for the sad, unfortunate victims of murder. And so the response you evoke from me is one of revulsion. I don't want to see the painting; I don't share the implied point of view. It repels me. Not the subject matter, but the attitude."

"You think they're pornographic."

"Your figures are too far away to be graphic. Too small to excite."

"Obscene, then."

"Not in the legal sense. They don't upset the general community the way they do me. Personally, I find them obscene, yes." Thorne said this with no animus whatever, as if they were discussing a Times Square movie. "Pardon me. I shouldn't talk to you this way. I always try to avoid it. But as it happens, I feel very strongly about your work, and so speak where I should be silent."

"Did you imagine you were doing me a kindness, by saying nothing in your review?"

"Possibly I spared you some pain, but that was not my concern. I didn't want to spoil the general trust of the review by launching into what could only have seemed an ill-timed fit of righteousness." The eloquent eyebrows came to rest. "I do hope I haven't spoiled your evening."

"No. That's not possible."

"If you'll excuse me, now, I'll—"

"Don't you think murder should be repulsive?"

"I do. But I look at your paintings, and I don't think you even know what murder *is.*"

Hood gave him a little bow. "Thank you for being so direct."

Thorne smiled briefly, and receded down the hall to replenish his empty glass.

Hood sat down in the front room, in a low-slung chair beneath a window. The noise of the party—the comings and goings, the shrieks of laughter—swirled far above his head like whitecaps curling miles above the head of a deep-sea diver. He found himself thinking of Nicholas Hood (1951–1986)—a minor artist whose work he used to know and admire, but admired no longer. A short, unimportant career.

Valerie Vale was coming toward him from the kitchen, a sexual princess in sweatshirt and jeans. She was saying something naïve; her arms were opening wide. Hood got up from his chair and darted away, like a fish.

FOUR

THE studio was dark, and cold as the street. Hood crossed the floor with hand outstretched until he banged into his work table. He felt for the lamp, switched it on. The bulb buzzed at him like a hornet.

He sat down in the little tent of light and looked in the drawer for the razor knife. He rolled up his sleeves, and set the cold blade against his wrist; his pulse was thumping like a tiny heart. He stroked it with the knife, drawing a dotted red line, but no blood escaped. When he stroked again the top layer of skin broke apart, stinging. Hood sucked in his breath with a sharp hiss. He raised the knife again, stared at his wrist, but knew he wasn't up to it.

"I need some anesthetic." He spoke out loud, then peered into the dark corners of the studio as if someone might be lurking there to catch him in this moment of cowardice.

The snow was already thick underfoot and still falling so heavily that it seemed to hang in the air like lace curtains. A car slithered to an ungainly stop as he crossed Hudson; a siren cried on a distant street. Gusts of wind blew snow into his eyes, froze his cheeks. He went into the Broome Street Café stamping the snow from his feet, wiping his face.

"Scotch, please." He drank it straight down. "Same again." The bartender poured the second drink, eyeing him. He presented Hood with a check.

"I have to pay now?"

"It's better if you do."

"I come here all the time—I live just around the corner."

"I don't know you."

Hood pulled out his money, nine dollars. "Keep it—I've enjoyed your company."

He was going to need more than two Scotches if he was going to kill himself. He wished he'd succeeded on the first try—it was humiliating to be a coward as well as a failure. Just three or four doses of whiskey, then he could face that knife. He wasn't at all afraid of death, but the pain was hard to take; he would cut his wrist before the night was out, if he could get enough to drink.

The bar was not as crowded as usual, no doubt because it was nearly two o'clock in the morning. Maybe it was not the ideal place to spend one's last night, but there was a kind of comfort in the subdued conversations, in the windows damp and opaque with steam. A large man in a fur coat and a cowboy hat kept saying, "Oh, Lordy! My Lordy!"

Someone was staring at him. Hood felt it on the back of his neck, and spun around on the barstool. At the far end of the bar, almost hidden by another stool, stood the hideous dwarf he had seen at the Novack show. There could be no mistaking that blistered face, the open sores. He was the ugliest being Hood had ever seen. The little man raised his glass at Hood, toasting him. Hood raised his glass in reply and silently they drank each other's health, like two gentlemen aboard the *Titanic*, Hood thought.

"Are you mad at me, or what?" Valerie Vale brushed snow from her hair. "Why'd you take off from the party like that?"

"I, uh, had something to do in the studio." Hood had trouble taking his eyes off the dwarf, finally managed to focus on Valerie's black friend. "Hello there, Bill."

The black man pursed his lips slightly, by way of greeting.

Valerie said, "I know why I bumped into you twice today. It's 'cause its' the fourteenth—two sevens. That's real lucky."

"Is it the fourteenth?"

"Guess by now it's the fifteenth."

Hood smiled without warmth. "How about that. It's my birthday."

"Oh! Happy Birthday!" She kissed him wetly on the cheek. "What's that you're drinking?"

"Scotch."

"Bill, honey—buy Nick a Scotch, will ya?"

Bill mumbled something, but moved closer to the bar. Another drink appeared in Hood's hand. Valerie had launched herself into an appallingly detailed description of her aims as an artist. Hood kept her going with a few nods and murmurs, but he was growing more distant by the minute.

All the faces in that smoky bar seemed to recede—faces made beautiful by yearning, by hunger for love, for fame and money, for goodness and an end to pain. Well, he would have his end to pain; it was approaching him now through the smoke and the night. A few pints of blood on the studio floor, and love and fame, money and tears would vanish. Already, they were distant cries—sounds of a faraway battle, an abandoned war.

The man in the corner wanted nothing; the ugly face held no hint of desire, and this seeming repleteness attracted Hood. He excused himself from Valerie and her sullen consort, and made his way toward this exemplar of contentment in a wanting world. "I want to buy you a drink," Hood told him.

The man looked up at Hood, his red eyes saying nothing.

"But I don't have any money."

The man looked away, bored.

"Don't go away. I have to get some money first, and then I want to talk to you. I feel I should buy you something first, even if it's only a drink."

Hood left the bar and hurried outside into a scene from a postcard Christmas. The snow had stopped falling, and lay silent and glittering under the streetlights. A grubby white moon skimmed over the city, trailing a wisp of cloud. Hood tramped impatiently through the drifts toward home. The old freight elevator, when he got there, seemed to take forever to haul him upward.

He tiptoed through the apartment by the light from the kitchen stove. He peered into the bedroom and saw Susan's sleeping form outlined on the bed, her back to him. Hood did not think of her as vulnerable, usually, but she looked vulnerable now.

He went to the kitchen, where a clock said three-fifteen. He opened a coffee tin, and pulled out a handful of bills. He counted out three hundred in fifties, and put the rest back.

An odd, stray thought formed as he moved soundlessly to the front door. He saw himself as if he were a picture in a collection of slides, and heard himself saying, "Here's me—a thief in my own home. It was cold that night! It was my birthday, I remember—I was a little short of cash. Later on, I killed myself."

He half ran back to the café, anxious to get there before the short man left. They had something going, Hood thought—he'd be a good man to spend his last hours with. He could get extremely drunk with no fear that the man would try to take care of him. They would share the blessed apathy of chance acquaintance.

Hood pushed past the man in the fur coat and cowboy hat, who was still parked just inside the door, exclaiming, "My Lordy! Oh, Lordy!" Valerie called out, "We thought we'd lost you!" But Hood wanted no part of her; he was all for the little beacon at the end of the bar.

"Bartender. I need another Scotch—and whatever that small blond man is drinking."

The bartender made an elaborate show of boredom. "I can't serve you—you're too drunk."

"I'm not drunk, you idiot. Besides which, today is my birthday, and if I choose to get drunk it's none of your business."

"It's against the law for me to serve you. You appear to be intoxicated." He said this by rote, like a cop.

Hood stood on the brass rail and leaned way over the bar. "I will have a Scotch. And a drink for him. Now."

"'Fraid not, buddy. You're cut off."

"And a drink for everyone else in here!"

"Get off the bar, asshole."

A silken voice intervened, almost shining like those bars of light in biblical illustrations. "Hold it now. Why all this noise? What is the gentleman's pleasure?"

He had not spoken loudly, but the dwarf's voice had a thrilling, seductive power. The bartender suddenly looked as fake as a Segal sculpture—a plaster figure surrounded by props from a world more real than he. He blinked at the blond man, who was now beside Hood, waist high. "You may serve my friend without fear. I assume full responsibility. And there will be significant profit in the transaction for all concerned—not least of all, your employer."

The bartender poured out a Scotch and a vodka. Hood laid out three fifties on the bar. "And one for everyone else." He turned to the stranger and raised his glass. "Thank you."

"You bought the drinks." Again the seductive voice, the rough pleasing texture between satin and silk. Hood judged the man to be about forty, but it was hard to tell with the face so destroyed by ancient infections. Hood was in awe of such ugliness, and the fearlessness it implied.

Hood said, "You were at the Novack on opening night."

"Yes, indeed. I saw you there." The voice was caressing Hood, soothing him. "A strange sort of meeting, is it not?"

Hood was too wrapped in the sound of the words to reply to their content.

"I know you so much better than you know me."

Hood shuddered. "How is that possible?"

"It's obvious. I've seen your work. Your paintings."

"They won't tell you anything."

"On the contrary. It was like snooping through the passport of your soul. One sees all the visas, the entry and exit stamps—a mark for every station on your travels. A fascinating document."

"I never go anywhere."

"Farther than most. But your paintings are beautiful, quite aside from any biographical import. The paintings themselves are remarkable."

"How many did you buy?"

"Is that intended to be rude?"

"I just can't figure out why you came to me."

"I didn't. You came to me."

Hood closed his eyes and tried to remember. He had the clear impression that the fellow had reached out to him. But it was true: Hood had crossed the room to offer him a drink. "Say something," he said, his eyes still shut.

"I want to help you, but you must make a choice: Before I say anything more, I must be sure you want to hear it—if you would rather I remain silent, say so—because what I have to say will change your life forever."

Hood opened his eyes and made a gesture with palms up. "Speak."

The man raised a finger in warning. "Think carefully, Mr. Hood. I said *forever*. Suppose you wish I'd never spoken? You may not like the way things change."

He had been in utter despair, ready to end his life. Any change, Hood reasoned, could only be an improvement. He leaned forward and looked deeply into the man's glittering, red-rimmed eyes and whispered, "I'm yours."

"Excellent! Your work deserves much more attention than it has so far received, and I can get you noticed."

"Are you a dealer? You have a gallery?"

The man shook his head.

"Are you some kind of agent?"

The man threw back his blond head and laughed. His mouth opened, showing rows of jagged teeth, but no sound came out.

"You *are* an agent."

"If you like. Let's just say I get people where they want to go. Smooth the way, so to speak."

"I'm already represented. Sherri Novack has been handling my work for some time."

"Mm. With a notable lack of success. But I'm not suggesting you switch galleries. All I'm saying is that I can help you. I *know* I can help you."

The man's words were as appealing to Hood as the rasp of his voice. He ordered another drink from the bartender, meeting no resistance this time, and added another fifty to the change on the bar. He tried to hand another vodka to his new friend, but the drink was declined with a gesture. Hood put the drink aside and said, "You know a lot of rich people, is that it?"

"I know a lot of rich people. Some of them well. But not just rich people—I have connections everywhere. I am also psychic. I tend to know what people will do before they do it."

"In that case, you should play the stock market."

"Doesn't interest me." He pointed a small, clawlike finger at the man near the door—the one in the fur coat and cowboy hat. "You see that man over there? That man will die within the hour."

Hood said, "I don't care."

"Why should you? Nevertheless, the fact that his incipient demise is visible to me might interest you. His life is unreeling like a spool of thread—I can see the approaching end."

Hood had never had the slightest interest in occult matters, but he played along. "Don't you have to go into a trance? Get in touch with the Other World?"

The man smiled. "It isn't something one slips in and out of. I am in *constant* touch with the other world, because it isn't, in fact, another world."

Hood finished his Scotch, and started in on the man's rejected vodka. He jabbed a finger into the man's shoulder. "I'll tell you one thing: You have the most beautiful voice I've ever heard. You should make records."

The man displayed his silent laugh, the pointed teeth.

Valerie Vale came over to them. The stranger seemed totally oblivious to her perfect breasts, which were about level with his eyes. "Excuse me, Nick?"

"Yes, my dear."

"Um, me and Bill are gonna go over to CBGB's and wondered if you wanna come along."

"No, thank you. I have some business to—"

"Okay, sure. Just asking." Her voice went small. "You take care now."

"Right." He watched her enfolded under the dark wing of Bill Lennox. She called over, "Hey! Thanks for the drinks!"

Hood gave her a little salute.

"You like her."

"Not her. Her body."

"The two of you look good together. As if you belong."

Hood lapsed into a silence, drinking another drink. He knew he couldn't make that last trip to the studio; he knew he couldn't face that knife. He was no longer sure he wanted to kill himself.

A blast of cold air slammed into the room, and a woman burst in, scarf flying, hands flapping up and down like little wings. "Someone call an ambulance! Call an ambulance! Where's the fucking phone!" No one in the bar moved. She turned around in a tight, hysterical circle. "I hit a guy! He came outa nowhere, right in front! Call a fucking ambulance!"

The bartender finally came to life and picked up the phone.

Several patrons rushed to the exit; others wiped clear circles in the steamy windows. The woman flapped her arms, opening and closing her mouth like a gull. Behind her, the corner was empty.

"He's gone," Hood said.

The short man showed neither surprise nor concern.

"It can't be him."

"Why not satisfy your curiosity? Go and take a look."

Hood ran past the distraught woman and outside. A small group of people stood shivering at the corner, where a bright yellow Toyota had spun completely around, its back wheels up on the sidewalk. Next to the gutter, a man lay dead—there was no possible doubt. He looked like a rolled-up carpet of blood and fur, from which an arm and leg stuck out like the broken branches of a swastika. A cowboy hat lay upside down, nearby. A woman was sobbing, and the words "He's dead" were passed in relay through the crowd.

The stranger appeared beside Hood, leaning on his walking stick. Hood whirled on him. "Why didn't you warn him! You saw it coming!"

"Nothing in this world could have prevented his death."

"You just let him die! You didn't make the slightest effort to give him a chance!"

"Will you walk with me a little? I live up that way." He pointed his cane to the north. "I don't blame you, if you're frightened."

Hood didn't move.

"Very well. But please remember I didn't *cause* any of this." The man turned away from him and started to limp across Broome Street. Hood stayed, trembling on the corner.

An ambulance came wailing around from Sixth Avenue. Two paramedics climbed out and rushed to the dead man. Hood watched them make efficient but futile efforts to save him. When a police car pulled up, he ran across the street and caught up with

the stranger who was hobbling up West Broadway. Hood slowed
to his pace, saying nothing.

"I'm sorry if I scared you." That strange, sandpaper voice.
"You of course don't believe in psychic powers."

"I don't think about them one way or the other. I've never had
any reason."

"It's the sort of thing you get used to."

"How? How can you get used to a thing like that? It's
horrific!"

"Perhaps you need another drink. Is there any place still
open?"

"I'm all right. I'll just walk for a while."

"If you want to be alone, say so. I've no wish to intrude on
your solitude."

"Don't worry. I spend too much time alone, as it is."

Despite the death they had witnessed, the night was calm
and pleasant. It was warmer now, though not warm enough to
melt the snow, and the streets were quiet and empty. A Yellow
cab hissed by them, hoping for a fare. They didn't speak
again until they reached Washington Square. The drug dealers
had gone, and the graffiti-scarred arch was covered in snow. The
little park looked as it must have in a time more civilized than
Hood's.

He said, "I should have brought my camera."

"What for?"

"I use it to record pieces of architecture."

They continued up Fifth, into lower midtown. Hood was
reminded of Susan when they passed the dark windows of a
discount store where she liked to shop for dresses. He remembered the image of her sleeping, her back to him, but banished
the thought from his mind. They passed the public library at
Forty-second Street, its twin lions made foolish by white topping.
Hood said, "I don't even know your name."

"Bellisle. Andre Bellisle."

"Is that French?"

Bellisle showed a ridge of teeth. "Originally."

Hood wondered why he wasn't feeling sick from the drinks, tired and used up. Somehow, in Bellisle's placid company he felt peaceful. The man was a mystery he felt no compulsion to solve. He felt little desire to ask questions, little desire at all.

Bellisle led him into Rockefeller Plaza, past the golden Prometheus, thief of fire, at the foot of the RCA Building. They stopped at a Fiftieth Street entrance. "There is a rather good view from the rooftop. Perhaps you are familiar with it."

"No," Hood said. "Anyway, it's not open."

A security guard appeared on the other side of the glass doors. He looked surprised to see anyone standing there, then suspicious. But then he suddenly smiled at Bellisle, lifted his hand in greeting, and unlocked the door. Bellisle thanked him as they stepped inside. "We'll just be going up for a little while."

The guard beamed. "Sure thing, sir. Just let me know if you need anything. You just buzz down."

Hood followed Bellisle into a massive, gleaming elevator, and watched him press the top button with his walking stick. In a moment they were shooting skyward, though Hood had the distinct sensation he was tumbling through the earth. He managed to say, "You must work here, or something."

Bellisle shook his head. "I told you. I have a lot of connections."

They got out at the top level, and Bellisle opened a door to the outside. The roof was a perfectly white rectangle, onto which Hood stepped with some fear. It was like treading among mountaintops. If the Himalayas were the roof of the world, this must be the roof of New York City. The Empire State Building, twenty blocks south, was only an equal here—a landmark among hundreds of concrete peaks. "My God," Hood said.

Bellisle produced a key from his pocket, and opened a gate in the fence, motioning Hood toward a chest-high wall. "Are you afraid of heights?"

"Not before now." There was a strong wind up here; Hood gripped the wall to steady himself. Below him the lights of the city blazed in brilliant clusters, like tiaras and bracelets scattered on white cotton. Everything was out of scale and the eye, no matter where it looked, was confronted by bizarre proportions. It was indeed "a rather good view."

They went back indoors and along a corridor. Then Bellisle led him into the Rainbow Room, an acre of restaurant surrounded on three sides by windows. Hood quickly sat down with his back to the view. Bellisle fetched a bottle and glass from behind the bar and set them before Hood, then sat down across from him.

Hood poured himself a drink. "How is it you have the run of the place at this ungodly hour?"

"I can pretty much come and go as I like—but I hope you're not going to ask a lot of questions. We're here to talk about you, Mr. Hood. You're much more interesting than I—particularly your future."

"Is that why the view from the mountain? Some day, my son, all this will be yours?"

"Accuse me of cliché, if you like. All true stories are old stories."

Hood wondered where Bellisle was from. He had pronounced "cliché" in the British manner, accent on the first syllable, but he didn't seem English. But he was not to ask questions. "You assume I have a future."

"Indeed. You wanted to dispense with it this evening—by the razor express."

Hood froze, his glass in midair. "How did you know that?"

"Doesn't matter. You have since decided otherwise, am I right?"

Hood thought a minute, turning his glass in the light from a chandelier. "Things don't feel as bleak as they did. But who knows? I don't want to go on painting in a closet."

"Nor should you." Bellisle leaned forward, speaking warmly. "There is a time for these things to come to fruition. Your time is now. I said I want to help you. And I can."

"Help me how? Why?"

"The 'how' is simple: I can give you . . . opportunities. Opportunities beyond your reach. What form these opportunities take you will learn soon enough."

"I'm asking now."

"I understand your impatience, but I will not indulge it. As to the 'why': The answer is, because I want to."

"What's in it for you? Sherri already gets fifty percent of everything I sell."

"I don't want your money!" Bellisle sat back in his chair, which was far too big for him. "I want you!"

"If it's sex you're after, you've come to the wrong guy."

"Mr. Hood, I am not homosexual. And when I tell you to keep your money, it means exactly that. Do I look in need of cash?"

Hood saw the black velvet, white silk, the accents of gold watch and cuff links. "No."

"Do I look at you with lust? Am I leering? Does my tongue hang out?"

"You seem highly excited, frankly. I don't know what it's about."

"Not sex—the very idea is laughable. Your *work* excites me. The prospect of making you famous excites me. It's entirely within our power. The only question is whether you really want it."

"Oh, I want it." Hood finished his Scotch, poured himself another.

"Then permit me a few remarks on your work."

"Go ahead—I'm ready."

Bellisle looked away from him, across the mauve room, the white tables. "It's as if you've traveled down a long corridor, at the end of which you reach an iron door. On the other side of this door? Freedom. Your subject matter takes you the length of the corridor; your technique is your ticket of admission to the other side. Yet you hold back. There is beauty in your work but little power. You take the bold step of tackling an unpleasant theme, but then you turn prim—you go all cool and shy. It is here that your technique works against you."

"Do you know how hard it is to do what I do?"

"I talk of effects, not methods, and the effect is cold. Your figures are so distant, one feels nothing for them. People cannot get involved in your paintings. If you were making a movie, would you not draw close, in a climactic scene? Instead, you hang back, breathless and afraid, as if death were a holy thing. Death is a bodily function, like any other."

"Except it occurs only once in a lifetime."

"All the more reason to close in! Anyone can consider violence from a distance. It takes an extraordinary man to stare it in the face."

"You're forgetting the thought behind my painting."

"Oh, please! We're talking about surfaces! Effects! I don't care what goes on before; I don't care what happens underneath. In art, your surface is everything. It's all you control. You stand on one side of a mirror, looking out, your audience on the other, peering in. And neither sees the other, except in bad art. In *real* art, the one *suspects* the other, but the conscious attention remains on the image, your surface."

"That is bullshit—pure, unadulterated—"

"Let me finish—I shan't go over this again. Can you tell me why, why your work is so relentlessly cold?"

"It's intended, you fool!"

Bellisle jumped to his feet. Hood thought he was going to stomp out, but the hideous little man just lowered his head, as if counting to ten. He said quietly, "The picture you *intend* to paint means nothing." He moved closer to a window, staring out through his ugly reflection. "In the end, your work fails because you don't know what you're talking about. Everything you paint is outside your experience. It's no wonder people sense your shortcomings, even if they can't articulate them. You've never seen a murder."

"God forbid."

Bellisle shrieked, "WHY DO YOU SAY THAT!" The words nearly shook the walls, rattled the windows. He pushed a strand of blond hair from his forehead. "Murder is your subject. You will never get it right until you know what you're painting. This is so obvious it has completely escaped your notice."

Hood said, "You're shaking. Why don't you sit down—I don't want a shouting match. And suddenly I'm very tired."

Bellisle came back to the table, which was nearly at chest height. "Good. Think about it in your sleep, or whatever the expression is."

"Sleep on it."

"Just so, yes." He passed a hand over his face, as if he could straighten the ruined skin. "Like you, patience is not my strong point. Did I frighten you?"

"I've no interest in committing murder for the sake of research."

Bellisle's eyes flashed, and Hood feared another explosion, but the dwarf only sighed. "That isn't what I said."

"You make it sound like some kind of spectator sport."

"It often is." He moved away from the table.

Hood said, "Did I offend you?"

"All human beings offend me." He picked up his walking stick and turned toward the hall.

"Wait!" Hood stood up too fast. He had to grab the table for support, and the Rainbow Room circled his head like a carousel. From across the room, he heard the elevator doors open, and then Bellisle's rough-smooth voice calling, "Happy Birthday, Mr. Hood!"

FIVE

"I thought you'd never wake up," Susan said. "Happy Birthday!" She came into the room and sat on the bed beside him. "How does it feel to be thirty-five?"

Hood groaned. "Hasn't hit me yet." He closed his eyes and lay back; bits of the night flickered before him: Bellisle's face, the dead man in the snow, Valerie. He remembered the cold blade on his wrist.

"Open your eyes." Susan held out a present. It was slightly larger than a pack of cigarettes, wrapped in paper with a pattern of little tigers. Hood held the parcel to his ear and shook it.

"Come on, I want you to try it out."

Hood tore off the paper. It was a Sony Walkman, small enough to fit in a shirt pocket. "What a perfect present. I won't be at the mercy of Leo's cowboy music."

Susan handed him a cassette recording of Scarlatti sonatas. He put the headphones on, and took a minute to figure out the machine. Then a harpsichord sprang to life in his head, frisking about in Renaissance exuberance. "It's wonderful! Thank you!" Susan smiled, and kissed his forehead, then left the room to make him some breakfast.

The music was a high-spirited display of virtuosity, a dazzling performance, and yet . . . Hood began to feel uneasy. He remembered the night, recalled the sight of Susan's sleeping back, behind which he had stolen her money. There was no reason for her to look into the coffee tin this morning, but Bellisle's prescience had rubbed off, because he knew that she would. He switched off the Walkman, and got out of bed. He got dressed quickly, skipping the shower he knew he needed, because he didn't want to be naked, defending himself.

When she came into the room, her face was pale. "I'm missing three hundred dollars."

Hood fumbled with shirt buttons, his back toward her. "Isn't it in your purse?"

"I put it in the coffee tin. I didn't want to carry that much cash around."

"Maybe you put it in the wrong tin."

Her voice was thin and distracted. "The other tins . . . the other tins are full. I mean, I use them. They have flour and stuff in them."

"Oh. Well, I'm sure it'll turn up." He squeezed past her, and slipped into the bathroom. He ran the water in the sink, and listened for the sound of her walking away. She didn't move; she must know it was him. He turned off the water, and opened the door. "I borrowed some money, actually, now that I think of it. Last night. When you were sleeping. I would've asked, but I didn't want to wake you up."

She squinted at him, a deep crease forming between her eyebrows. Hood pulled some grubby bills from his pocket and held them out to her, but she made no move to take them. He counted it out—four twenties and several smaller bills. "There's ninety-two dollars here." He reached past her and placed it on the dresser beside the yellow Walkman. "I owe you two hundred and eight dollars."

Susan stepped back when he reached across, as if to avoid being touched by him. "That's great. How am I supposed to make the rent now? What do I do—take it out of my savings?"

"You'll have it back before the end of the month."

Her voice was flat, numb. "What did you spend it on?"

"Actually, I think I lost some in the bar. I didn't realize I'd taken that much and I must've dropped some. I bought a few drinks, I know that."

"A few drinks. There's two hundred dollars gone."

"I know. I'm sorry. I can't—I must've lost it. I had an awful lot to drink."

"Oh, that makes it all right, then—I mean, if you were drunk."

Hood could count the number of times she had been angry with him on one hand, never without cause. Unlike himself, she was not given to irritable moods, fits of unreasonableness. "Look," he said. "Why don't you take the Walkman back, and get a refund. That should just about—"

"That was a present. I'm not taking it back." She turned away and went down the hall.

Hood followed her slowly, and watched her sit down at the harpsichord, where she began thundering out a series of scales. He went over and placed his hands on her shoulders. Susan struck out blindly with the back of her hand. The blow caught him in the solar plexus; pain seeped through his belly like dye. Amazing how much she could hurt him, without intending to.

The sun was pale and watery; the snow lay gray and soggy on the streets. Everything, from the soot-streaked cars to the cast-iron buildings with their filigree of rust, looked ready for the junkyard. Hood stopped into a news vendor's and picked up a copy of *Artforum*. But when he went to pay for it, he found no money in his pockets.

Leo was working in his corner, and didn't look up when Hood entered the studio. The thought of painting made Hood want to retch, so he started tidying up his half of the studio. He cleared off the worktable, put the razor knife away, and set his paints and brushes in order. The canvas he had smeared with paint was stuck to the floor, and left a tacky patch when he ripped it upward. He got down on hands and knees and scraped the black sludge from the floorboards.

"It's a cleaning lady you've become, I see." Leo was behind him now, bending over to stretch the kinks out of his back.

"Actually, I've turned into an asshole."

"Hmph. Quite an image."

"I had a fight with Susan." Hood set his easel back in place.

"Tsk, tsk. What did you do to cause this?" There would be no sympathy from Leo, clearly.

"I borrowed some money without asking."

"I can lend you some money. Thirty or forty dollars, if you need." That would probably empty his bank account.

"Thanks. I don't think it would help."

"Well, it's there, if you want it." Leo sat down again to work. Hood went to stand by the window, looking down on the docks. He listened for a time to the whisper of Leo's brush; then he said, "I met a very strange man last night."

"Oh?"

"Maybe I shouldn't even tell you about him."

"Everybody's strange. To me, at least."

"Not like this guy. He can see the future."

"Oh. *Ja?*"

"I don't mean he *claims* to see the future. He sees it—as clearly as you or I see the past. He gave me a demonstration."

"Bending spoons, was he?"

Hood told him about the man in the cowboy hat—the sudden, foreseen death.

Leo put his brush down, and looked at Hood. "That is damn scary, Nicholas."

"He knew it was my birthday, without my telling him. And my name. He could have picked those up at the gallery—he was there on opening night. He also knows this address."

"He does? You didn't tell him?"

"No. And he's outside, right now."

Leo looked out the window. At the end of the pier stood

Andre Bellisle, a dark Rorschach against the pewter Hudson. "The ugly little bastard with the cane? The way he's standing, he looks like a man with an appointment."

"I don't want to see him. If I hadn't met him, I wouldn't have taken that money from Susan."

"Ha! The devil made you do it!"

"He didn't *make* me do anything. But there's something . . . wrong about him."

As if to encourage further speculation, Bellisle turned slightly and gave them a better view of his face. Leo pointed. "My *Gott*, he's ugly! And phony, too! He looks like an actor—playing *Phantom of the Opera*, or something! Why waste your time with such a fellow?"

"He said he could help me—get my work seen by the right people, et cetera. He's not a dealer. I don't know what he is."

"If he can help, fine." Leo sat once more at his easel. "But don't waste your energy."

"I don't think I should even see him again."

Bellisle turned from the water and headed toward the building. Hood thought he would come straight up the stairs, but he stepped around an iron barrier and started walking away. Let him go, Hood thought, let him go. But he pushed the window open, and called out, "Bellisle!"

Leo swiveled around. "Shut the window!"

Hood called out again. Bellisle came back and stood below the window, where he saluted Hood with his cane. Hood invited him in.

"You're sure I'm not disturbing you?" he said, when Hood opened the door. The torn-silk voice had lost none of its seductive power.

"Not at all—I was just tidying up. Will you have coffee?"

"If it's no trouble, yes. Delightful."

Hood took his coat. Underneath, Bellisle was wearing the

black velvet getup of the night before. "Perhaps your friend would prefer not to have visitors."

Hood looked over at Leo, who was resolutely concentrating on his work. "It's all right. As long as we're quiet."

"Leo Forstadt, if I'm not mistaken." Bellisle kept his voice low.

"Yes. We've been sharing this space for a couple of years."

When he had made the coffee, Hood led him over to his side of the studio, where he pulled out his sketchbook. "These are things I might do. Haven't decided yet."

Bellisle flipped through it quickly. "Your standard product, I see."

"Pardon me?"

"Nothing really new in there."

Hood took the sketchbook, and turned to a drawing of two Puerto Rican hoodlums circling each other with knives. Dark faces floated in the background. He handed it back to Bellisle, who put it on the table without looking. "Have you thought any more about my offer?"

"Aren't you going to look at it?"

"Don't evade me."

"Frankly, I don't understand your offer. You get my work to the right people, and I do nothing."

"You will do many things. It's not a simple agent-client relationship."

"We should get it in writing then—before there are any more misunderstandings."

Bellisle opened his mouth in his silent laugh. "If it has to be in writing, Mr. Hood, it's not worth having."

Hood didn't know what to say.

Bellisle shifted slightly, turning his back to the window light. "The relationship that will develop, if it does develop, will be a matter of choosing all the time, not of a brief signature. Things will be required of you—not for *my* sake, but for the sake of your future. I cannot make it any plainer than that. The truth is, the relationship will become clear only when it has developed."

"No contract."

"No written contract."

"No verbal agreement?"

"About what?"

Hood fell silent. He was drifting on the edge of gloom; the man's face was so hard to take. Bellisle suddenly smiled. "You should be happy! Since there is no contract, you can back out of it any time you like!"

"Suppose you sell all my work, and then I want out?"

"Then you shall be out."

"There has to be a catch somewhere."

"No contract, no fine print—how can there be a catch?"

"Either you can't do what you say, or you'll—"

"Oh, but I can. I will."

"Or you'll do it and then demand some exorbitant fee."

"On what possible ground? Really, I had no idea you would be so cynical. In my experience, artists are a trusting lot."

"*Young* artists. I've been around the block."

"I find it quite tiring." Bellisle put the back of his hand to his forehead and pretended to swoon. The gesture was so out of place that Hood laughed out loud. He pushed the sketchbook back to Bellisle, who glanced at it. "What is it—*West Side Story?*"

"Look at the movement in the two figures! Don't you think it shows—"

"It's fine. You draw very well." The tone was dismissive.

Hood turned a few pages and stopped at the scene of a killing in a corner store. A thief with a stocking over his face was shooting a man behind the counter. Blood gushed up from a chest wound, so that the victim's face was also hidden. Hood said, "This might have some impact, when it has color."

"It's a good idea."

"But?"

"But it doesn't add anything to what you've already done. There's no development, no movement. You're treading water. I agree it's as good as anything you've done. Not a negligible thing."

"Christ."

"If I thought you were going along perfectly well, I would never have made an offer. The reason we are together is because I can help you. These drawings confirm it."

"What about this?" Hood thrust out a drawing of suicide by hanging. In an angular, suffocating room, a single tormented figure dangled among sparse details.

"Same again."

"And this?" A domestic dispute. A muscular man, a shotgun exploding, a fat woman surprised as the rage in her belly became death.

"Good." Bellisle conveyed no pleasure with the word. Hood pulled the sketchbook away and tossed it into the trash can where it landed with a clang.

"What the hell is going on here!" Leo had come around the partition, sounding very German. He looked from Bellisle to Hood. "You're throwing out your work now?"

"I'm going to do something different."

"You treat your work like garbage? Like trash? What's wrong with you!" Leo reached into the can and retrieved the sketchbook. "This is not something you toss out like moldy bread."

"They're all wrong, Leo."

"So, now you bury your mistakes? You used to learn from them."

Bellisle spoke. "Perhaps I should be going . . ."

Leo thrust his chin out at him. "Yes, I think so. Why do you come to tell the man his work his garbage! Who do you think you are!"

"I invited Mr. Bellisle to come in," Hood said. "I also invited his opinion."

"Whose opinion could be so important?"

"Leo, go back to work."

"Who can work! Malicious bullshit floating around. I was going to leave, but why should I? I make things in here. This man does nothing but spit."

Bellisle got up. "Mr. Forstadt, I apologize. I had no idea we were disturbing you so profoundly." His red eyes glittered. "Please forgive the intrusion."

The elegance of the apology made Leo even angrier. He pulled Bellisle's cloak from its hook on the wall and threw it at him. "Get the hell from here. Don't come back."

Hood stepped in front of Leo. "You have no right to talk to my friend that way!"

"A friend it is! He has you throwing out your sketches, your thoughts, your ideas, and this is a friend! Pity you!"

"Shut up, Leo!"

Leo stood there, his nostrils flaring, breathing hard. Then he turned his back on them and went to his easel.

Bellisle picked up his walking stick. "Really, Nick—I'm sorry."

"It's all right. It's not your fault."

"I upset a lot of people, I'm afraid." He pointed the cane at a dusty Nikon on a shelf, and said, "That thing will come in handy, if things go the way they should."

"I've been meaning to clean it off, now that spring's coming."

"Spring is indeed coming. And by the way"—he buttoned his coat—"I've already got things moving for you. You should see some results very soon. Possibly this afternoon."

Hood opened the door for him. "How did you know my studio was here?"

"Not worth mentioning. See you again, I hope."

Hood closed the door, and turned to Leo. "I've never seen

you jump on anyone like that before—it was disgusting."

"What is he—some rich, ugly asshole who thinks he knows everything. You can still feel him in the room—it's like a terrible smell."

"You're being ridiculous."

"Maybe. It's *your* work in the garbage, however."

Hood opened the sketchbook to the hanging man. The loneliness, the sheer despair of the scene reached out. The picture was about subjects not included in the frame—foremost among them, love. Yes, it was wrong to throw it away, but it was he, and not Bellisle, who had done that. Suicide. A gob of spit in the eye of the world. He had been at that point—balanced on a cliff edge, about to jump—and Bellisle had saved him. Hood no longer wanted to end his life; he wanted to change it.

He spent the rest of the afternoon cleaning the camera, and left the studio about four o'clock. He didn't want to face Susan, so he turned uptown, toward the gallery. When he got there, Marcia sprang up from behind her desk and beckoned him to follow her to Sherri's office. Sherri was concluding a conversation on the phone with her usual jocose series of threats. She motioned excitedly for Hood to sit down, and a moment later slammed down the phone. "Where the hell have you been?"

"I was at the studio—"

"I just sent a messenger over there to get you!"

"He must've just missed me. I—"

"You've sold three paintings, petunia."

Hood laughed. "Petunia?"

"Didn't you hear me? I said three of your paintings are bought and paid for."

"Jesus Christ."

"Jesus Christ is right. Who've you been fucking?"

"I don't— You're sure about this? There's no mistake?"

"Honey, I wouldn't tell you about a nibble. I'm talking cash on the barrelhead. That was my bank on the phone. They've received wires crediting the gallery with"—she put on her half glasses and peered at a scratch pad—"twenty-four thousand dollars."

Hood flopped back in his chair. "I don't believe it."

"That ain't all, pigeon." She removed the glasses and jabbed them at him. "I got another one on the way, over thirty thousand dollars. Talked to the guy ten minutes ago—some baron in Lucerne. He's buying the big one out front. So you got roughly forty grand coming to ya, and honey it couldn't happen to a nicer guy or a better fucking artist. I'm over the goddam moon myself, and believe me Sherri Novack after twenty years in the business does not excite easily."

"God, Sherri—how did you come up with all this?"

"Honey, I wish I could take responsibility, but the truth is I never set eyes on these guys. I mean, we got the baron—he's a fucking scream—right out of the movies. And there's an oil guy from Texas—Baxter Millwright the Third, if you can believe that. And the other one's a banker in Paris."

Hood thought for a moment. "It's so different from what I expected. Oilmen, bankers . . . people like that don't buy a lot of art, do they?"

"People with *money* buy art. You want to wait till some poet makes an offer? I can send the money back, and—"

"No thanks!" He gave a nervous little laugh. "I just always thought it would happen differently."

Sherri shrugged. "Happens different ways for different artists—it's one a the things keeps it interesting."

"But aren't you curious about these people? Don't you wonder how they got on to me?"

"What's with you! You want me to run a Standard and Poor's on 'em? The money came through, all right? I'm not gonna ask 'em if they really meant it!" The telephone rang, and she snatched it up. She listened a moment, then said, "Tell him I'll call back."

Hood sat forward in his chair. "Well, I guess it's obvious you met Andre Bellisle."

"Met who?" Her plump face creased like dough.

"Andre Bellisle—short, blond guy. Ugly as sin."

"Never heard of him. What is he?"

"He's interested in my work. Says he has all sorts of connections, and—"

She tapped the scratch pad. "This is not him. Guys like that'll talk ya to death. Take it from me, doll, sincerity is money." She reached into the desk drawer and pulled out some stickers marked SOLD.

Hood followed her out of the office and down the hall to the alcove where his smallest picture hung. He recognized the compact man standing before it—the grubby raincoat and the checkered pants. Hood said hello.

"We meet again! I couldn't get enough of this guy. Had to come back for a second look."

"I'm glad."

Sherri reached in front of the man and replaced the price tag with one of the stickers. Hood said, "I don't see how this adds up to fifty thousand dollars."

"Easy, sweethot. After the first one sold, this one became worth a lot more."

The raincoat man rubbed the clearing on top of his head. "Wait a sec! Are you this guy Hood?"

"Yes, I am."

"Hah! And here I was raving on about your stuff the other day and the whole time I didn't even realize I was talking to the man himself!" He stuck out a hairy hand. "Glad to know you, Mr. Hood. Gary Lauzon, kinda like ozone with an el." He cocked his head at Sherri. "Guy's a real artist here."

"He wouldn't be here if he wasn't." She said to Hood, "I'm gonna leave the others till the wire comes through. Don't wanna jinx the deal or nothin'." She waddled off down the hall, leaving Hood with Lauzon.

"Prices like these, you must make a hell of a living."

"It doesn't happen very often."

"Well, you deserve a lot, in my opinion—not that I know anything."

"Thank you. Excuse me, I have to—"

"Oh, sure, I know you're busy."

Hood left Lauzon and rejoined Sherri in the office. She wrote him out a check for twelve thousand dollars, tore it off, and handed it across the desk as if it were a ten-cent stamp. "*Mazel tov.*"

"Actually, um, I'm a little short of hard cash at the moment."

"Say no more." She swiveled around and fiddled with the combination on the safe behind her desk. She removed a cashbox, opened it, and counted out five hundred dollars. "Have to gimme a receipt for that. We'll put it against the next one." She handed him a receipt book, and Hood filled out a slip.

When he had signed it, she said, "Not bad for a day's work, huh?"

"Not bad at all."

"Now you gotta haul ass outa here. I got calls to make."

"Sherri. Thank you very much."

"Oh, no sir! Thank *you*!" And she bowed deeply, mocking him.

Lauzon hailed him as he was about to go outside. "Mr. Hood! Let me buy you dinner! I gotta go back to the shop later, so I was about to stop off for a quick bite."

Hood was quite taken aback. "I don't know, I—"

"I saw a sign once! 'Support the arts, take a painter to lunch.' I'd hate to miss the opportunity."

"It's very kind of you, but I should be getting home."

"Okay—another time, then." He held open the door as if Hood were a visiting dignitary. "Which way you going?"

Hood pointed toward Broome Street.

"Me too. Greek place I always go for lunch." Unlike most New Yorkers, Lauzon was not a fast walker. He strolled as if they were touring the main street of a small town, shooting the breeze. "Art is just the latest thing I got into. Not that I plan to become an artist, or anything. I just suddenly realized there's a whole new world out there I know nothing about—just waiting for me. I'm taking this art history course once a week. Fascinating. Fascinating."

"I don't imagine there are many cops in the class."

Lauzon barked out a short laugh. "Dead right. Did you know—when a kid wants to become a cop they give him an aptitude test with a couple of questions about Shakespeare and Michelangelo. The story is, if you answer them correctly, you don't get in."

It was Hood's turn to laugh.

"Makes sense! How is a guy who knows all that going to fit in with a bunch of flatfeet from Flatbush? He's going to be severely depressed! I gotta say, I envy you. Must be a relaxing line of work, sloshing paint around."

Hood was taking baby steps in an effort to stay beside Lauzon, when more than anything he wanted to run home and tell Susan about his sudden wealth. He said, "Painting may be a relaxing hobby; it's not a relaxing life."

"Huh! You should try homicide!"

"Homicide? You're a detective?"

"Ten years this month."

"You must've had some interesting cases."

"Not many mysteries, if that's what you mean. Most times, the guy's standing there with the gun in his hand, crying. Almost always know who did it within three hours. If not, you have a serious problem."

"I thought police files were full of unsolved cases."

"Unsolved means unprovable, usually—not enough evidence, too many liars for an alibi, et cetera. It's not as dull as I make it sound, but it's not like in the movies. Don't get me wrong"—he raised a finger in warning—"I like my work. It just leaves a few gaps—particularly in the intellectual arenas."

Hood sized up this compact ball of energy. "So, you must be a tough guy, right?"

"A naïve observation, if I may say so. Think about it: In all likelihood, the first people a homicide cop is gonna talk to are the recently bereaved. Tact is required. Sensitivity. You gotta deal with the family, the medical examiner, the press, crazy people, social workers, you name it—can't have some gorilla going in. Toughness is not a high priority."

They reached Broome Street, and once again Hood shook the pudgy, ring-studded hand. "It's been a pleasure, Mr. Lauzon."

"Oh, hey—it's been an education." Lauzon's smile was big as a Times Square billboard.

A boy was beside Susan at the harpsichord, crying his eyes out. As Hood walked by toward the bedroom, he heard Susan speaking in that low, compassionate murmur she used to comfort others, primarily Hood himself. The boy looked about twelve years old, with little pointy shoulders that quivered as he cried. Hood undressed, and went into the bathroom to take the shower he'd skipped that morning.

When he came back to the front room later, buttoning his shirt, he was surprised to see the boy still sitting beside Susan. Damn it! Hood couldn't wait to tell her his good news, and here he was locked into some music therapy. He felt like telling the kid to beat it.

It felt good, however, to restore exactly two hundred and eight dollars to the coffee tin. He heard Susan saying the words "practice" and "scales." He wanted to yell out, "Money! Success!" He wanted to tap dance on the harpsichord, but instead he stood in the kitchen, tense, waiting for the kid to leave.

Finally, he heard the door open, and Susan was saying good-bye.

"My God," Hood said. "I thought he'd never leave!"

Susan folded up some music and slipped it into the bench. "You're not the only one in the world with problems," she said, and left the room. Hood followed her into the bedroom. This wasn't going the way he had imagined. Susan sat in front of the mirror, her brow creased with thought.

"Look," he said. "I have some news to tell you. I'm sorry if I seemed insensitive."

"You did."

"Please!" He raised his hands in surrender. "All I want is to take you out to dinner!"

"You want to spend sixty dollars in a restaurant? When I can't even make the rent? We can eat here." She started brushing her hair with angry swipes.

Hood sighed. "I've sold a couple of paintings."

"Oh?" Her interest was mild. She was no doubt remembering times when Hood had sold canvasses to fellow artists for as little as fifty dollars.

"You don't understand. Sherri has sold three of my pictures. Take a look at this." He unfolded the check and dropped it onto the dresser. "That's just for two of them. The third isn't even paid for yet."

Susan stopped brushing her hair and squinted at the check. "This is your money?"

Hood looked at her reflection, trying not to smile too widely. "And I've already replaced the money I borrowed. It's in the coffee tin."

"It's a lot of money," she said, and resumed brushing her hair.

"I know it doesn't make me virtuous, but the fact is I've paid you back the money, and we don't have to worry about the rent, and I want to take you out to dinner. Maybe you could start getting dressed while it sinks in." Frustration crept into his voice.

She looked up at him, and her face softened. "I'm sorry. But for some reason, I don't feel very happy about it. I guess it's so sudden, I just feel . . . confused."

"Susan, I've been painting for over fifteen years! This is not overnight success! Nothing has dropped from a clear blue sky! This is what I've been working for all these years, and it calls for a modest celebration."

"You're right. I'm just having a delayed reaction." She stood up and kissed him on the cheek, and said, "Congratulations." It was like being kissed by the mayor's wife. "Give me a few minutes," she said, and disappeared into the bathroom.

The telephone rang.

"That you, sweet pea?"

"Sherri. What's up?"

"The baron came through. We pulled down another thirty thousand bucks."

"Fabulous. Sherri, you're a phenomenon."

"Got nothin' to do with it. Have you been up to something I don't know about? Have you been humping some deposed princess, or what?"

Hood laughed.

"I mean it, twinkletoes. This is an unusual turn of events here. For someone in your position, this is un-fucking-heard-of. The more I think about it, the more I get the shivers. Something's going on."

"What do you mean, Sherri? What can be going on?"

"I don't know! That's what gives me the willies!"

Sherri Novack—for all her bluster—was cold-blooded and iron-nerved. Hearing her admit to fear made Hood uneasy; he wondered if he should elaborate about André Bellisle.

She plucked the thought from his head, her voice suddenly calm. "Who's this guy you mentioned today?"

"Andre Bellisle?"

"Yeah. Talk to me."

Hood told her about meeting Bellisle in the Broome Street Café. He didn't mention any psychic powers, jumping straight ahead to the proposed deal. ". . . Apparently, he liked my paintings and wanted to help me."

"What does that mean, may I ask?"

"That was my response, exactly. But don't worry—he's not a dealer. I told him I was already represented by you, and had no intentions of changing the arrangement."

"You done the right thing there, pal."

"He's very mysterious, frankly, and very ugly. But I believe he really wants to help, and he really has connections. He said he'd already made a start—that we should have some good news very soon."

"When did he say this?"

"This morning. He came to the studio."

"You saw him this morning."

"Sherri. He's not a dealer."

"So you said. You think he's spotting for the baron?"

"It wouldn't surprise me. He hasn't told me what his plans are, though, or who he knows. Maybe you should meet him."

"Rich guy?"

"Looks it."

"I should meet him."

Susan came out of the bathroom, wrapped in a towel. Hood wanted to end this conversation, which should have been so cheerful but was not. "I'll see if I can bring him round to the gallery. Don't forget—we don't *know* he had anything to do with this."

"What's his end?"

"Pardon me?"

"His *end*—what's he get outa this?"

"I don't know . . . personal satisfaction?"

A raucous laugh came over the line. "Sure honey!" The laugh had roused her bronchitis, and Hood waited out a series of hacks and barks that left her voice weak and intermittent, like a distant radio station. "Listen to me now. Ya listening?"

"I'm going out to dinner, Sherri. I—"

"I don't wanna think you're diddling around with other dealers behind my back, y'unnerstand?"

"Sherri—"

"Lemme finish. If you are fucking around with some other dealer, I will not take it lightly. I shouldn't have to remind you that we've shared some pretty lean years, and I will be up-fucking-set if you fly the coop. Do not, repeat, DO NOT fuck with your Aunt Sherri."

Hood was irritated, and wanted her to know it. "I told you about Bellisle right away. Don't let the first sign of interest get you paranoid."

"You angry now?"

"Frankly—"

"Don't be. I just want everything out in the open. No surprises down the line."

"Fine."

"Welcome to success, Mr. Hood. Cold up there?"

SIX

THEY had chosen a small French restaurant in the east Fifties, and Susan kept looking around at the formal decor, the solemn waiters, and the sheer Frenchness of the place, as if she were still a young girl fresh from Wisconsin. Hood ordered a white Burgundy, and they toasted his good fortune, and a future suddenly brighter. When the waiter came to take their order (he had a thick mustache and disapproving eyes), Hood chose an expensive veal dish, and Susan asked for a salad.

Hood knew he had been more than a little self-involved of late, so he made an effort to steer the conversation away from himself. He asked about the boy who had been crying at the harpsichord.

Susan thought for a moment. "Paul's difficult for me. He has a very good ear, and he's a quick sight-reader. He only needs to hear something once and he can do a very convincing job on it. Consequently, he never practices—his gifts turn out to be handicaps."

"I don't know how you can teach someone like that."

"He has all the gifts! And none of the joy of it! That's what I can't teach him."

"You can only do your best."

"I should have just become a nurse—something absolutely useful and uncomplicated. Music never stops judging you." She tossed her head, dismissing her life.

Hood leaned forward and touched her arm across the table. "There's nobody like you, Susan. You must be the most gentle, purest, best . . ."

"Of course, you don't go out much." She could never listen to praise without protest, and looked relieved that the waiter interrupted it by bringing their food.

Hood was feeling wonderful. Amazing what a little money could do—allowing wine, and a fancy meal, a reprieve from worry. He felt the fracture between them knitting itself together, the pain being borne away. Susan asked about the sale of his work, and Hood told her about the odd assortment of buyers. He mentioned Bellisle, and Sherri's suspicions, only briefly.

Susan gave him a quizzical look. "And none of these buyers was at the show? They haven't been to the gallery?"

"Not that I know of."

"They must've talked to someone who was there, then."

"Probably. Yes."

"Bellisle, right? The man who wanted to help you."

"Not necessarily. It could be someone else."

"Who else? You said Sherri doesn't even know them."

"I don't know."

"He said he had contacts. He was going to help. Why are you resisting the idea it was him?"

The waiter came to take their dessert order. Neither of them wanted dessert, so Hood ordered a cognac for himself and a Grand Marnier for Susan. When the waiter left, she said, "It seems you don't want to think this Bellisle character helped you."

"Maybe I don't. I've always envisioned people just seeing a painting, falling in love with it, and buying it on the spot. The idea of someone making a deal over international long-distance, sight unseen, sort of takes the—" He broke off, and stared over Susan's shoulder.

"What's wrong?"

"Bellisle."

"He's here?" She was too polite to turn and stare.

"Quite a coincidence, him showing up." Hood saw the ugly

Bellisle was accompanied by a tense-looking, gingery man dressed in a chalk-stripe suit. The maître d' clutched two menus, and led them through the dining room toward a private alcove on the far side. They had to pass by Hood's table, and as they did so, Bellisle gave him a barely perceptible nod.

"Jesus Christ."

"Guess he didn't see you."

"That was weird. Normally he's—he's rather gracious, almost courtly. I have to speak to him."

"Oh, don't get up. He's probably—"

But Hood was already on his feet, making his way over to the alcove.

Bellisle and his ginger-colored man were each surveying a menu—Bellisle without a trace of interest. When Hood approached he said, "Hello," in the cool tone a celebrity might adopt to discourage a persistent fan. The ginger man gave him an equally cool glance of appraisal, as if he were a mannikin in Bellisle's control.

"I, ah—" Hood was suddenly nervous. "I just wanted to thank you for . . . what you did."

Bellisle waved a languid, gloved hand. "The real work was yours. I did very little."

"I'd like to talk to you, if—"

"Another time, sir."

Hood rejoined Susan. "He didn't even bother to introduce me! It's so bizarre! First it's like he adopted me, and now he doesn't want to know me! It's ridiculous! I hope he's not going to start playing games."

"God, Nick—you sound jealous."

"And why should he show up just when we're here?"

"Stranger things have happened. Will you stop turning around?"

"It's just such a change! This morning he hung around the studio until I invited him in!"

"Susan rubbed her forehead and looked dejected. Hood knew he had forced the evening off the rails, but he was too upset to apologize. The ginger man went by their table then, toward the men's room. Bellisle was suddenly at their table, his disfigurement split by a smile. "Forgive me, Nicholas." That rough-smooth voice again.

Susan looked alarmed, shrinking back in her chair. Hood had forgotten how repulsive the man was on first sight, and he moved rapidly to cover her loss of poise with a swift introduction. "Andre, this is my wife Susan."

"An honor." Bellisle bowed slightly, his hands behind his back. Susan managed a faint smile—a trace of moon on an overcast night.

"I couldn't speak in front of the, er, gentleman. Business, you understand. I didn't want to divide my attention. That sounds pompous, doesn't it?"

"You were very frosty all of a sudden. And just when I wanted to thank you."

"The money came through, I take it?"

"It came through, all right. How did you know I'd be here?"

Bellisle looked irritated with the question, but covered it quickly. "I don't even know what the weather's going to be from one day to the next. Had I known you'd be here, I would've gone somewhere else—not to avoid your company, I hasten to add, but only to keep things . . . focused. Anything else is death." As if sensing the heaviness of the word, he turned to Susan and spoke gently. "Susan, I understand you are a musician?" Hood hadn't told him that; he watched her nervously twisting the ring on her finger.

"Yes. I play the harpsichord."

"How lovely. Are you a Bach enthusiast?"

"Very much so. Among others. Scarlatti, Rameau . . ."

"And Lully? D'Anglebert?"

"You know D'Anglebert? Not many people have heard of

him." She kept her face averted, an uncharacteristic posture for her.

Bellisle said, "I've been fortunate enough to know some very gifted musicians in my time. Piano, violin—but never a harpsichordist. I wonder why that is."

"They're a different breed." Hood spoke up, sensing Susan's discomfort.

"I believe it. You must excuse me now—mustn't let my, er, friend return to an empty table. I'm sorry if I appeared rude a moment ago—I wouldn't upset you for the world. So nice to have met you, Susan." With another small bow, he was gone.

Hood said, "Strange guy, don't you think? I find him fascinating."

Susan toyed with her coffee spoon. "I don't know why."

"What's wrong? You look pale." He touched her hand: it felt cold and clammy.

"I feel awful—terribly depressed all of a sudden." She put a hand to her forehead. "It's like someone is dying somewhere."

Her mood descended on the table like a pall, smothering them. Hood signaled the waiter for a check. Susan said, "Was he in an accident of some kind?"

"You mean his face?"

"I've never seen anything so ugly."

"Susan!"

"I'm sorry. He scared me, I think."

"Now you're depressed."

"I know! And I was so happy!"

Hood paid with two fifty-dollar bills. The tip was not as munificent as he had planned, because the celebration seemed to have lost its point; the atmosphere had turned funereal.

Hood sat up in the living room, after Susan had gone to bed, avoiding the contamination of her depression. Why did she have to go into a foul mood now? Why now? She'd been fine until Bellisle showed up; she was stone blind to his good qualities. Taking stock of his own feelings he found, where happiness should have been, only an absence of hunger, a hollow. He fell asleep on the couch.

He was awakened some time later by the ringing telephone. It must have rung a long time, because Susan was in the room answering it, her hair tangled from sleep. She rubbed one eye with her knuckles and held the phone out, waiting for Hood to take it. He got up stiffly. "Hello?"

"Are you awake?"

"No. What is it."

"You must come immediately. The Belair Hotel—Broadway and Ninety-fourth." Bellisle sounded breathless.

"I'm sleeping."

"Well, sleep if you want. You don't *have* to come—but this is one of the opportunities I promised you."

"What's going on?"

"I can't go into details, but if you get here fast enough you'll have your next painting. Broadway and Ninety-fourth. Bring your camera."

"It's at the studio."

"You should have time. Sorry to wake you, but I have no control over the timing of these things. You'll have to trust my judgment. Are you coming?"

"It's cold out there, and I'm half-asleep."

"It's up to you." Bellisle broke the connection. Hood put the phone down and rubbed the back of his neck.

"What does he want?" Susan was sitting on the arm of the couch. Her eyes were closed, and her voice was furry with sleep.

"He wants me to meet him uptown."

She opened her eyes. "At this hour? You're not going, are you?"

"No." He took her by the elbow, and helped her up from the couch. "Let's go to bed."

As Hood got undressed in the darkness of the bedroom, he wondered what Bellisle could be so excited about. Broadway and Ninety-fourth? The area was a mixture of old decay and new high-rises. A place like the Belair would be inhabited by struggling actors and Puerto Rican families. What was Bellisle doing there in the first place?

He got into bed beside Susan, and closed his eyes. Immediately, Bellisle's gargoyle face swam into view—"You'll have your next painting," he had said. Did he think of Hood as a welfare case? True, he hadn't finished a painting since before the show had opened, or even started one, but that didn't make him a beggar. He turned over, and tried to relax. Sleep was what he needed.

Then he was on his feet and getting dressed. Susan stirred. "Oh, God—you're not going, are you?"

"He's been right about everything so far. I'd be an idiot not to trust him."

"You're crazy." She punched her pillow twice, and turned away from him.

He was lucky enough to catch a cab right away. He gave the driver the studio address, and when he had picked up the camera, he was whisked up Tenth Avenue to Broadway and Ninety-fourth. Bellisle was standing beside a small crowd that was gathered on the corner, staring up at the hotel across the street. He didn't even glance at Hood. "Have you got your camera?"

Hood looked up and saw a boy perched on the edge of the hotel roof, eight stories up. It was hard to tell from this distance, but he appeared to be fifteen or sixteen. "Jesus. Did anyone call the police?"

"They're inside. On the way up. You should have come sooner."

One heard that such groups of spectators tended to yell "jump," but there was no such ghoulishness here. Theirs were almost the faces of followers, disciples—expectant and fearful— faces about to see miracles.

"Do you have the right lens?"

"Are you kidding? You want me to take a picture?"

"You have the opportunity." Bellisle spoke as if they were at the zoo, observing an interesting variety of ape. A grim heat began to grow in Hood as he fitted a long lens to the camera. He tried to ignore this mixture of dread and anticipation, and set the film speed at 1600. If he took a picture, it would be very grainy.

"He's terrified!" Hood had his eye at the camera now, shifting the boy in and out of focus.

"That's not unusual."

The boy turned slightly, and nearly lost his grip on the rooftop wall. He was saying something to someone behind him. The words reached the ground a second later. "Stay back!"

Hood said, "Jesus. He's gonna jump."

"Oh, yes."

"They're scaring him."

The boy waved back whoever was trying to approach him on the roof. He screamed, "Get the fuck away from me!" Then he did a strange thing. He stretched out his arms, cruciform, as if bearing up the sky. Hood shifted focus; the crowd drew in its breath. The boy raised his arms in unison and sprang upward, like a high diver. Then he hung in the air for a moment, perfectly still, before he dropped. Hood clicked the shutter.

He followed the boy downward on his plunge, and fired the camera again just as the boy's hands pierced the umbrella of light beneath a streetlamp. This was followed by an explosion. The boy had landed on top of a car, slamming into it with such force that the roof was destroyed. A pale hand hung over the edge, gleaming whitely.

One man took a tentative step toward the car; a woman screamed; several more were moaning, but most turned away in silence. Hood was stunned. He couldn't seem to breathe; the camera dangled from his neck like an albatross.

A cop began to clear them away from the scene.

"Are you coming?" Bellisle tapped his cane on the sidewalk impatiently. Hood's mind remained a blank as he crossed the street with Bellisle.

Neither of them spoke for a while. They walked toward downtown, past the shuttered shops, the ragged drunks, the all-night vegetable stores, and Hood found his legs were quivering. He carried the boy's terrified face inside him, like a pallbearer. What could have driven a boy so young to—

"You were at that point, not so long ago."

"He couldn't have been more than sixteen!"

"Perhaps he saw something you didn't."

Hood stopped, and looked at Bellisle. "This is what you wanted me to see? You wanted me to see some kid kill himself?"

"Not in the spirit of entertainment. I'm sure it's an experience you'll put to good use."

"I'm going home, Bellisle."

"Very well. Shall I take the film?"

"Take the whole fucking thing. I don't want it." He pulled the camera from around his neck and handed it over. "Keep the fucking thing."

Next morning, Hood felt a tight circle of pain around his head. It stayed with him through a scorching hot shower, and only began to ease when he ran the water as cold as he could stand it. He was trying hard not to think of the boy, but the sounds came back to him: "Stay back!" and the terrible explosion that had blasted the soul from that young body.

Susan was out somewhere. Hood was glad to have a quiet breakfast alone. Watching the boy's death had opened a seal in his character; something vital was leaking out of him, never to come again, and poison fluid was seeping in. He couldn't face anyone, not even Susan, laid open like this.

Outside, it felt like it was going to rain any minute. Hood stopped in at the bank to pick up two rolls of quarters, before heading for a small restaurant where he always used the pay phone—anything to stop thinking of the boy. The restaurant was serving an unusually late breakfast crowd, but the phone, an old-fashioned one with folding doors, was situated downstairs away from the noise.

He called Marcia first, and got the information he needed, then dialed a very lengthy number that connected him with the Switzerland Free Trade Association, located in Lucerne. A mechanized voice demanded he drop an endless series of quarters into the slot, and then a phone began to ring, half a world away. He spoke to three different young women, all of whom spoke heavily accented but perfectly grammatical English, before being put through to the office of Baron Fritz Von Gletscher. An apologetic voice, youthful and male, informed Hood that he could not speak to the baron because, alas, the baron was out of the country. The baron was visiting the United States—New York, as it happened, where he might yet be reachable at the Swiss consulate. When he called the consulate on Madison Avenue, no, they were sorry, what a shame, the baron had just boarded a morning flight for London.

He had better luck with Texas. He got through to Emco Oil and in no time at all had Baxter Millwright himself on the phone. "What can I do for you, Mr. Hood?"

"You've already done it. You bought one of my paintings last week."

"You the owner, or the artist?"

"Artist."

"Well, hot dog! I'm just tickled to death! Wish I could say I've seen the painting, but that'd be a mistruth. Never laid eyes on it! Friend o' mine knows the art world made a pitch I just couldn't ignore, and I bought it! You callin' for the dang thing back?" The question was followed by a cowboy hoot of laughter.

"No," Hood said evenly. "I'm very happy you bought it. I was just wondering how you heard about me."

"Friend o' mine tipped me off. Old, old friend—clever as a snake. Good eye for a bargain."

"Can you tell me who it was?"

There was a brief silence.

"Mr. Hood? You familiar with a certain expression concerning a gift horse?"

"Yes. I'm not complaining. I just want—"

"Sign of a truly stupid person—offer to do him a favor, he gets irritated some way. I didn't get where I am by turning down every offer of help came down the pike. What I know about art you could write on a skeeter's behind, but my advice to you is paint what you gotta paint, and sell what you gotta sell."

"Your friend's name wouldn't be Bellisle, would it?"

"Nosir. It would not. Y'all have a nice day."

So much for Texas. Hood opened his second roll of quarters and spread them out on the metal shelf. An image of the falling boy appeared in his mind, but he forced it aside by saying the number aloud as he dialed Paris. The woman who answered sounded American—it was hard to tell, because she spoke very quietly, without a trace of animation.

"My name is Nicholas Hood. Could I speak to Mr. Lefevre? Does he speak English?"

"No, he—" The woman broke off. Tried again. "My hus-band—" Her voice seemed to catch, and then there was a rustling sound, as if she buried the phone in the folds of her dress.

"Hello? Are you still there?" Hood waited a moment, considered whether to hang up and try later.

Then a deep male voice, very cultured, came on the line. "Hello, this is M. Girard. I am attorney to M. Lefevre."

"My name is Hood. I'm an American painter. Mr. Lefevre bought one of my paintings last week, and—"

"Yes, I believe it. He's never before bought a painting in his life, but he was behaving very erratically last week. Can you tell me how much was the purchase price?"

Hood was surprised by the question. He had to think a moment. "I believe in the thirty-thousand-dollar range."

"You received this amount?"

"My dealer did. But I just wanted to ask Mr. Lefevre—"

"Yes, I see the notation here. Your transaction will not be affected in any way."

"Affected? Affected by what?"

"By his death. M. Lefevre shot himself last Friday."

"Oh."

"If there's nothing else . . ."

The sky was darker and the air heavy when Hood went back outside. The calls had only served to increase his anxiety, and he could not escape the feeling that Andre Bellisle had somehow affected each of the buyers, even if he had not met them in person. It was just a feeling, he realized; the calls themselves proved nothing. Nevertheless, a queasiness lurked inside him, and he hoped that the studio would be empty.

This turned out to be the case, although it was unusual for Leo to be anywhere else on a weekday morning. The place was unnaturally quiet. Hood paused just inside the door, and bent

down to pick up a large manila envelope that was lying on the
floor. He immediately knew what it contained. He dropped it
onto the worktable and went to stand by the window, half
expecting to see Bellisle standing out there. A thin gray drizzle
hung like a web around the pier, where a few pigeons and gulls
waddled disconsolately. When he had made himself a coffee,
Hood sat at the table and tore open the envelope. A cold hand
closed around his heart. In the first photograph, the boy was
hanging in midair. It was the moment when he had bent forward
and touched his knees, doing the "tuck" part of his swan dive. His
face was outthrust, teeth clenched, chin jutting out, and the
whites of his eyes were enormous.

The boy's expression changed in the next picture. Terror had
boiled away—indeed all emotion was now distilled into tranquility. His hands plunged into the grainy streetlight, and behind
him, the windows were blurred, streaked upward—the merest
glance would tell you the boy was a split second from death. And
yet, his face was now relaxed, the eyes no longer wide but almost
sleepy, as if the spirit had already departed, carrying with it all
pain and desire. Hood couldn't be sure if this was tranquility, or
emptiness.

He put the photo aside. To stand there and allow a boy, a
child, to perform his death for you! One would have to have a
headstone for a heart. Hood did not see himself as that kind of
man; he didn't feel the pictures were his. But he knew he had
triggered the camera.

And Bellisle. Hood shuddered, remembering Bellisle's cold-
blooded attitude.

He set a prepared canvas on his easel, and laid out tubes of
acrylic. This was not a painting to labor over for weeks; he would
forgo the subtle shadings of oil for the speed of acrylic. He
selected several reds, mud yellow, grays, off-whites, and several
shades of black. He pulled three of the wider brushes from the

coffee tin that bristled like a quiver of arrows. "I could paint this picture with my thumb," he thought.

The window light was soft, cottony gray, as it filtered through the rain. Shadowless. Hood picked up a tube, and squeezed out some charcoal gray.

Morning dissolved into noon, and Hood slipped into what he liked to consider a state of grace. The feeling reminded him of those long summer evenings of childhood. He would be outside playing; the air might smell of fresh-cut grass, as he and his friends played on into darkness—climbing trees, hiding in bushes. And somewhere in the distance, he would hear his mother's voice calling him home, a voice from that colder world of clocks and grown-ups. Painting was a return to that magic hour when the moon slowly overtook the sun, and a game could last forever.

Sometime in the afternoon, Hood heard the door of the studio open, and Leo's heavy tread. There were footsteps in the room, the clank of a kettle, the sounds of another life—of Leo dropping something, or clearing his throat. But these sounds came through to Hood the way a conversation filters through the fringes of sleep.

He felt he was flying away from the studio, held to it only by the most tenuous thread, like a kite. But Leo's footsteps came closer, close enough to threaten Hood's flight with a sudden plunge to earth. "Stay back!" He heard his own voice far below himself, still on earth. The footsteps halted. "Get the fuck away!" The footsteps went away.

He began to come around when the light was nearly gone. His fingers were cramping; his back was aching; Leo was long gone. He reached out and snapped on the overhead lights. With a dab of white on the end of his brush, he added highlights to the windows in his paintings, reflections of the streetlight. But the world had penetrated now; he was Nicholas Hood once again,

and Nicholas Hood was dead tired. He rubbed his eyes and stood
back from the work.

A lump rose in his throat. For on his easel, in the last of the
window light, a masterpiece was shimmering. It blessed him; it
spoke his name and called him worthy, and it shone in the room
like a grail.

SEVEN

ALTHOUGH it had left the snow a mottled gray mess, pocked and cratered, the quiet rain had rinsed the atmosphere. Hood stood for a moment, after stepping out of the studio, and breathed deeply. Even New York City air could taste good after a day of paint fumes.

He made his way home on aching legs and found Susan curled up on the couch, watching Jimmy Cagney. Hood knelt in front of her and draped his arms around her, resting his head in her lap.

"What's all this for?" She sounded both pleased and suspicious. "You're not having an affair, are you?"

"You are so good to come home to." He had Susan, he had a masterpiece, he had money, and Hood was feeling grateful.

"Take off your coat, and I'll bring you some supper."

Hood went to change into his dressing gown, washed himself quickly, and came back to the living room where Susan had set out some shepherd's pie and a bottle of English beer. He ate ravenously, having gone the whole day without food. He had a second helping, and another bottle of beer, as Jimmy Cagney abused his girlfriend by squashing half a grapefruit in her face. Hood lay down and fell asleep with his head on Susan's lap. She woke him later, when the movie was over, and he followed her blindly into the bedroom.

When Hood was having breakfast, Susan was rushing around getting ready for a day of rehearsal. "You won't forget the concert tonight, will you? This one's special."

"What're you playing?"

"The harpsichord."

"Very funny."

"I told you about it last night! It's at Merkin Hall!" She was stuffing music and apples into an enormous bag. "How could you forget? It's the most important thing in my life!"

Hood got up and hugged her. "I'll be there. Eight o'clock?"

"You better be."

"Last night I was in a state of . . ."

"Why? Your weird friend?"

"It's hard to explain, really—but I painted the best thing ever. Ever."

"Was it worth getting up in the middle of the night?"

"Oh, yes."

"And annoying your charming wife?"

"I'm afraid so."

She stuck her tongue out, and Hood laughed. "Wait till you see. I'm taking it to the gallery today."

"Just don't forget my concert, buddy."

Hood was left staring at the door in the sudden silence of her leaving. He vowed to spend more time with her.

"*Gott in Himmel*, the Demon Painter comes!" Leo was parked in front of Hood's painting, hands on hips, as if considering whether to give it a ticket.

"What do you think?" Hood went to stand beside him.

"You were like a possessed person yesterday. I come to take a peek and you tell me fuck off!"

"Did I?" Hood didn't remember.

"Yes, did you. You hurt my sensitive artist's soul, too."

"I'm sorry."

"Now I go to work."

"Wait!" Hood grabbed his arm. "You haven't told me what you think!"

"It's good! Do some more!"

"Good? All my stuff is good!"

"In that case, you don't need my opinion. Good-bye." Leo was playing with him—getting even for yesterday's brush-off. He sat down before his own painting.

"Of course, I don't *need* your opinion. But don't you think this is better? Don't you find this . . ."

"Nicholas, it's very good. But I think you've taken some sort of holiday. Instead of your usual detail, you've done everything in a blur."

"Well, look at the subject!"

"I know. But you painted this in one day. Why you think it should be better than work you actually *thought* about, I don't know. It hits you over the head. That's all."

"Fuck you, Leo. You're blind."

"*Danke schön.*"

"You look at it for two seconds and think you know everything."

Leo stayed silent after that. Hood looked at the painting for a long time, hardly believing he'd finished it so fast. Toward lunchtime, he wrapped it in brown paper, tied it with string, and left the studio.

It was colder now, and a stiff wind buffeted the canvas like a sail. By the time he could flag a cab, Hood's temper was on edge and his hands were frozen. The taxi lurched across Sixth Avenue.

"Hey! Let's take it slow and smooth—I've got a painting here."

"You tell me how to drive?" The driver glared at him over his shoulder. He had eyebrows thick as mustaches, and sounded Middle Eastern.

"Look," Hood said. "Stop the car."

"Relax, my friend!"

"Stop the fucking car!"

The driver jammed on the brakes. "Two dollar!"

Hood pushed open the door and struggled onto the street with his painting. The driver jumped out of the other side and swiftly came around to Hood. "You give me two dollar!"

Hood leaned his painting against the rear bumper. "You want your money, come and get it."

"I no wanna punch you. Give me money, or I call some cop."

Hood pushed him hard in the chest with both hands. The driver lost balance, and swung at him ineffectively. When he swung again, Hood stepped aside, grabbed his arm, and twisted hard. He forced him facedown against the hood of the car and banged his face against the metal for emphasis. "You're a piece of shit—got that? You're a worthless piece of shit, and you don't deserve to live. Got it?"

The man was crying, out of fear and humiliation. The tears stopped Hood instantly. He released the man, who went smartly around to the other side of the car. He spat at Hood. "I hate you. I hate America. All you know how to do is violence. Kill people. Fucking sick country."

Hood placed two dollars on the hood of the car. The man snatched the money and threw it into the air, and the wind carried it down the street. He got into the car and peeled away, so that Hood's painting fell over in the street. He picked it up, and trudged toward the gallery, taking deep breaths to calm himself down.

Marcia looked up from her typewriter when he struggled through the front door. "Does Sherri know you're coming? Is that for us?"

Hood put it against the wall and shook the cramps out of his hands. "Is Sherri in the office?"

"There's someone with her—I better not interrupt."

Hood was panting, and rubbing his hands. "There any coffee?" Marcia fetched him a cup, and sat down again at the typewriter. Whatever Sherri had hired her for, it wasn't her typing skills. She pecked erratically, each clack echoing distinctly through the gallery. Hood sat down and picked up a copy of *Arts Magazine*.

He turned to a feature on Peter Laszlo, read the first paragraph, and then turned to a sidebar on Andy Stark. It was a brief sketch of his career, with one or two quotes, accompanied by a small black-and-white photo of one of his portraits, which conveyed nothing of his talent. There was no mention of Hood, unless you counted the phrase "several other Novack artists."

Marcia's inept click-clack was getting on his nerves. "Can you give Sherri a buzz and tell her I'm here?"

"I better not—I think this guy is pretty important."

"I wouldn't have come if it weren't important."

Marcia frowned slightly, but she picked up the phone and spoke very quietly, as if she were in church. "Sorry to interrupt, Sherri—Nicholas Hood is here, and . . . Yes, but he—" She hung up and sighed. "Now I'm in trouble."

"Oh, for fuck sake!" He tore the wrapping from the picture and left it in a heap on the floor, then carried the canvas through the back gallery and rapped on Sherri's door, before opening it. "I've got something you have to see."

There was a man seated opposite Sherri. He turned slightly in Hood's direction, while Sherri turned slowly to stone. She said, coolly, "Mr. Fisk, this is Nicholas Hood."

"Gosh, yes!" The man leapt to his feet and proffered a freckled hand. He was dressed in rumpled tweed, and had one of those freckly, serviceable English faces. "Delighted! I was looking at your work earlier—most impressive."

"Maybe you'll be interested in this one, then." Hood set the picture on top of a filing cabinet.

"Just now, of course, I'm talking to Miss Novack, but . . . I *say!*" Mr. Fisk took a step closer to the painting. "This is *very* . . ."

Hood had painted the boy on his deathbound plunge at that

moment when his hands broke into the streetlamp light. The windows of the hotel in the background were fringed, blurred upward; there was a terrific sensation of speed. "My goodness," Mr. Fisk said. "Look at his *face*. If it were turned upside down, you might think he was rising to heaven! Such *peace!*" His head bobbed closer to the picture. "Is that a little cross round his neck? I believe it is. What d'you think, Miss Novack?"

She hadn't looked at the painting. "I think Mr. Hood is being very rude, and I will look at his work later."

"Mm. Yes. I see." Mr. Fisk coughed uncomfortably. Hood watched the back of his neck turn deep red, the fair skin a thermometer of the emotions. "Good piece of work," he muttered, and promptly sat down.

Hood reached for his canvas. "I'll get it out of Miss Novack's sight."

A freckled hand darted out to restrain him. "Please. If it's all right with . . ." Fisk looked over at Sherri, who merely shrugged.

Hood went back to the front of the gallery where Marcia was still typing, and slumped down in a chair. He closed his eyes, and called up every detail of his painting, every dab of color. Marcia's typing stopped.

"Just because you're an artist, doesn't give you the right to abuse people, you know."

Hood opened his eyes and found Marcia looking down at him.

"Just because I work as a receptionist, doesn't mean I don't rate some sort of respect. You make me look like an idiot! Do you know how many maniacs we get in here, all lugging their sketches and slides and even paintings? They all think they're geniuses, and they all want Sherri to drop everything at once and look at their work. Well, it's my job to keep them out of her hair."

"And you equate me with them?"

"I'm just saying it's part of my job to keep people out of Sherri's office when she's busy! You stepped over the line!"

"I apologize."

"You sound really sincere, too." She went back to her desk and started stacking papers and slamming drawers with excessive noise.

"Did it ever occur to you that maybe one or two of those people have talent? God knows who you drove away!"

"It's my job. I didn't say it was right."

"People like you made me want to kill myself, when I was starting out. Petty tyrants . . ."

"I don't have to listen to this!" Marcia grabbed her coat and was out the door before she even put it on. Hood didn't want to fight with Sherri, so he left a moment later.

He wandered around SoHo for a while, staring absentmindedly into shop windows and wishing he had a friend to visit. But he didn't really have any friends. He had realized long ago that most people make of friendship a secondary career, devoting many hours a week to restaurant outings, telephone calls, and other social pursuits. Over the years, painting had taken over his life, and his marriage to Susan had quelled the desperate need for human contact that in earlier years had caused him to spend time with people he despised. And Leo was always working.

He stood for a time in the biography section of a bookstore, reading a volume of Van Gogh's letters. The book had been an inspiration to him, in his early twenties. All that talk of going after the Truth, it had to affect you. But times change. These days, you couldn't mention Truth without laughing.

In a coffee shop near the Village, he ate a tasteless hamburger, and read the *Daily News*. There was a small article about the boy's suicide, suggesting that the police had been ineffective. Hood bet they would have paid handsomely for one of his photographs.

It felt painfully bright when Hood came out of the restaurant, though in fact the sky was overcast. The streets were beginning to fill up with rush hour traffic, and everyone looked harried or sad. Hood's earlier righteousness had ebbed, and now he was angry at himself. He would have to apologize to Sherri and Marcia. He didn't want to apologize to anyone; he just wanted to erase the day.

He was back on his way to the studio when he caught sight of Andre Bellisle. He was striding purposively uptown, across the street, the cane aswing at his side like a tail. Hood dodged cars and pedestrians, slipping in the slush as he crossed the street. He tugged on Bellisle's scarf that flapped in the wind like a black pennant. "How did you know about the boy?"

Bellisle stopped and turned, and Hood was startled by the change in him. The smaller man looked as if he had been away at a spa. The skin, formerly so warped and mottled and blistered, was much smoother, healthier-looking. The eyes were not nearly so red and watery. Bellisle was a very ugly being, but his aspect was no longer fearsomely distorted. Hood said, "Jesus. What happened to your face!"

"Is something wrong?"

"No, no! You look different! Better! You look a lot better, that's all."

"Thank you. I feel better. But I'd really rather not discuss my appearance."

"All right. How did you know about the boy?"

Bellisle touched a healed patch of skin on his cheek. "The same way I knew about the man who got hit by the automobile."

"And how did you know that?"

"I simply perceived it without benefit of sight or hearing. May we walk? I have an appointment."

Bellisle swiveled an eye at him as they walked. "You seem distracted. Are you upset?"

"No. Maybe. I've been behaving badly."

"You? You haven't the capacity."

"I may surprise you."

"I doubt it."

"Tell me about the boy! Were you asleep? Dreaming? Did you have a vision of the kid diving off a roof? What were you doing?"

Bellisle made a slight, impatient hiss. "Questions. Just take my word for it: These things *occur* to me. I know them with absolute certainty. It doesn't come in a flash. There's nothing interesting about it."

"How long before he jumped did you see it?"

"No exact time. Are you going to suggest I should have prevented it?"

"Why didn't you! He was just a boy!"

"All right." Bellisle adopted the tone of a math teacher explaining fractions to a recalcitrant child. "Suppose I had prevented him. Suppose I had climbed up to that roof, and physically hauled him back from the edge. What would I have seen beforehand?"

"Obviously, you would have seen yourself doing exactly that."

"And what, pray, does that look like?"

Hood didn't respond. They stood at a corner waiting for a light to change. When it turned green, Bellisle said, "If an event is *not* going to occur, then I do *not* see it. The concept is not obscure. I saw the boy's leap in my mind, and knew that nothing on earth could prevent his death. It looked like something you might paint, so I gave you a call. You're not feeling guilty, are you?" Bellisle looked sincerely worried. As if nothing mattered more than Hood's peace of mind.

"I don't know. My feelings are out of control."

Before Bellisle could respond to this confession, Hood

remembered something else. "That fellow you were with in the
restaurant. That was the baron from Switzerland, right? Von
Gletscher?"

"Life will become impossibly dreary for both of us if you insist
on playing detective. Yes. The man in the restaurant was Baron
Von Gletscher. Why this should be of any interest to you—"

"Of course I care who buys my work! Did he want to buy it,
or did you pressure him into it?"

"He bought it on my recommendation. There's every reason
to think he will be happy with his purchase. As to your other
patrons . . . my involvement was less direct. Friends of
friends."

"The man in Paris is dead."

"Yes. A suicide, I'm told. I've never met the man."

"Never? Would you swear to that? You've had no contact
with him?"

"Believe me or don't. I shan't repeat myself." Bellisle looked
at him, sadly. "What else do you want to know? Let's get all these
questions behind us, shall we?"

"How does it happen I keep bumping into you!"

"Coincidence?"

"I've lived in this city eight years. I could count on one hand
the number of times I've run into people I know."

They had reached the south edge of Gramercy Park. A lone
jogger towed a tiny dog around the fence, and from Third
Avenue, a block away, came the bleatings of evening traffic.
Bellisle came to a stop at the corner. "I told you I would make
myself available, and so I have. If you have any objections, I can
vanish forthwith. Just say the word, Mr. Hood—don't worry
about my feelings."

Faced with Bellisle's reasonable manner, Hood suddenly felt
in the wrong. "I don't know what I want," he said, and chipped
with his heel at a filthy crust of snow. "Except to feel better."

"We all want that." Bellisle pointed toward Third Avenue. "I'd rather continue on my own now. I have to meet someone. But I do have another project for you."

Hood kicked a lump of dirty ice into the street. "Like the boy? No, thank you."

"Midnight tonight. Washington Square Park."

"I won't be there."

"As you wish," Bellisle said, and turned along Eighteenth Street, the cane flapping at his side.

Hood was one of the first to arrive at Merkin Hall, the auditorium was nearly empty. The harpsichord gleamed in the spotlight like a new car. Hood was reading the program for the third time when finally the house lights dimmed and Susan, accompanied by her two colleagues, appeared on the stage to generous applause. There was a good crowd in the hall by then.

They began with a trio sonata by Telemann, a pleasant work with a somber adagio section, but it felt to Hood like harmless background music—the sort of stuff he liked to have playing while he worked, because it had no power to distract. Susan's lengthy rehearsals had paid off handsomely, however—the three performers harmonized perfectly. Every nuance, every trill was under unified control, as if they were a single performer. When they finished the perky allegro, the audience clapped loudly.

Susan looked pretty up there on stage. She was wearing green velvet, with a touch of lace at the throat and cuffs. She raised her hands for the beginning of a suite by Handel, the audience quieted, and the music began again. Concentration lent an appealing seriousness to her features, and Hood knew, had this been his first experience of her, it would have been love at first sight. He wondered how many of the beak-nosed, balding gentlemen in the audience were lost in fantasies less than musical. Again, the music had failed to transport him. Hood suspected that he was a bit of a philistine about anything other than painting.

He dozed off during the Bach suite that ended the program, and was only awakened by the cascade of applause that followed. Quite a few people stood up, but Hood thought this ovation business completely uncalled for. He wondered how much Susan had to do with their being so excited. Was it not the very essence of her art to humble herself before another's creation; in effect, to disappear? Well, to each his own.

Hood waited for her in the cramped little lobby, where he stared at advertisements for concerts to come. A hot sickly feeling began to radiate from his stomach—a feeling quite divorced from his reaction to the concert. He was flooded all of a sudden with something like fear that was not fear—like disgust, but not disgust. It was what he had felt the night he watched the boy dive from the hotel roof, just before the boy dove. Part of him had wanted the leap, the fall, the death, and this hot, sick feeling was desire. He was feeling it because Bellisle had given him a date and a time: midnight, Washington Square Park. It was nearly midnight now.

The feeling abated a little when Susan came into the lobby looking vulnerable and small, her eyes pouched with fatigue. In the backseat of the taxi on the way home, she leaned over and rested her head on his shoulder. Hood started talking about the concert, asking questions about the program, why they'd chosen those selections and not others. He asked about the flutist, about the rehearsals—it was practically an interview. He was stacking question upon question like sandbags, as if he could build a wall and hold back that dark flood of desire.

But Susan tired of it. She said, "Why are you so chatty tonight? It's not like you."

The fragile wall was breached, and Hood was lost. "I'm a

little distracted, actually. I may go to the studio."

"All right."

He kissed her temple, where a wisp of hair curled down across her cheek. Her sleepy acquiescence frightened him; there was nothing he could do at the studio at this hour. Nothing good.

EIGHT

AFTER kissing Susan good night at the apartment door, he told himself he would not keep the appointment with Bellisle. He stepped back onto the street with no intention of going to Washington Square. He told himself that he was walking aimlessly, just taking a stroll, no harm in that. But one block later he turned north once again and took the shortest route toward the park. The throbbing in his stomach came back in full force; his heart began to pound. "Such nausea, such disgust—you'd think I was about to rape a child, torment a blind lady," he thought. "And yet at worst I'll be meeting a man in a park."

He stopped at a corner in the Village where a greasy young man in a torn overcoat was haranguing a rough semicircle of people who looked at him without interest. The whining voice was amplified through a torn speaker that rattled with every consonant. In an effort to be provocative, the man pointed at Hood. "You!" he said. "You think the world is a stinkhole! You think the world is a mess! You think that God don't care about the AIDS, the drugs! The pornography and perversions! But I tell you God so loved the world he gave his only begotten Son! Jesus Christ our Lord died on the cross so you and me and all us sinners could enter the kingdom of Heaven."

Hood smiled.

"And what've you done for Jesus Christ lately? He died for your sins, man, and you stand there, smiling! Greater love than this hath no man! And you stand there smiling!" He flicked the microphone cord, leaned forward confidentially. "He died for our sins and what does He ask in return? Two things. Two things.

First, we must love God above all in the world. That's one. And two: You gotta love your neighbor as yourself—no better and no worse. Love your neighbor as yourself."

One by one, individuals detached themselves from the group and wandered away. The preacher pushed back his greasy hair, trying to recapture a thought. Finally, he said, "The world is a test, man. That's why there's so much evil in the world."

"What was Hitler testing?" Hood said it quietly.

"What? What was the question?"

"What was Hitler testing?"

"He was testing our patience, man!"

Hood laughed.

"He was testing our fortitude! Our courage! Our resolve!"

"And the children he murdered, did they pass the test?"

"What? What's the question?"

"You heard me."

A black man with wrists as thin as pencils nudged Hood. "Ver' good question."

The preacher was sweating heavily, despite the cold. "Jesus said, 'Suffer the little children to come unto me'! They were called home, man, 'cause they were ready to live in Heaven. Unlike us here. You and me."

"If they cried in the gas chamber, did they flunk the test?"

"Got nothin' to do with it! The test is, can you go through this vale of tears with your soul intact—loving your neighbor, loving your God. 'F He was nice to you alla time, there wouldn't be no test! He gives you a lotta money and you say why thank you Lord, I love you, how's he gonna know you really love him?"

"You've got all the answers."

"God has all the answers. Jesus Christ has all the answers."

"Everything makes sense to you, right? No mysteries in your universe."

"Everything I need explained was explained to me a long time ago by Matthew, Mark, Luke, and John. You own a Bible, man? When's the last time you read that book?"

"I bet you were a junkie. You've found a new drug."

"I admit it! I admit I was one of the lost ones. I sold my soul for a needle in my arm. But faith in the Lord cured me of that affliction."

"So, now you're an asshole on a corner, screaming at the wind."

"Spit in my face, man! Go ahead! I'm not the first to suffer insult and degradation for my faith in the Lord!"

"You love it. You invite it. You're just showing off."

The preacher suddenly changed tactics. He leaned forward and displayed dirty teeth in what was meant to be a loving smile. "Come forward, my brother. Come forward and shake my hand."

"No, thank you."

"Come forward and accept my friendship. I offer you an end to all your painful searching. I am not your enemy."

"You're not anything. You're nothing. You're a mouthful of clichés."

"Brother, come forward. Shake my hand."

Hood turned away and started walking.

"You can't hurt me!" The whining voice rattled the speaker. "It's you! You! It's your soul, man!"

Hood kept walking until he was a block away from Washington Square. He stopped and looked at his watch. A quarter to twelve. He was poised at the edge of the curb, feeling like that boy at the edge of the roof, about to leap. Except no one was watching. Except he wasn't going to die.

Clusters of drug dealers loitered on the perimeter of the park, but there was nothing going on inside the park itself. An idle wind tossed soggy flags of newsprint around the arch. There was no sign of Bellisle. Hood walked through the arch and followed one of the paths that formed an X across the square. In the exact center, he came to a stop, and the heat surged in his belly.

Raucous laughter flew up from the drug dealers, and Hood stiffened. This was no place to be at this hour, five to twelve, alone and without purpose. He would have left then, but a man was approaching from the southwest corner of the park. He was carrying a shopping bag, and his walk was uneven, as if the bag were very heavy.

The man put the bag down at the edge of the center circle where Hood was waiting. He too looked around, as if he had an appointment with someone. Hood noticed that he was unshaven, but not altogether unkempt. His clothes were tidy, and clean enough. Hood started back toward the arch.

"You Baker?"

Hood only half turned, leery of another pointless conversation.

"You Baker? Guy I'm supposed to meet?"

"No." Hood walked back to the arch and looked up and down the street. Still no sign of Bellisle.

The man began shouting from the middle of the park. "Baker! Baker! I'm not gonna wait all night!" He was pacing around in a tight circle like a tense man waiting for a bus. Hood wondered what his midnight business with Mr. Baker might be. Clearly, he didn't know Baker very well, since he had mistaken Hood for the man. And then it occurred to him that "Baker" might be none other than Andre Bellisle. He walked back toward the man.

"Better stay back," the man said. Hood was about ten yards away. There was a smell of gasoline in the air.

Hood said, "I'm supposed to meet somebody here. Who is Baker?"

"Never mind who he is. Don't come any closer." The man sneezed. "Christ. I'm fucking freezing."

"Is Baker a short man—ugly face? Blond hair?"

"How would I know? I never met the guy." The man laughed.

"You're sure his name's not Bellisle."

"His name is Baker. I get the feeling you're him."

"No."

"You're Baker, aren't you."

"No. I'm not."

"What am I supposed to do? I can't stand around all night. Now I don't know if you're Baker or not."

"You've never met this guy? Never talked to him?"

"Talked to him once. On the phone. He only said a couple of words."

"Did he have a kind of British accent?"

"No."

They stood facing one another, Hood on the circumference of the concrete circle, the man with his shopping bag in the center. Hood kept smelling gasoline, as if there were an open tank nearby. Finally, the man said, "Suppose it doesn't matter, really. I just don't know why you pretend to be someone else."

"It may be Baker is pretending to be someone else. I think I know him as Bellisle."

"Double-talk. All double-talk. Maybe I should just go home." He hung his head, as if addressing his heart. "I can't go home. I'm soaked in gasoline."

"What?" Hood wasn't sure he'd heard correctly.

"I said I'm soaked in gasoline! Ya deaf?" The man drew something from his pocket, stood there poised like a gunfighter.

Hood started toward him. "Don't!"

He flicked the lighter a couple of times, getting only sparks.

"For Christ's sake!" Hood ran for him, but the man hugged the lighter close. A long flame uncoiled from his hands and slithered up his chest, setting his face and hair ablaze. Suddenly, orange pennants flapped across his shoulders and down the length of his body. The shopping bag exploded with a bang and twirled into the sky, sending Hood reeling back.

When he opened his eyes again, he saw a bonfire darting back and forth, shrieking terribly. The thing would take a few steps and turn, flapping its orange wings, and then would come the hideous scream. It took off across the park and ran smack into a tree and fell to its knees, where it was hugged and caressed by flame, until it tipped over, and the screaming stopped.

By the time Hood recovered from his shock, a black man had reached the prostrate figure and put out the last of the flames with his coat. Hood came up behind him, and recognized him as one of the drug dealers. He was muttering, "Oh, geez. Geez." He yelled to someone, "Call a ambulance, man! Call a ambulance! O my God in heaven!" Footsteps scurried away.

The stiff, blackened thing on the ground was silent, except for intermittent wheezing. It raised a forearm like a flag scorched in battle, then let it fall back with a small defeated thud.

Hood knelt beside the black man and scooped up a little snow, sprinkling some where a face had been. He rubbed a little more on the top of the head. The black man beside him was saying an Our Father. The dying man's stomach pulsed up and down, faster and faster, and then went still.

"He's dead."

"You right. I think so, too."

"I can't stay here."

The black man leaned over the body and removed a wallet and some plastic bags of powder from the coat pockets. "I ain't stealin'," he said. "This my coat here."

"I know. I'm leaving now."

"Ain't nobody stoppin' us, is there?"

"No." Hood tucked his head down and walked under the arch to the street.

"Not quite the same as the boy, was it." Bellisle stood in front of him. He wore his coat draped over his shoulders like a theatrical impresario, and he smiled like a very old cat. Hood pushed him aside, and ran.

He didn't stop running until he reached Broome Street, and was still in a panic when he locked the apartment door behind him. For a wild moment, he thought that Susan was gone. He threw open the bedroom door and found her sleeping, chatting to someone in the depths of a dream. He closed the door again and paced around the living room, not knowing what to do.

He picked up the phone and dialed 911, asked for an ambulance in Washington Square.

The voice at the other end was calm. "Is this in reference to an individual who set himself on fire?"

"Yes! I think he's dead now."

"We already sent a crew out, sir. Could I just have your name?"

"What do you need that for?"

"It's just for our records, sir."

"But somebody else already—"

"I need the information, sir. Your name and address?"

Hood hung up. What if they thought he'd set a match to the dead man? Suppose they thought he'd just stood and watched him burn, a part of some wicked cult ceremony? He felt he had committed a great evil, but was not certain where. "Did I hurt anybody? No—he set himself on fire; he'd had it planned. Could I have prevented it? I tried, I told him to stop, I reached out, but it all happened so fast."

He had a vivid picture in his mind: He was in the witness stand, explaining how this terrible event had occurred. Judge and jury were eyeing him, waiting for him to say something true, should he be capable. He shook the image from his head and poured himself a brandy. "The only place I went wrong," he thought, "was in being there in the first place. I had no business being in that park at that time."

But that had been Bellisle's doing. Bellisle had foreseen it. Bellisle had got him there. Christ, he probably thought Hood was going to paint the damned atrocity.

Images of the flaming man were spinning in his head. "I'm going crazy," he said aloud. "I've lost my mind." He drank another brandy and felt it soothe his nerves. He still saw the burning man, the silent trees, the empty park; but he saw them in frames now, not in the real world.

He got out of his clothes and into bed, where he curled up in a tight ball. Susan muttered a few words in her sleep and rolled over, as peaceful as the moon. As far away.

Hood woke up when Susan got out of bed the next morning but he couldn't face her and pretended to be asleep. As he listened to her going through her morning routine, he considered telling her about the whole night—right from Bellisle's first mention of the time and place to his sudden appearance at the end. But it made no sense. Things like that just don't happen in the world; she would suggest he see a psychiatrist. He heard her go out the door and waited another ten minutes before getting out of bed.

"If I act normal, everything will *be* normal." Thus Hood reasoned to himself, and to some extent it worked. By the time he had showered and shaved, he began to feel more of a human being, less of an incubus, less of a ghoul.

After breakfast, he dialed the gallery. He made what he thought a handsome apology to Marcia, and then held the phone away from his ear while Sherri treated him to some vivid Brooklyn diction.

"Will you let me apologize?"

"There ain't enough apologies in the world, Mr. Hood!"

"I'm sorry, Sherri. Really, I—"

"I'm so mad at you I don't know where to begin! Let me count the fucking ways, doll!"

That was a good sign, when she called him doll. He had to wait out another squall as she detailed the torments she would heap on his head should he ever venture uninvited into her office again, and then she got down to business, out of breath. "Now," she said. "That painting. The falling kid."

"You like it?"

"This is not something you like. You like a little doggie. You like a trip to the country. This painting takes my breath away."

"Really?"

"I kid you not. And you fucked up a sale."

"Oh?" Hood expected another blast of vituperation, but Sherri went on calmly.

"Mr. Fisk was gonna buy a Laszlo. We were in the middle of a deal when you burst in—the sixty-thousand-dollar range."

"Oh."

"Now he wants to buy the falling kid."

Hood waited a moment. "You said he *wants* to buy it. How much did you turn down?"

"Seventy-five thousand."

"You turned down seventy-five thousand? You're supposed to sell my work!"

"No, I'm not. I'm supposed to sell it for the highest price I can get, and honey, when that thing is framed and on the wall there's gonna be so many offers your head'll spin."

"You just turned down more money than I've earned in my life!"

"Two weeks, sweetie. Just gimme two weeks, and if you don't have fifty grand in your personal pocket by then I will pay you that much myself. I'd be stealing it."

"Just don't let Fisk get away."

"He'll be back. He was hot."

Seventy-five thousand dollars. On his way to the studio, Hood wondered if maybe he should change his dealer. Maybe he should sign with Amy Dunne. But he decided to let Sherri have her rope. If she could get more for the picture, so much the better.

He stopped at a fruit store and bought an apple. As he stood on a corner waiting for the light to change, he took the first bite and made another resolution to avoid Bellisle. He was feeling healthy and whole again. He wanted none of the sickly guilt that followed his meetings with Bellisle, or the unwholesome throbbing urgency that preceded them. He could see enough violence on television.

The light turned green, and several pedestrians pushed by him to cross the street. Hood was standing motionless, the once-bitten apple in his hand. At the precise moment when he had made his resolution, he was instantly rewarded by a vision. A painting appeared in his head, complete and whole, a finished work of art.

There would be three canvases, three frames—a triptych. By working on three canvases simultaneously, he could finish in record time. There would be no delays waiting for paint to dry. He tossed the apple into a trash can, and hurried to the studio.

"Leo! How are you!"

Leo turned from his work.

"Don't look at me like that! I'm happy for a change!"

"You're going to be obnoxious?"

"I've got a monster in my head I have to get down. It just came to me like a, like a visitation! I swear! I'm pregnant! It's glorious!"

"Such fanfare, Nicholas. You should hire a brass band."

For the next hour Hood clattered about with hammer and nails, getting his three canvases in order. Leo made no overt objection to the noise, but he slipped a tape of Patsy Cline into the cassette deck. Hood escaped from this via the Walkman Susan had given him. He put on the headphones and listened to Philip Glass.

In the center of the first canvas he drew the man with head bent, hands clutched to his chest. On the perimeter of the circle where he stood, he placed the second figure (who was Hood with an altered face) with hand outstretched—whether to beg or to help was not clear. The faces were to be all but invisible, the first with his head down, the other in profile.

On the second canvas, he drew the central figure, particularly the face, more heavily, in anticipation of his robe of flame which the viewer would have to see through. The other man stepped forward, his hand lowered, his mouth open. The background figures drew closer.

On the third, the burning man had levitated a foot off the ground, despite the heavy boots Hood had drawn on his feet. And his witness fell to his knees like Saint Peter at the calming of the storm. The background figures dispersed in panic, as if a bomb had exploded.

The picture was so clear in his mind that the process was almost like painting by numbers. He took up gray for his second run through the triptych, coloring the concrete and the sky. This was the same for all three sections, and took very little time.

By four o'clock, when Leo had left for the day, the work was well advanced. Hood was aching all over, and he badly needed the bathroom, but nothing would tear him away. His face was sticky with a benign fever that burned like painted fire, without heat.

He worked on through the supper hour, shifting from one frame to the next, and the pictures grew beneath his brush. He worked on until his eyes began to hurt, and he was forced to switch on the overhead lamps. The ache in his back, the pain in his arm grew worse, but sometime in the evening these passed over into numbness, and Hood felt he could paint forever.

The music of Philip Glass spun around and around in his head. He had set the machine on automatic reverse, so that time was not divided into any measure at all. He had no idea of the hour when Susan knocked on the door. He knew it was Susan, although she rarely came to the studio. His hand kept painting as he spoke. "Who is it?"

"It's me!"

"Not now, Susan! Working!" His brush dipped into orange, and brought the burning man's agony to a finer pitch.

"Aren't you going to let me in?"

"I can't! I just can't! I'll see you in the morning!" He covered his ears once more with the headphones and turned the music up, banishing his wife with the touch of a dial.

He finished the fire in all three sections—the first with its tongue of flame lapping at the man's chin, the second where it spread out to form a cross about his shoulders, and the third where the figure rose skyward in a blaze. The man's face took on a look of ecstasy here, his eyes turned upward to his cruel, invisible god.

Hood filled in the fringes of the sky with mauve and purple, as if dawn were breaking at midnight, a morning without sun. And when the feathery strokes of mauve and fuchsia were done, the scene became a ceremony, a mass from some religion too old to have a name. Hood turned from the work and tossed his brush into a can of turpentine.

He closed up the studio and clumped stiffly downstairs. Outside, the real dawn flooded the sky with tarnished silver, and it began to rain—large, heavy drops, big as pearls. He walked home through the empty, wet streets, the only survivor of some cataclysm that had wiped out the rest of mankind.

By the time he got home, Hood felt as if he'd been hit by a

truck. He lowered himself gingerly onto the couch and sat there, stunned. Susan came out of the bedroom, hauling two large bags of laundry. Without a word to him, she went into the kitchen. Hood heard her running water into a bucket. She started washing the floor then, scrubbing by the front door where Hood had left wet footprints. He looked at her through half-closed eyes, and she seemed terribly far away. "I'm sorry I couldn't open the door last night." He found it difficult to speak. "It would've been like you stopping in the middle of a concert."

"You're not a performer." She squeezed out the mop, determined not to look at him.

"No. I'm not a performer."

"You treat me like an employee."

"I can't explain. You'll have to see the work."

"It doesn't matter what you were painting. You said you'd be home early. I was worried."

"Susan, there's no phone in the studio."

"I *know* that. I was worried! I couldn't sleep! Jesus, what would you do if I stayed out past three in the morning!"

"Was it that late?"

"Oh, spare me." She attacked another section of the floor. Hood saw then that she hadn't slept at all; she probably hadn't even gone to bed. She stuck the mop into the bucket, and finally looked at him. "How would you feel if I locked you out?"

"It was different last night. The work was—"

"You sent me away! I needed to see you, understand? I was worried about you, and you sent me away! You couldn't even open the door!"

"No, I couldn't. I was working."

"God, you'd think it was a cure for cancer." She squeezed the mop as if trying to kill it, and started back in on the floor.

Hood thought for a moment, closing his eyes so as not to see her engaged in manual labor—a sight that always made him uneasy. Finally, he said, "You know I don't use words like 'genius' very often . . ."

"I hope you're not going to start now."

"My work, up to now, has been the result of thought. Thought, and experience, and practice. My painting has always been very . . . deliberate. I've always been completely in control."

"Well, so you should be. It's not a picnic."

"It's changed. It changed the other night, when I painted that boy who dove off the roof."

Susan stuck the mop in the bucket and stared at him. "You painted that boy? The one who killed himself?"

"Yes. And the whole experience—"

"You painted a picture of a boy killing himself. I don't be-lieve it."

"Why shouldn't I?"

"Why should you! Jesus, Nick, do you really think that's a good thing to do? How would you feel if I killed myself, and Leo painted a picture of it the next day? Being an artist doesn't give you the right to do anything you damn well please."

Hood looked at her standing there, mop in hand, like an allegory of a clean mind. He wondered if it were worth pursuing the point, but he couldn't believe she felt strongly about his subject matter. She was just giving him a rough time because she was hurt. "Regardless of any problems of taste, the fact is that the painting came out of me as if it already existed. I painted it all in one shot, without stopping. I *had* to paint it that way. If I'd stopped, the whole thing might've fallen apart. And I did it again yesterday. Another whole painting, Susan. A huge project! Three canvases! Done. Finished in less than twenty-four hours. I'm talking about a breakthrough so big I wasn't even looking for it."

"Fine. Good for you. Just don't start treating me like dirt now that you have a taste for the term 'genius.'"

"I only meant to describe the *process*. For the first time in my life I have reason to believe in inspiration, and maybe you should take a look at the fucking paintings before you pass judgment on them." He got up and went into the bedroom.

As he was getting out of his clothes, he thought, "Why is it every time something good happens, people start to hate me?" He began to get angrier and angrier as he lay in bed remembering Susan's words. Then he rolled over and summoned his painting in his mind's eye. Oh, he would give everything, everything he had, to paint like that again.

NINE

HIS triumphant bout with "The Burning Man" had left Hood exhausted. Painting was out of the question, so he set himself the task of building frames for the triptych. The carpentry was relaxing work that left him pleasantly tired at the end of the day. He spent the rest of his time reading and watching television.

Susan remained distant from him and hardly said a word as he lounged around the apartment. Since she was by nature an affectionate person, her withdrawal was all the more dramatic. Hood tried to think of ways to please her.

One night after supper, he asked her to play for him. When they had first married, he used to ask her often, almost every night, but as he became familiar with her repertoire, he asked less and less frequently. It had been well over a year since he had asked her to play. Susan looked up from the letter she was writing at the kitchen table. "You're sick of my playing. You hear it all the time."

"But I don't *listen* all the time." He drew the curtains against the evening sun. "Will you play?"

She looked at him a moment before getting up and crossing to the harpsichord. She was wearing faded blue jeans, and a red T-shirt that said MEL THE MOVER. When she was seated with her back to him she said, "What would you like?"

"I don't know. Something simple."

She chose Bach's Prelude in C, and Hood went to stand behind her. Her eyes were fixed on a point somewhere in space, as if she looked into the eyes of a stern, invisible muse. The bones in her hand rippled delicately as she played the arpeggios; the rest of her body was solemn and still. When the piece was over, she placed her hands in her lap.

Hood touched her shoulder. "That was beautiful. Perfect."

"Good piece, isn't it?"

"You always say that—as if you had nothing to do with it."

The bony shoulders were lifted in a shrug.

She played a ruminative, lilting piece next, which Hood didn't recognize. It was serious and slow, tinged with melancholy, as if the composer were remembering a great loss from long ago—far enough back that he could now face both past and future with equal resignation, if not tranquility.

"Who wrote that?"

"Lully."

"He must've been a wonderful man. Really a good man."

"Actually he was far from it. He was ruthless—really Machiavellian in getting what he wanted."

"You wouldn't think he could write like that."

"Who knows? Maybe he lifted it from D'Anglebert. Would you like something else?"

"Yes." He bent low, and spoke quietly into her ear. "I'd like your shirt."

Susan raised her arms, and Hood pulled the red shirt off, over her head. He ran his fingers lightly over her shoulders and down her back, making small circles where he knew she liked to be touched. Susan made a low sound in her throat, and tipped her head back against him. She pulled his hands round to her chest.

They went to bed and made love as they hadn't for months. When it was over, they lay damp and hot in each other's arms, and later they slept the sleep of the innocent and the young.

Their life together was very good over the next few weeks. Hood worked on a small painting (lovers in a clearing, no violence) and took up a long-dormant interest in ink drawing. Susan sat for two of these drawings in the apartment, and they finished the afternoons in bed.

They visited the Museum of Modern Art, where they saw a Douanier Rousseau exhibition, and spent another afternoon touring the medieval section of the Metropolitan. They were considerate of each other, gave each other little gifts, and, in short, behaved as a married couple will when, after long complacency, they remember why they love. It was a happy time.

On one of their afternoon excursions they stopped at a small midtown restaurant for espressos. Hood was reflecting, during a comfortable silence, on why he had been so relaxed recently, and ended his train of thought aloud. "I haven't seen Andre Bellisle for some time," he said. "Thank God."

Susan just wrinkled her nose.

"I hope I never see him again."

"I hope so, too," she said. "There's something wrong with him, if you ask me. That time he showed up when we were having dinner . . ."

"Go on. What were you going to say?"

"It sounds melodramatic . . . but I felt like I was in the presence of an evil being. I don't think anything good would come of knowing him."

Hood signaled the waitress for two more coffees; then he leaned toward Susan and said, "Let me tell you a story."

Susan listened as he told her how Bellisle had arranged to meet him in Washington Square. He told her of the victim's appointment with "Baker," and his death moments later in flames. Susan said nothing the whole time. But when he got to the part where the man set fire to himself, she leaned back in the booth and stared at the table, as if something inside her had caved in. She didn't look up again as he told her of the magnificent painting that had grown out of these events.

Hood had started the story by way of illustrating his agreement with Susan's assessment of Bellisle's character. But as he got
to describing his painting, the horror in his voice diminished,
leaving the unmistakable sound of wonder.

Susan said quietly, "You were there."

"What? I didn't hear you."

"You were actually there. When that happened."

"Well, I didn't know what he was going to do. It's not the sort
of thing you expect, is it?"

"What exactly *do* you expect when you set out in the middle
of the night to meet a person you have no reason to trust?"

"I don't know. Anyway, the only reason I told you all this is
simply to explain why I don't want to see him anymore. In some
way, I think he caused those deaths. I don't believe he's simply
psychic, that he simply foresees these things. He has some sort of
control over people."

"He certainly controls you."

"Oh, bullshit."

"Who else could drag you out of bed, keep you up all night
watching this . . . carnage? Think about it, Nick. He has some
sort of hold on—"

"Bullshit! I went because I wanted to. And because I didn't
know what was going to happen! Whatever else he may be, you
have to admit Bellisle is interesting. And you seem to forget that
he managed to sell three paintings. He's not a man you dismiss
lightly."

"The worst thing is that you paint these horrors."

"What am I supposed to paint, Susan? Sunflowers?"

"Nick—"

"You haven't even seen them. Admit it—you're being idiotic,
criticizing work you haven't seen. Who are you to say what can
or cannot be painted? Why are you so quick to judge?"

"So why don't you show them to me?"

"Fine. Let's go." He signaled for the check.

"Where are we going?"

"They're at the Novack. I think Sherri's going to show them sometime soon." He used a pay phone to call the gallery.

Sherri had left for the day by the time they got there, so Marcia took them to the third floor. In the elevator she said, "You two ought to go around together more often—you look nice together." The remark made Susan smile, but Hood just stared at the floor numbers above the door.

Marcia unlocked a storage room attached to the work space where pictures were framed and prepared for shipping. "They're in there," she said.

"Look," Susan said. "It's your friend Bellisle!" She was looking down through a window facing West Broadway. "And look who he's with!"

Hood joined her at the window. Two floors below them, Andre Bellisle was standing in front of the Amy Dunne Gallery, deep in conversation with Sam Weigel. Bellisle was emphasizing a point with graceful hand motions. Somehow, he looked taller from above.

"I'm surprised you recognized him—he looks so much better."

"What are you talking about? He looks exactly the same!"

"Look at his skin! Look at the way he stands!"

"I don't know, Nick. He looks the same to me."

"You haven't seen him up close. Believe me, he's not nearly as repulsive as he was."

Marcia looked over their shoulders. "That man was at the group show opening. I didn't realize he was a friend of yours."

"He wasn't then. Don't you think he looks better?"

"No." Marcia shuddered. "Not at all." She went back to the elevator and pushed the button. "Make sure the door's locked before you come down."

Hood was somewhat taken aback that neither woman could

see the dramatic improvement in Bellisle's face. But then again, he was an artist—his very life depended on seeing beauty and order where others beheld only chaos, or banality, or nothing at all.

He stayed by the window, and let Susan look at the paintings alone. It was very warm for an April afternoon—the people below took their time strolling home. The men carried their suit jackets over their shoulders, and women stopped to peer into shop windows. Nobody seemed in a rush.

Bellisle and Weigel disappeared into Amy Dunne's gallery, where there was a display of Giacometti's drawings. What was it Bellisle had said? "I chose to make myself available." Well, he could make himself as available as he liked. Hood wasn't having any. He watched the street scene for a while, and then went to find Susan.

She was standing in front of "The Burning Man" triptych. The paintings were on the floor, leaning against the wall, and Susan peered down at them as if she were thinking, rather than looking. Hood waited beside her for a while, but she said nothing. Finally, he said, "What do you think?"

She moved farther into the little room and looked at the boy diving gracefully into the depths of his nonexistence. Her face looked strained and sorrowful, as if her own future were ending with his. "I think—" She started to speak, had to clear her throat. "I think I'm going to lose you."

Hood put his arms around her, but received no hug in return. "Does that mean you don't like them?"

"It means I think people will love them and you'll make a lot of money and I wish you hadn't painted them."

Over the next few weeks he worked steadily, but not obsessively. He turned out two oils, minor things depicting ambiguous situations. The first was two men, apparently quarreling, in a small boat on a rough sea. The second showed a man entering a house, where a woman waited with a violin case on her lap. Neither piece satisfied Hood. But he knew others would be drawn into them by their narrative possibilities.

He now had four canvases in storage at the Novack, and gradually, without their saying anything, the idea grew between Sherri and Hood that he would soon have a one-man show. When he trundled in the latest picture, Sherri removed her half glasses and said, "Whatcha got?"

He showed her the man entering the house; the woman waiting.

"It's good. We can use that. Whyn't you put it upstairs, or have Marcia do it—I gotta make some calls." She pulled the telephone across the desk. "Bring me a few more like that and I think we're ready to roll."

Hood didn't want to leave right away. He leaned against the door and said, "I think I'm on the verge of something really big."

"Like 'The Burning Man'?" She was squinting into a little address book, not really paying attention.

"Maybe bigger. It's just a buildup of energy at this point."

"Don't stop the little things, meanwhile. They're gonna get snapped right up. I don't know what's got into you, but it's comin' out gold. Tell me if this is an eight or a three." She pushed the address book across the desk and poked at it with a stubby finger.

"It's a three. Did Fisk change his mind about 'The Falling Boy'?"

"He wants it. But he's still lowballing. If you want, I can take his eighty thousand, but it's nuts not to wait till your own show opens. You're gonna be big, Nick."

"You don't call me doll anymore."

"Doll."

Hood was feeling uncomfortable, as if Sherri were a complete stranger. "I don't know how soon I'll be able to fill the place up."

"I got a slot coming up October three, and another one middle a January."

"October's way too soon."

"Thing is, you get this on a wall by October, you got one hot bid in for the Whitney show come New Year." Sherri was referring to the Whitney's biennial New Work show. It was the absolute pinnacle for the young artist. Reviews would be written across the country, and dealers would travel from all over the world to get in on the next trend, a piece of the next genius. "'The Burning Man' will blow those characters away. But you gotta show'em you got legs. If they think it's a one-time thing, forget it."

"October's impossible. I won't have enough."

"Give it a shot. Don't kill yourself. I'm just tellin' ya what *could* happen. Did you say a three?" She tapped out a number on the phone. "Problems?"

"It's all so serious."

"It's a business. What'd you expect?" She hung up the phone. "No answer. I notice wealthy people don't go in for tape machines."

Hood didn't know what he was hanging around for. He said, "I've changed, haven't I?"

"Everybody changes." She buzzed Marcia, spoke into the phone. "Honey, find me a real number for Manby. Buzz me right back." She flipped through the address book. "Your work's better."

"And that's what matters, right?"

"That's what matters." The intercom buzzed, and she started firing questions at Marcia. Hood left without saying good-bye. He couldn't say when, exactly, but some time ago Sherri had ceased to be a friend.

*   *   *

He was determined not to brood; he refused to let Susan's reaction to his paintings, and Sherri's coolness keep him down. He settled into a routine of work and relaxation that carried him through the rest of the spring and into early June. He went to the studio every morning, except Sunday, promptly at nine. He and Leo would work quietly until one o'clock, when they would adjourn outside to the pier for lunch. Then back to work until six o'clock.

He renewed his effort to prove to Susan that he was not a monster. She was delighted to come home from jogging one Sunday and find he had prepared a picnic lunch for them to take to Central Park. The leaves were nearly in full bloom, at the peak of their emerald green. Hood rented a boat and they rowed across Belvedere Pond while it was still morning. There was only one other couple on the water, and one or two black men with fishing poles.

Hood brought the boat in under a huge willow that hung low over the water, and poured them each some white wine. They sat with their backs to the buildings on Central Park West, and faced the bridge, where another couple strolled with a little boy. "Oh, I could become addicted to this," Susan said. "We could move out of SoHo, and live in the park."

"We could live off roots and berries."

"Or fish—there's a man over there with a fishing pole."

It wasn't long before the park began to fill with people. Boat after boat nosed around the bend, and shouts of children pierced the quiet. Susan said, "Wouldn't it be nice if we were the only ones here?"

Hood reached out and stroked her hair. "We *are* the only ones here. We're the only people in the world."

"I can't imagine living without you, after all these years." She kissed his forehead. "I bet *you* can."

Hood looked up through fronds of willow at the brilliant blue
sky. "I can imagine it," he said. "But I would hate it. Hate it." He
put his arms around her, held her close. "Maybe we should have
a child."

Susan immediately pulled away, her brown eyes completely
round. "You mean that?"

"Yes. I do."

"It would have to be soon. I'm thirty-two, don't forget. I don't
even know if I can have one!"

"Yes you can."

"When did you have in mind?"

"Right now. Right under this tree."

Susan laughed. "I wouldn't mind one bit. Except for the
crowd." She rested her head on his chest. "My God," she said.
"An actual baby."

And then Bellisle appeared. He was walking slowly across the
bridge with Sam Weigel, his blond hair flashing in the sun.
Happiness flew from Hood, instantly. An electric current came to
life in his gut, and his heart began to thud. He said, "Let's go
back now."

"But it's so nice!"

"Getting too crowded." He packed up their lunch things, and
sat down between the oars. Susan sat in the stern, but clearly
didn't want to leave. Hood pulled them out from under the
willow into the sunlight. Sam Weigel was leaving Bellisle on the
bridge. Susan was saying something. "What? I'm sorry?"

"Do you feel like seeing a movie? The Biograph's not far.
They have a Bette Davis series running."

"You go ahead." They were near the bridge now. Bellisle was
leaning on the railing, staring into the water. "I think I have to
take a walk."

"We can go for a walk, if you like."

"No. You go to the movie. You'll enjoy it."

"You don't want me to come with you." The realization hit her like a blow to the stomach. Her face had been bright and happy just moments earlier.

"I know it's sudden," he said. "I have to think about some things."

He pulled in at the boathouse dock. When he had paid at the ticket booth, he handed her the empty picnic basket. "You know your way to the subway up here?"

Susan's voice quavered slightly. "I can't believe you're doing this, Nick. You open me up with this lovely day, and your talk of a baby, and then you shove me away."

"I'm sorry. Really." He moved to touch her, but she whirled away from him. A boy on a bicycle had to swerve to avoid her.

Hood turned and ran along the fence that surrounded the boathouse. He came up behind Bellisle on the bridge, panting. "Are you looking for me?"

Bellisle straightened up and faced him. Hood was so taken aback by the change in Bellisle's appearance that he literally took a step back from him. Where pustules and blisters had all but obliterated Bellisle's features, the skin now healed over, the sores dried up. While no one would have called him beautiful, he was no longer the singularly repellent entity of before. He had high, aristocratic cheekbones, a noble, slightly beaked nose; the formerly red, watery eyes were now clear, and icy blue. True, the skin was still lined and dotted with scars and pits, but it only gave him a worldly, slightly dissolute air; he might be taken for a drunkard poet, a man intent on pissing his genius away. He said, "Good of you to find me."

Hood couldn't speak. Because Bellisle was not only now possessed of an attractive face, he was considerably taller than before. Hood could've sworn the man had only been chest-high beside him, but now he was quite equal to him in stature. Bellisle showed his sharp teeth in a smile. "You needn't be so alarmed.

I happen to suffer from a recurring condition, that's all. As you see, it's momentarily in remission."

"It's not just your face." Hood kept his distance, looking at him. "You're taller than you were before."

"A trick of psychology, I assure you."

"No. You are definitely taller than you were."

"How would that be possible?"

Hood shook his head. "Forget it. I must be out of my—"

"It's nothing to worry about, I'm sure."

"Maybe you're right. Mr. Baker."

Bellisle squinted at him. "Oh dear. Oh dear. You have things very wrong. Is that why you've kept away from me these past weeks? I underestimated your capacity for jumping to conclusions."

"The man who burned himself in the park thought I was you. He called me Baker. You called yourself Baker with him, didn't you. You arranged to meet him in the park, and sent me instead."

Bellisle pointed with his cane—a gesture made regal by his striking new appearance. "Can we walk in the shade? I hate the sun."

"You knew what would happen. You let him die."

Bellisle reached inside his jacket and pulled out a neatly folded bit of paper. "You never read the papers, I take it."

Hood took the clipping and unfolded it. The article was titled, CALL FROM A STRANGER, written by C. Randall Baker, columnist for the *New York Post*. The first sentence read, "Last Tuesday I received a call from a guy who announced the intention of setting himself on fire. I thought it was a joke."

Bellisle said, "You see I'm not Mr. Baker, nor did I pretend to be. The unfortunate victim of self-immolation had tried to arrange an audience with C. Randall Baker, columnist and newshound. No doubt he was a publicity seeker of the more flamboyant stripe. And you showed up instead. Can we *please* get out of the sun?"

They walked to the end of the bridge, and along a shaded area by the pond. A black family sat nearby, around the racket of an oversized radio. Hood finished reading Baker's column, which was written in that combination of cynicism and sentimentality beloved of old-time reporters. Baker lamented his own obtuseness and marveled at the dead man's pain, clearly moved by the event.

Bellisle perched on the edge of a bench, very erect, with the cane propped between his knees. "You see. It was no different from the boy. I foresaw the event; I told you about it."

Hood shoved the clipping into his pocket. "And I painted it."

"Yes. Thought you might." He looked Hood up and down, as if wondering whether to buy him. "I'm very happy you've come."

"What's the story with you and Sam Weigel?"

"Nothing that concerns you, my friend. We go to bars together."

"You and I had a deal. You led me to believe our relationship would be unique. But you seem very tight with Weigel."

"We drink together!"

"Are you sleeping with him?"

"Hah! Listen to yourself!"

"He's homosexual."

"That is meaningless to me, as you should know by now. Why do you care whose company I keep?"

Hood sat on the end of the bench and watched a boy heave a large stick into the water. A woolly dog leapt gamely into the water and swam out to fetch it. "My painting is better than it was before I met you. Maybe I'm afraid you'll have the same effect on Weigel. Help the competition."

"I shan't people the earth with great artists, if that's what you think. The chances of there being two of your magnitude are infinitesimal. Wait for your one-man show."

"How did you know about that?"

Bellisle shrugged. "Miss Novack is a smart woman."

"It has to be in October. But there's no way I'll have enough substantial work by then. Not new work."

"Nonsense. That's three clear months."

"Since 'The Burning Man,' all I seem able to come up with are smaller things. They're not bad, but they won't raise a storm."

"The storm will break, if you stick with me. I promise."

Hood looked at Bellisle's healed face, into the cold blue eyes. "Promise you won't help Weigel."

"Forget Weigel." Bellisle touched his forehead tentatively, as if checking to make sure the skin were still there. "Besides," he said. "For coming back to me, I have a little reward for you."

"Yeah," Hood said, and looked out across the rowers on the pond. "That's probably why I feel so scared."

He finished several small pictures over the next two weeks. Leo worked in the studio as well, but they rarely ate lunch together now. Hood's meal consisted of a sandwich wolfed down at the easel. In the evenings he went to the gallery and worked on the frames.

He was thrown back into himself the way he had been before his rapprochement with Susan; he was distracted, irritable, ready for a fight. Bellisle had given him a time and a place, and the knowledge of its approach kept a low-voltage fear trembling inside him. Luckily, Susan was busy preparing for a recital, so they were kept by their schedules out of each other's way. No fighting broke out, but they lived with barbed wire around their hearts.

His date with Bellisle was for Wednesday morning, three A.M. On Tuesday evening he scrawled out a note for Susan on the kitchen table. "Very important meeting. Will be home tomorrow morning or evening. Please do *not* worry."

Susan might come to the studio anyway, when she found the note, so Hood wanted to avoid the place. He walked up to the village and had a solitary dinner in a quiet café. Afterward, he watched a movie in a Fourth Street cinema. That took him to eight-thirty. There was a large bookstore just up the street that stayed open until midnight, so he strolled up there. He found Valerie Vale at a discount table, leafing through an illustrated history of the nude. Hood said, "Straight for the dirty stuff, eh?"

Valerie's face turned deep red. "I just thought—if I'm posing for this stuff all the time, I should know more about it."

"The models were never as pretty as you."

She flipped the pages back to a Rubens. "Sorta heavy, huh."

"I don't think jogging was the thing back then. How've you been?"

She shrugged. "Okay, I guess. I just been up to Connecticut to visit my folks and that. They're taking a big tour of Europe comin' up."

"How nice."

Valerie put the book back on the table. "If you want to know the truth, I been lousy. I broke up with Bill."

"Bill?"

"The black guy!"

"Oh, him! That's all to the good."

"He's a terrific artist."

"And a nasty man. What are you doing tonight?"

"Nothin'."

"Feel like a drink?" He gave her a lascivious wink.

"Nick. You're married. You shouldn't tease me."

"I'm not. I need some company for a few hours, and then I have to meet somebody at three in the morning."

Valerie looked over her shoulder as if they might be arrested at any moment. "Where did you wanna go?" She didn't question the appointment at three A.M.

When they were seated at a table in McTaggart's, a grubby little beer joint on Cornelia Street, Valerie leaned forward and said, "I feel like a sinner, being with you."

Hood laughed. "Only a Catholic would say something like that."

"The nuns hated me. They thought I was seducing all the little boys. I was always older than the other girls, 'cause of this reading problem I had, so I was a little more, um, developed. They thought I was dumb, too, but later on it turns out I was dyslexic. Letters and that don't look the same to me."

The waiter came for their order—a swarthy young man with an oversized Adam's apple, who was none too pleased that they ordered no food. When he had turned on his heel and gone, Hood asked Valerie about her painting.

"It's coming along," she said. "It's fine. I been doing still lifes, mostly. They don't cost anything, and you can take as long as you want. Trouble is, how exciting can it be—bananas on canvas."

Hood smiled.

"What's wrong?" She looked worried.

"It sounds funny, that's all."

"Bananas on canvas?" She furrowed her brow in an effort to see the humor. "I guess so."

The waiter slammed a couple of beers on the table and veered off to more lucrative ground.

Valerie said, "Sometimes I sit for hours in front of this empty canvas and it just seems to get bigger and bigger till I feel like I'm falling into it. Then I start to paint on it just so I stay in this world and don't get sucked into the Twilight Zone."

"It's the other way round with me. I prefer the Twilight Zone. Anything that takes me out of this world. I'd like to see your work."

"You'll just laugh. It's not as good as yours."

"Anyone as innocent as you must come up with some interesting stuff."

"I'm not innocent! I'm real bad. You wouldn't believe the
stuff I done."

They talked for a while about Hood's work. Valerie showed
an extraordinary recall of his pictures, remembering many small
details. Hood began to find it quite embarrassing, so he asked if
she wanted another beer. She said, "Yeah, if that waiter'd get the
poker out of his ass."

She couldn't get his attention, so she got up and crossed the
room and tapped him on the shoulder. He whirled on her, and
said loud enough for the whole restaurant to hear, "I'll *get* to
you!"

Valerie sat back down. "Boy, he's kind of a jerk." She
remained subdued for the next couple of minutes. The waiter
finally approached the table. "Did you need something?"

Hood examined his face. "Are you an actor, by any chance?"

"Yes!" The waiter beamed. "Trying to break into Broadway.
It's not easy, though."

"You have a good face for an actor."

"I think so. But a lot depends on who you know."

"It has the blank stupidity they like for commercials— nose
drop ads. Of course, you have a potbelly, and your hair's
receding, but they can do wonders with lighting. Now bring the
young lady her beer, before you lose the rest of your teeth."

The waiter's Adam's apple bobbed, and he opened his mouth
like a fish. He retreated to the bar.

Valerie said, "Jesus. You really did a number on him."

"I don't like him."

"Yeah, but—geez."

She lived five floors above the Donkey's Head Tavern, on
Hudson Street. Hood was gasping for breath by the time she
opened her door and turned on the light. The room was hardly
nine feet square, and had no window.

"It's poky," she said. "But it's home."

Hood glanced into the cramped corners. "You're very brave, aren't you."

"It's not that bad. At least, I don't think so. But my sister came down from Darien a couple of months ago, and when I opened the door, she just burst out laughing. It really upset me—I mean, it's not very nice to laugh at someone's *home*."

"You've managed to make it look all right," Hood said, though it was not true. The overstuffed chair looked as if the Salvation Army had turned it down; the spavined bed looked near to collapse.

Valerie reached into a closet that had no door and pulled out a large black portfolio. "You promise not to laugh?"

"No," Hood said. "If it's funny, I'm going to laugh—that's a risk you take."

She pulled out a small sheet of drawing paper. "This isn't one of my best, but—"

"Never apologize." He took the whole folio from her. "If it needs an apology, throw it out. Or keep it for yourself." He sat on the cavernous bed and opened the portfolio across the pillow. Valerie plunked down in a chair and stared at her feet.

"I want to apologize for everything I draw. I wish they were all better."

Hood was searching the first watercolor for signs of character but found none—it was a stiff, unlifelike arrangement of flowers. The next showed a bowl of fruit by a window. The wash of light was not bad, but she had been defeated by the fruit itself. He put this aside, and examined an ink-and-watercolor rendering of a cat. The animal was slinking down from a table, about to leap from the frame. No close observer of animals, even Hood could see that the anatomy of the haunches was wrong. Still, Valerie had caught the gleam in the eye, the taut alertness in the body.

"That's Bill's cat. I hadda keep puttin' him back on the table."

Hood rapidly went through the remaining works; all had a

worked-over look that was death to a watercolor. He sighed and said, "Don't try to save paper. If you get it wrong, start again, or pick another subject. Don't belabor the point."

"No good, huh."

"You don't trust yourself—it shows in all of these, except the cat. I assume you had to work fast because he kept moving."

"Yeah! I couldn't get his legs right!"

"But it feels like a *cat*. There's some life in it that you didn't have time to obliterate."

"You really hate them."

"How long have you been painting?"

Valerie shrugged, still looking at her toes. "Four years. Off and on. I get discouraged and quit every few months. But I always go back to it. I got nothin' else."

Hood folded up the portfolio. The work was not good enough to get her into the least demanding art school; it would be wrong to encourage her. He couldn't imagine why Leo had let her continue in the class—but then, it would be hard to look into the heart-shaped face, those dark blue eyes, and say no. Indeed, her sheer sexual presence would probably always open doors, gain her entry to places she didn't belong.

As if sensing he was about to demolish her, she knelt on the chair to reach over the back, giving Hood a favorable view of her backside. She pulled out a sheet of paper three times the size of the others, and handed it over. It was a full-length charcoal sketch of herself, seated on a bed, leaning back against a wall. Her eyes looked straight out at the viewer; her legs were wide open.

Hood felt his aesthetic judgment drowned by the appeal to his erotic sensibilities. "Well," he said. "Now you have a subject!"

"You like it?"

"It's the best one. Easily. I like the way you've done the face." He was not in fact looking at the face.

He could feel her sense of victory change the atmosphere in the room. She wanted him to look longer. "Do you think the legs are all right?" She left the chair and leaned down on the bed beside him. He could feel her breath on his neck.

"The legs are fine." He shifted now, so that, still without touching her, he could feel the heat of her cheek next to his. They both were perfectly still.

Her voice was almost a whisper. "I can hardly breathe, I want you so bad."

He placed a hand on the back of her neck. He said, "You're very hot."

The room and all its tawdry furnishings had disappeared in a vortex of physical rapture. When once again they were separate persons in a particular place, a particular time, Valerie turned her face to the wall and cried.

"You don't have to feel guilty."

"I do!"

"Well, don't. Susan doesn't live with me. She lives with someone I used to be."

Valerie pulled a Kleenex from a box on the floor and wiped her eyes, making raccoon circles of mascara. She blew her nose. "Why do you still live with her?"

"I don't know." He was distracted by a sudden memory, an image: Valerie, naked, singing in some mysterious place, with clouds of fog rolling in from all sides. From out of the fog, a pair of outstretched hands about to encircle her neck. Hood looked at her throat now, where an artery pulsed with life. She was a sexual athlete, yes, but all in all a fragile being. He had a sudden urge—the way one might on seeing a translucent, porcelain cup—to break her. He reached for his watch and saw it was three o'clock. "I've got to rush. I'm already late."

Valerie opened her eyes. "What for?"

"My appointment, remember?"

"Oh. Yeah." She propped herself up on one elbow and watched him getting dressed.

Hood didn't want to look at her again. He felt like a diver, struggling up toward the glittering surface, desperate to breathe the air again. And Valerie was pulling him down.

As he hurriedly combed his hair, she looked at him in the mirror. "Guess we killed the time, huh?"

TEN

THE address was on East Seventy-third Street, between Madison and Fifth. By the time the cab turned left off Madison, Hood was gripping the edge of the seat. Electricity pulsed through his body like never before; he felt panic, excitement, fear. As he was paying the driver, a man emerged from the town house, wearing a full-length tweed coat and a wide-brimmed hat pulled low to hide his features. He brushed against Hood as he got into the cab.

Hood said, "Is Andre Bellisle in there?"

The man tucked his face deeper into his collar, and shut the car door. Hood realized then that he was about to enter a brothel.

He rang the doorbell, and was admitted by a buzzer. The foyer, which was deserted, was decorated in very expensive good taste. There were fluted columns, a marble floor, and hanging above the fireplace a painting by Remington. It might have been the home of an ambassador. Hood opened a pair of double doors and peered into a huge den, also deserted. He closed the door and went up a thickly carpeted staircase.

The upstairs hall had five doors leading to what presumably were bedrooms. All five were closed, the hall silent. The stairs continued, narrower and uncarpeted, toward the third floor. Hood climbed these and knocked on a small door at the top. He heard footsteps, and the door was thrown open.

"You're late." Bellisle loomed in the doorway, his nostrils flared in contempt. There was nothing left of the ugly dwarf he had been. In place of that creature stood a proud, patrician, beautiful man, whose eyes and skin glowed with health.

Hood was left quite breathless and could only manage to
stammer out something about having a lot of work to finish.

"In future, either come or don't come. Don't be late." He
motioned Hood to enter.

The small attic room contained a desk, a couch, and six
television monitors stacked on a table. Each screen showed a top
view of a bed.

Hood sat on the edge of the couch, his fear gone, his wonder
at the change in Bellisle subsiding. He was not entirely sure he
was not hallucinating, but he spoke in a cool tone to hide any
uncertainty. "I can't imagine why you brought me here."

"Oh? Not interested in sex?"

"Not in watching it."

Only one of the TV monitors contained any people. A man
was on top of a woman, his buttocks gleaming in the light from
a Tiffany lamp. Bellisle pointed. "From *his* position it probably
seems like a wonderful experience."

"I'm glad you don't have the sound on."

"I can turn it up, if you like."

"No."

Bellisle folded his arms, and turned his cool blue eyes to the
screen. The smirk on his face said he'd seen it all before. The
man was moving up and down with no more passion than an oil
pump.

Hood settled back on the couch. "What technique this guy
has. It's soporific."

"You think it less ridiculous if the couple is in rapture? It's the
opposite. Human beings are absurdly serious about their plea-
sures."

"You, of course, are not human."

"It's only a temporary condition."

Hood yawned. The man continued up and down like a
clockwork toy. "Does the girl know about the camera?" Her face

was partly obscured by the man's shoulder; her eyes looked unfocused.

Bellisle didn't answer. He stared at the screen, his fingers fluttering over his face.

"Why are you wasting my time?"

"I'm not. Wait and see."

"This is not my idea of a laugh—watching some guy's ass all night. And it has nothing to do with my work."

"Ah, but people change, Nicholas. I'd despair altogether if I didn't know that."

The man removed himself from the girl, and disappeared from the screen. He came back and tied one of her hands to the bedpost, while she lay there unresisting. He went round to the other side, his potbelly shaking with each step, and tied the other hand. The girl said something, but showed no fear when he moved to the foot of the bed. His torso blocked their view for a few moments.

"He has to pay her *and* tie her up? You'd think one or the other would be enough. What's he doing now?" The man bent over the woman's head. "Not a blindfold, too!"

The man folded his arms and stood back to admire his composition. He had tied her feet together, not apart, so that the girl was cruciform. She turned her head in his direction and said something. The man remained motionless, his bald head glistening, his round stomach thrust forward. The girl spoke again. He bent forward and kissed her belly. There was no sound, but Hood saw her laugh. The man went out of view.

"Uh-oh," Hood said. "Gone to get his flippers?"

The girl jerked her head up, as if frightened by a sudden noise. Her mouth was moving, her neck straining, but the man must have made a soothing noise, because she settled back on the pillow.

The man appeared at the edge of the frame.

"What's he got now?"

Bellisle put a finger to his lips and smiled.

The man shifted his weight slightly, and there was a gleam of metal.

"What is that? A knife?" Hood sat up on the edge of the couch. The man still hadn't moved fully into the light. "I can't quite see what he's—"

"It's a knife." Bellisle's voice was dry, stating historical fact. "Watch the screen, Nicholas."

The man took a step toward the bed; there was another glint of steel.

Hood leapt to his feet. "What room are they in!"

Bellisle raised an eyebrow. "There's nothing you can do."

"What room are they in!" Hood grabbed him by the lapels, but Bellisle was iron, heavy as a battleship. "Tell me!"

Hood ran down the stairs. He burst onto the second floor and threw open the first door he came to. A bed, a mirror, an empty room. He opened another. An identical room, also empty. He ran the length of the hall, and opened each door one after another. He called out, "Scream! Scream! Tell me where you are!"

Silence.

He ran down to the first floor and through the double doors into the huge drawing room. At the end of this was another door. Hood ran for it.

Locked.

He took a few steps back and threw his weight against it, but the door hardly budged. Something to ram it with—he needed something to ram it with. He grabbed a wooden chair and swung it. Two of the legs snapped off; the door was barely scratched. He swung it again. Another leg splintered, and Hood fell to the floor. And on the floor was a key, the brass streaked with blood.

He got to his feet, and fitted the key into the lock.

The thing on the bed was no longer a girl. The bed was no longer a bed. The wall at the head of the bed was not a wall; it was a study in red by Jackson Pollack. Strings of droplets were flung up the wall, even to the ceiling. The killer had raised his knife again and again, dipping it into his living female palette again and again. Arterial spray had filled in any parts of the wall he might have missed.

Hood took a step closer. One didn't think about blood having a smell, but he smelled it now—thick, musky, intensely human. He should be throwing up, he knew, he should be sick, but he wanted to see. He wanted to see.

She might have been twenty-three or twenty-four. There was a thick red streak across her forehead, but other than this her face had not been touched. The eyes were rolled up into the head. Her chin rested on her chest, her head turned slightly to one side, as if she had dropped off to sleep.

The rest was red devastation—the torn-open body and the bed were soaked in blood and utter silence. So much gore should whimper, it should cry, it should have a particular sound. But it was silent as a painting.

Hood closed the door behind him and ran back up to the two flights of stairs. The attic was empty; Bellisle had gone. He turned around and looked at the TV monitors. Five of the screens were just as before. But the sixth showed the room he had just left, and in that room a man was killing a girl. Her ripped and bleeding form bounced with each blow, but not with life. With each stroke his arm made an arc backward over his shoulder throwing blood into the air. He bobbed up and down, as mechanical in murder as he had been in sex, stabbing a girl who could not respond, could no longer even care.

A telephone rang, and Hood let out a short scream. Every muscle quivered. He fumbled for the receiver and dropped it, his eyes locked on the monitor. The man had removed himself from the girl. Hood watched him button his shirt and pull on his pants, ignoring the fact that he was covered with blood. He flung a long tweed coat over his shoulders, and placed on his head a wide-brimmed hat. Then he left the screen, left what remained of the girl, just as Hood had found her. The picture burst into a blizzard of electronic snow, and Hood was released from its grip.

From a nearby cabinet, he heard the click as a machine switched itself off. The monitor screen went dark. Hood realized then that he had been watching a videotape. All of it—both the sex and the murder—had been over before he had even set foot in the house. The killer was the man who had come out of the house just as Hood had arrived. He knelt and picked up the telephone receiver, holding it to his ear without speaking.

That satin voice. "Do you understand now, Nicholas?"

Hood's throat was dry. "Understand what?"

"How I see things. I couldn't prevent it any more than you could. In my case, of course, I saw it *before* it happened. If I were like you, perhaps I would try to play hero, but I am not like you—I know what I can, and cannot, do."

Hood was rocking back and forth on his knees. A sob broke from his throat. "Why did you choose me?"

"You came to me, remember? In a fit of jealousy over Sam Weigel. I gave you a time and a place."

"It's a spell! A trance! I'm compelled!"

Bellisle chuckled. "Where would be the fun in that? Don't come to me if you really don't want to. My feelings will recover."

"If you had any."

"I am nothing *but* feeling. You would see that, if you were not totally blind."

Hood struggled to his feet, swaying slightly. "What do I do now? About the girl. The police."

"The killer will be caught without your assistance. He will confess, and the police will believe him. They won't come looking for you, assuming you do nothing to warrant their interest. What did you see, after all? Some electromagnetic impulses. An image of the past."

"This is hell." Hood's voice was a whisper. "Hell."

"Call it what you will, Nicholas. It's your world."

A brief rain had fallen while he'd been in the house; the streets were slick and shining. He walked down Fifth Avenue and eventually caught a cab. A shudder passed through him in the car, a sudden fear that he reeked of blood.

The studio was desolate. He sat on a stool in the thin veil of moonlight, curling and uncurling his hands. The blood, if any, was invisible. Leo's coffee cup was on the edge of the worktable, and Hood stared at it for a long time. It seemed a symbol of innocence as blatant as a lamb, a reminder that it was possible to be a fine artist, to spend your life working, worrying about technique, about money, and have life by daylight, not death in the black of night.

"I'm sick," he said aloud and wished it were true, wished he had someone to sympathize, to tuck him into bed and bring him soup, someone to cool his brow. Going home was out of the question: He would start to babble, the night would spill out of him, and Susan would be horrified. How was it he lived with a woman who was good? If she lived to be a hundred, she would never be in trouble, no one would ever dislike her. Nicholas Hood was her only vice. He said her name aloud, a sweet word.

Night dissolved slowly into dawn; the Hudson River outside his window turned from black to gray, and a thick, heavy rain hammered on the glass. Hood constructed his biggest frame ever, nine by six, and stretched the last of his canvas across it.

Leo came in around nine-thirty. When he approached, Hood told him to stay back. The outline was coming along quickly.

When there was a knock on the door, later in the day, Leo left his easel to open it.

"Leave it," Hood said.

Leo looked at him crossly, then opened the door.

"Hi, Leo. Is Nick in there?"

Leo let her in. He must have seen from her face that trouble was coming. He discreetly picked up his lunch bag and went out.

Hood didn't look, but he heard her footsteps approach. "Don't look," he said. "Stay back. I don't want anyone to see until it's finished."

She stopped at the edge of the frame; her voice was gentle. "Please tell me what I've done wrong."

Hood dipped a thick brush in black, and worked at something on the other end of the picture.

"Did you hear me? Just tell me what I've—"

"You haven't done anything wrong. I have to work."

He heard her sharp intake of breath, as if he had stuck her with a needle. She continued quietly. "Something about me drives you away. Something you need, that I don't give you. Tell me."

"Susan, I have to work."

"You weren't working at four in the morning. I came down here to find you."

Hood stopped. "I was sleeping. I set the alarm for three, and went out to see Bellisle."

"I don't believe you."

He dipped his brush again and stepped up on a chair to reach the top of his frame. "I told you, I had an appointment."

"He's evil. You said so yourself. Why on earth would you—"

"Susan! I'm trying to work! Now, please go!"

He glanced down at her sad, uptilted face. She had the eyes of a deer caught in the sights of a high-powered rifle. "I guess there are marriages where people don't believe each other—that go on and on, and they never believe each other. But I'm not used to it. Maybe you lied to me before, but I didn't know it. I wasn't suspicious. But it hurts so much—to not believe you." She waited for some response, and received none. "Are you fucking someone?"

The word was like a scar across that mild voice. Hood looked down at her. "No. Now let me work."

She burst into tears then, suddenly as a child. He had seen her cry like that only once in their years together. She had been making tea, when the kettle's handle broke, spilling boiling water all over her dress. It clung to her legs, scalding her, and the tears had sprung from her eyes. Hood had taken her by the hand and held a cool facecloth to the injury—it had been sweet to comfort her so easily. He had no comfort for her now.

She said, "It hurts so much! I need a best friend! But you're my best friend!"

"Look," he said, brush in hand, "this is going really well. When it's done, we can talk all you want. I'm going to be sleeping here, so don't wait up."

Over the summer, Leo had begun to take a book with him out to the pier when he had lunch. Hood had stayed indoors, working ceaselessly, so the books were all Leo's company. He was surprised one day in August to see Hood coming down to the pier to join him.

"I'm working on the top border," he said. "Can't eat and jump up and down at the same time."

"Dilettante." Leo bit into a fragrant sausage.

"I haven't taken a break in a month!"

Leo put aside his novel. "I was joking, Nicholas."

"Your sense of humor is Germanic."

"When do I get to see the monstrosity you're working on?"

"When it's finished. A couple of weeks."

"It takes up the whole studio."

"I really don't want to talk about it."

Leo read a page of his book. Hood nibbled on a sandwich and watched the pigeons that pecked hopefully nearby. Leo and he had become strangers. "How is Susan these days?"

"Fine. I suppose. Same as usual."

"Tell her I asked after her."

"I will."

Hood finished his lunch and leaned back against a piling. The sun soaked into his skin, and for the first time in weeks he felt reluctant to get back to the painting.

"So this is how the great artists spend their time, huh?" Valerie appeared at his elbow, shielding her eyes with a salute.

"Lunch break only—not a vacation." Leo offered her some unidentifiable dessert, which she declined with a shake of the head.

Hood opened his eyes lazily. At his eye level, Valerie's crotch was displayed beneath her skin-tight shorts with the detail of a botanical sample. She tugged a lock of his hair and said, "You look beautiful in the sun."

"And you," he said, still looking at her crotch.

She held up a sketchbook. "My new resolution. Gonna do some kinda work every single day. I'm gonna go down there a little bit 'n' see if there's a boat to sketch."

Hood leaned forward and bit her crotch.

"Nick!" She jumped back. "My God!"

"Sorry." He picked up his lunch bag and empty milk carton and tossed them into a garbage can. "Inspiration."

Leo got to his feet and walked back toward the studio. When he was out of earshot, Valerie said, "I don't think Leo liked that."

"You did, though."

"Yeah, but . . ."

"So don't worry about Leo. I have to get back to work."

She walked with him along the pier. "How's it going?"

"Coming along."

"I don't think I could ever work on the same thing for that long. Too hyperactive, I guess."

Hood kissed her on the forehead. "See you later."

She backed away, slowly, as if she couldn't take her eyes off him. With a final wave, he went inside.

He picked up where he had left off working on an ochre-gold nimbus above the murdered girl's head. It was nearly complete when Leo's voice came through the canvas. "If you must have affairs, it's your life. But please keep them to yourself—I don't want to know these things."

Hood was too irritated to reply.

"It's impossible for me. I won't lie to Susan for you—it's clear, I hope."

"What makes you think I'm having an affair?"

"She looks at you like a little cow. You bite her in her, in her—"

"That was just a joke."

"You wouldn't do such a thing to Susan. Not in public."

"You're over the line, Leo. Mind your own business. What are you—SoHo's moral arbiter? Cardinal Forstadt?" He heard Leo's chair scrape, and then a curse as he upset a can of something. Hood finished the halo. "If you weren't so repressed with females, you wouldn't resent a little flirting when you see it."

"Oh, the great psychologist here! I have some respect at least for women."

"Is that why you don't have one?"

Leo came around the edge of the frame and gestured at the painting. "Better not to have one that treat them with contempt. You tear out their intestines!"

"This is a painting! If you paint a murder, someone has to be dead in it. This time it happens to be woman. If it makes you sick, it's because I have contempt for murder, not for women. Not contempt—fear. And you weren't supposed to look at it, anyway."

"You take over the whole studio with this gory shit, how is one supposed not to look here?"

Hood just shook his head and looked back at the halo. He tried to recall how Fra Angelico did them, but he couldn't think with Leo yapping at his heels.

"Some things should not be painted."

"Fine," Hood said, and got down from his chair. "Don't paint them. Go get yourself elected in some third-rate country and tell all the artists what to paint."

Leo sighed, and seemed to deflate. He turned his back on Hood, and went back to his own work. "My *Gott*," he said quietly. "You have changed."

Hood called over his painting, "Yes! Like anything living!"

Hood was usually first out of bed, but that evening Valerie rolled away from him and was pulling on her jeans before he had a chance to catch his breath. "What's wrong?" he said. "You have a date?"

"I have to do some work."

Hood struggled to keep a straight face. She wore her new dedication like something fashionable but uncomfortable.

She pulled a sweatshirt on. "I know it's just sex with you. You don't have to pretend it's anything else—lie there pretending you're interested."

"Don't be silly. I'm very fond of you."

"But I *love* you. You're everything, you're like a hero to me. I think about you all the time—when I get up, when I go to bed, when I'm eating, working—even when I'm thinking about something else, I'm thinking of you."

"Well, you shouldn't. You've got more important things to worry about." He found his trousers in a tangle of blankets, and tried to straighten them out.

She stood with her arms folded protectively across her chest. "I don't know, Nick. I thought it would be different. I thought you'd start to, like, respect me or something. But you're ashamed to be seen with me. You don't want to take me anywhere. Lemme finish! I know Susan is classier, and prettier, and smarter and more talented and she's probably better in bed, but—"

"Don't talk about Susan."

"Well I *think* about her!"

Hood buttoned his shirt. "Let me worry about Susan. She isn't your concern."

Valerie sat on the arm of a tattered chair. "Maybe we better not do this anymore. I have a feeling I'm gonna get hurt."

As Hood was putting on his shoes, she dug out a sketchbook. "Take a look at this," she said. "Your face is on every page."

Hood took the book and glanced at the top drawing. His face was turned slightly away and down. The hair was matted, damp-looking. It was almost a deathbed portrait. "Not bad," he said.

Valerie said, "Yeah. It sorta captures that just-fucked look."

Hood quickly combed his hair, and bent down to kiss her. She grabbed his collar and held his face close for a moment. "Except I'm the one that's getting fucked."

The painting was finished at the end of August. Hood invited Sherri Novack to the studio for her first viewing. He draped the picture with two bedsheets and went out and bought a bottle of wine.

"What, am I opening a shopping center?" she said. "Should I cut a ribbon?"

"Have some wine first." He poured her a glass of Chablis. "Leo, will you have some wine?"

"No, thank you—still working here." Leo remained tucked in his corner of the studio, irritated by the intrusion.

He had hoped to get Sherri relaxed and in a receptive mood before unveiling the picture, but they stood facing each other sipping wine in silence. He couldn't stand it. He pulled a cord, and the sheet tumbled from the painting. The vehemence of her reaction shook him.

"Jesus Christ!" Her head jerked back, as if the painting had physically struck her.

He had painted a crucifixion. The bed was upright, and the horror graphically displayed. Blood and entrails spilled from the torn abdomen. It was hard to distinguish the body from the bed. Sherri's mouth fell open.

He had painted her face as he remembered it, tilted down to one shoulder like the dead Christ, a stripe of blood across the forehead. In the background, where the old masters would have put hills of Italian countryside, he had outlined New York skyscrapers.

In the foreground loomed the murderer's face, immense, bloodstained, beads of sweat on the brow. He held a telephone to his ear; he was speaking into it. The cord traveled out of the frame, connecting him to the real world. The eyes were deep and black; terror shone beneath the surface, barely submerged. The whole painting was nine by six, and the killer's face took up nearly a third of the space.

"Nick, I gotta be honest with ya—I cannot take this in. I could give ya my first reaction, but I don't think that matters."

"Fine."

"Don't be offended—I didn't say it was bad." She waddled a little closer to the picture, stretching her neck to examine a detail. "One thing I do know: Nobody is gonna ignore it."

"Good."

"Thing hits ya like a freight train. I dunno how many people're gonna get past that first. . . . This is a stomach-turner, Nick."

"It should be—given the subject."

"I gotta get away from this. Go home and think about it."

Hood snapped, "It's on canvas, Sherri, not in your head! If you think it's garbage, just say so!"

"You want it in the show, it's in!"

"Fine."

"If that's all ya wanna know, I coulda toldya right off. I thought you wanted to know what I *thought*! What I felt! My mistake. You don't give a shit what I think."

"Probably not."

She picked up her purse, and took her coat from the back of a chair. "Listen. I got a sister in show business, and she has a little thing she likes to tell the up-and-comers: You be kind to people on your way up, they'll be kind to you on your way down."

"You don't need kindness. You need paintings."

"Paintings I got. Coming out my ears I got paintings. Kindness, everyone can use."

Hood snorted. "You treat me like shit all these years, and suddenly you develop feelings."

"Five years I been showing your stuff I didn't make a dime! This is treating you like shit? Stay sensitive, kid—but don't get paranoid."

Hood watched her stomp toward the door. "I don't know why you're so upset. I actually like you."

"Do us all a favor, Nick. Don't you never start hating nobody, or you're gonna leave a mess."

Hood smiled. "Come on, Sherri. Let's be friends."

She looked at him from the doorway. "Okay. Truce."

Hood crossed the room and gave her a little hug. He wondered if she felt the same revulsion as he. A truce was something between enemies.

Summer had passed without his noticing. Except for the single excursion to the park with Susan, the past three months might have been dead of winter for all the difference they had made in his life. He had planned to take it easy, just before the opening of the show, but he was now too obsessed with work to slow down. Susan was wary of him, and this made him all the more tense and scrappy, eager to get back to work. And Valerie provided no solace—her yearning for him was as palpable as fever.

He set himself the task of finishing four more paintings—one a week—by the beginning of October. He painted Leo as a shopkeeper, with a patch over one eye. The sign behind his cash register said, NEVER MORE THAN FIFTY DOLLARS IN THIS REGISTER. Leo managed a good-natured smile when he saw it, but Hood detected a glint of suspicion in his eye.

He painted Susan at the harpsichord, alone in a courtyard. He painted Bellisle as a vampire, fresh from the murder of a young girl who lay bleeding in the background. And he painted Valerie, standing at the end of the pier in her skin-tight shorts. The glitter of the Hudson River was reflected in her laughing face. Yet it had a tragic quality to it—like a high school photo of a girl who goes on to commit suicide.

The last was a self-portrait. He held a James Dean, vulnerable tough-guy pose—three-quarter profile with a cigarette, slouched on a fire escape. He preempted the charge of self-flattery by painting cataracts over his eyes. He added a few highlights to the hair, signed his name in the corner of the canvas, and went home to call Sherri.

He opened a beer as soon as he got home, and carried the phone over to the couch. It rang in his hand.

"He's comin', Nick. The little bastard is gonna show!"

"I was just going to phone you."

"You know who I'm talkin' about?"

"No. Detective Lauzon?"

"Who? What, are you gettin' picked up for something?"

"Forget it. Who's coming?"

"Gerald Mallon."

"Great!" He took a pull on his beer.

"You don't know who he is, do ya."

"He own a gallery?"

"The Whitney Museum. He's the curator for new work."

"Good person to know, I guess."

"He has invitations to six other shows onna same day, Nick. And he's going to exactly two. Yours first."

"You must've charmed him to death, Sherri."

"A nudge here, a pinch there. I did okay. He'll drop dead when he sees 'The Crucifixion.'"

"'The Confession,' you mean."

"Sorry. 'The Confession.' He'll wet his pants."

"Is that a reaction you look forward to?"

"You bet I do! He's puttin' together the January show, and if you get in there the sky's the limit. There'll be no stoppin' ya. This is *The Show*, remember? If you don't get in now, it's two years before the next one, so we're sittin' pretty for this one, not so hot for the next one."

"You've been very clever, Sherri. Thank you."

"Don't get so excited."

"I'm sorry. I just got in, and I'm tired. I've got four more things for the show."

"Jesus, you're supernatural."

"Just industrious. I'll bring them in, tomorrow."

"Good. Now. Somethin' I wanna get off my beautiful chest. That time in your studio, about 'The Crucifixion'—sorry, 'The Confession.' I gotta say, Nick, I musta been blind that day. It's a great picture. A *great* picture. And that is not a word I use. Not for anybody living."

"Sounds ominous."

"Whaddaya mean?"

"Nothing. Just mumbling to myself."

"It's also gonna make you famous."

"Well, let's hope so."

"Gotta run, Nick. Bring the new stuff round, first thing. Otherwise, it's gonna screw the whole—"

"I'll see you then, Sherri."

"Right. 'Bye."

He lay on the couch, and finished his beer before reaching once more for the phone.

"Detective Lauzon, please."

"He's very tied up. Can I tell him what it's in reference to, sir?"

"Just tell him Nick Hood called."

"Hold on a sec."

He heard a meaty hand clamp itself over the mouthpiece, then Lauzon came on the line. "Well, I'll be damned! I want to thank you for the invitation, Mr. Hood. Particularly for sending it to the precinct."

"Must've done wonders for your reputation as a highbrow cop."

"I'm now known as an asshole cop, and I owe it all to you."

Hood laughed. "So, will you come?"

"I wouldn't miss it for the world."

ELEVEN

THE gallery was already crowded when Hood and Susan arrived shortly after eight o'clock. Above their heads "The Burning Man" flared across the wall in brilliant orange glory. Hood had a brief attack of panic—perhaps it was not his; perhaps he had stolen it. Could he really have made such a beautiful thing?

"Certainly dominates the room," Susan said. "It makes everyone look small."

They moved closer, through the press of tuxedos and evening gowns. Hood looked over his painting, the strokes and swirls of orange and red and black. "It came so easily, this thing. I can't believe it's mine."

Susan looked thoughtful. "It would be truly beautiful," she said, "if I didn't know it was a real man."

"Oh, for Christ's sake, Susan—it's pigment on canvas. That's the only real thing about it."

"But it isn't!"

"Don't be so literal!"

Sherri clapped them both on the shoulder. "About time, sweethots! Susan, honey, lemme take ya coat. My God, this dress! You look gorgeous! Whaddaya think of this paintah? Ain't he somethin' else?"

Susan allowed that he was, indeed, something else.

"Nick, how you get any work done is beyond me, gorgeous woman like Susan around the place!"

"We all have our cross to bear, Sherri."

"Some cross! Enjoy the show, kids." With that, she waddled off into the crowd. Leo spotted them, and crossed the room.

Susan kissed him on the cheek. "You never come to see us anymore!"

"You're never home anymore!" His eyes disappeared in the crinkles of a smile. "If you want to see me, you'll just have to sit for a portrait."

"Nick would never let me in the studio."

Hood ignored them. He was anxious to see how Sherri had arranged the paintings.

Leo said, "I could paint you anywhere. It doesn't have to be the studio."

"You always say these things when you've had a glass of wine."

Leo's face went serious. "No. Truly, Susan. I'm thinking I could do something."

Hood made a quick circuit of the gallery. He found "The Confession" hanging all by itself in the backroom where Andy Stark's portraits had been. The walls were otherwise bare. Hood looked at the thing in wonder; it was so huge! Violence spilled from it in torrents of purple and red. Sherri had been right to place it back here—people would come to it having seen his other work, would approach the crucified girl psychologically prepared. He went to find Sherri, and told her he liked what she had done.

She craned her neck to look over his shoulder. "Who's this guy comin' in?"

"Where?"

"Baldy with the ring a hair."

Detective Lauzon looked relieved to find a familiar face. He came up to Hood, smiling. "Some gathering you have here! I've never seen so many limousines!"

"That's Sherri's doing." He introduced them.

"Quite an artist you have here in Mr. Hood. I'd buy some of this stuff myself, if I had any money."

"You tryin' a tell me the police business don't pay well?" Sherri punched his arm.

"Not unless there's something I don't know."

"C'mon. Let's get you a drink." She took his arm and winked at Hood. "Never know when ya gonna need the law on ya side."

Hood parked himself at the table in front where catalogs of the show were laid out. For the next hour, he devoted himself to the not unpleasant task of signing his name and accepting compliments. "The Burning Man" turned out to be a great favorite, though many people mentioned "The Falling Boy." No one brought up the thing in the back room, and Hood wondered whether hanging it there hadn't been a mistake, after all.

A very drunk man reeled out from a group of people and latched on to the table, nearly toppling it. Hood was shocked to see it was Sam Weigel. His hair was dirty, his face bloated. He swayed like a willow in a high wind, breathing fumes across the table. "Jus' wanted t'say you're doin' fine, Hoody."

"Thank you."

"Jus' fine."

"Maybe you better get some coffee. You look a little—"

"A little!" Weigel's head reared back, fell forward. "That is an understatement, Hoodsir. You're doin' fine, though, right?"

"If you say so."

"Fuckin' brilliant, really. I hadda future once."

"You better go home now."

"I hadda future once." Weigel pushed himself off from the table and teetered toward a bowl of punch where he collided with a fat man—an accident he remarked with a roar of laughter. Sherri gestured at the bartender, and he stepped around the punch bowl and steered Weigel firmly but gently toward the exit.

An image flashed in Hood's mind: Weigel and Bellisle on the bridge in Central Park. Bellisle had said, "We go to *bars* together!" But he was rapidly caught up again in smiles and congratulations. This show was going to put him over the top, he could feel it. The smiles and handshakes, the compliments were all extended in genuine excitement. These people knew he was going to take off; they were truly happy to meet him.

Another sour note occurred later in the evening, when a woman dressed in expensive overalls grabbed Sherri by the shoulder and spun her around—a feat requiring considerable strength. "That thing in the back room is disgusting. You should be ashamed of yourself!"

"Easy, honey. It's just a painting."

"It is *not* just a painting! He butchers the girl, and drapes it in this rosy romantic glow—as if she's just fallen asleep or something! It's extremely violent towards women! It's a piece of hate mail!"

"That may be your opinion, but—"

"It's a fact!" The intensity of her voice drew stares. Conversations stopped around the room. "It's not a matter of opinion that her guts have been ripped out. It's not a matter of opinion that it looks like a fucking stained-glass window with this slaughter in it! This is garbage! It says women are garbage! Dead meat!"

"You're free to leave, if ya that upset." Hood could tell Sherri was making a tremendous effort not to clobber the woman.

"I'm going to upset a lot more people, before I'm through with this! How long are we supposed to tolerate this stuff!"

"No one's forcin' ya to look at the thing!"

"It's on public display! Begging for approval! You're no better than a Times Square pornographer!"

Hood did not think himself a pornographer, but he felt his face flush at being called one. He slipped away into the back room, where he found Lauzon standing before the murdered girl, hands clasped behind his back, apparently oblivious to the commotion out front. Hood shrugged and said, "No accounting for taste."

"Yeah, she's pretty steamed."

"I suppose I should be glad it got a reaction."

"Bound to do that, wouldn't you say?" Lauzon blinked at him, then turned his attention back to the picture. "This is a very interesting painting."

"You like it?"

Lauzon took a deep breath. "No. I don't believe I do."

Hood didn't say anything.

Lauzon kept his eye on the painting. "I hope you don't mind if I'm candid."

Hood said, "Be as candid as you like. I just thought, as a homicide detective, you'd find it a little easier to take than most people."

"You don't actually see many things this bad. A bullet, after all, just makes a little hole—unless it's through the head or an artery or something. Usually, it's just a puncture. Mind you, I have seen a few instances where the killer got carried away. But it's different, seeing it in a painting. In some ways, it's worse."

"Why don't you like it?"

"Lots of reasons . . ." He suddenly grabbed Hood by the arm and looked into his eyes. "This is very rude of me. You invite me to your opening, and here I am insulting your work and it's really ill-mannered. I apologize."

"There's no need to apologize. I asked your opinion; you gave it."

"Some of the ones out front now—I love the 'Girl on a Pier.' That one nearly made me cry!"

Hood laughed. "Cops don't cry."

"It's a very sad picture!"

"Sad! Why?"

"Because she looks like she's going to die."

"Well, put your mind at rest. I can assure you she's very much alive."

Lauzon took his arm and steered him slowly toward the exit.

"Please forget what I said about this one here. I can't believe I was so— I'm going to feel bad all night."

"Not on my account."

A young couple came around the corner. The girl's reaction was immediate. "Ick!" she said. "I don't want to look at that!" Her boyfriend squinted at the painting on the far wall, then followed her out of the room.

"Been a lot of that," Lauzon said.

"Didn't give it much of a chance, did they?"

"Like you say—no accounting for taste." The detective took out a small notepad and pen. "Listen. I'd really like to talk to you about all this, but you're occupied right now, and I'm busy most of the time. Give me your number and I'll call you. We'll go out for coffee, or whatever . . ."

Hood gave him the number. "Thanks for coming. I get tired of the blue-haired ladies."

Lauzon shook his hand. "I'm really glad I came. It's been an education."

Hood saw Susan looking at one of the smaller paintings and was about to join her when Sherri called his name. She was beckoning him over to "The Falling Boy" on the opposite side of the room.

"Nicholas Hood—Gerald Mallon. Mr. Mallon is the Whitney's curator for new work, I'm sure you know."

"How do you do," Hood said, and looked Mallon over. He was sleek and prosperous-looking; his brown hair flopping neatly over to one side. He was one of those people who can smile without looking at all happy, but Hood supposed it might be facial structure, rather than temperament.

"I've been admiring this 'Falling Boy,'" he said. "It's a very interesting thing you've done with the light—almost like a grainy photograph. And of course the facial expression is beautiful."

"Thank you."

"Do you have any others like this?"

Sherri excused herself, and waded through a crowd toward Nigel Thorne.

"You mean people jumping off buildings?" Hood was put off by the question.

"No, no." Mallon grimaced like an irritated teacher. "Pictures with this monochrome effect. This palette."

"Not really. I have other night scenes, but—"

"No, this technique fascinates me. It always seems the best thing to do with color—get rid of most of it. Otherwise it always looks like Kodachrome."

"You think Raphael looks like Kodachrome?"

Mallon's eyes slid around to him like twin guns in a bunker. "I wasn't confusing you with Raphael."

"I thought you were making a general observation." He *had* made a general observation, Hood knew, and a damn stupid one. Any hope of getting a place in the Whitney show vanished; the man was a fool.

Susan came over. "Everybody seems very impressed," she said. "I've been eavesdropping on people."

Hood introduced her to Mallon. "Susan's the interesting one. She plays the harpsichord."

"Of course!" This time Mallon's whole face lit up. "I saw you at Merkin Hall! A splendid program! You were marvellous!"

"I'm glad you enjoyed it."

"Enjoyed it! I was jabbering about it for days! I'm a baroque music buff, you see—can't get enough of it. Tell me all about yourself, Susan. Tell me everything. How did you start? Why the harpsichord?"

Hood left them to it. He went once more to the back room. The crucified girl had no witnesses; her killer confessed to an empty hall. Hood sat down on the bench facing the picture and rubbed the back of his neck. He felt a slight depression coming on.

By midnight, all the limousines had gone, leaving Sherri, Susan, and Hood alone with the catering staff, who were cleaning up. Sherri invited the two of them into her office for cognac.

"So tell me how ya made out with Mallon."

Hood shrugged. "He liked Susan, anyway."

"That's good. Anything so he remembers ya's." She bent over with some difficulty to remove her shoes. "I talked to'm again on his way out. You're definitely in the running for the New Work show."

Susan took a sip of brandy and coughed. "Is that an important show?"

"It's make or break, sweethot."

"Do we know who else he's looking at?"

"I can guess—Laszlo for sure, Sam Weigel I'm almost positive—did you see him tonight? Disgusting! Anyway, Mallon'll also be looking for a few surprises. He likes to think he's ahead of the world, which is why the last show was a bust. Frankly, at this point he'd be a moron not to include you."

Hood said, "But he *is* a moron."

Hood slept in the next morning, and after a late breakfast wandered over to Valerie's apartment. But on his way up the filthy stairwell, he had second thoughts and turned back downstairs. The faint pulsing of dread faded when he stepped out onto the street. It was a beautiful autumn day, clear and cool, so he bought a paperback murder mystery and spent what was left of the morning reading in Washington Square. He gave barely a thought to the man who had destroyed himself there, but "The Burning Man" flashed several times in his mind's eye.

He ate a half-cooked hamburger in the Greenwich Tavern, and afterward strolled home through Chinatown and Little Italy. He was no longer bothered by his encounter with Gerald Mallon. He felt confident, proud, almost content.

Susan was ushering out her last pupil of the day—it was the boy who had cried that afternoon last March. She was handing him his cap and his music when Hood came in. The boy slipped out past Hood without a word.

"Maybe I'm not totally useless, after all," Susan said. "He's actually beginning to practice. He has a recital coming up, and I think he just may amaze them all. Did you talk to Sherri?"

Hood was taking his boots off. "No. Should I?"

"She's upset about something. She called three times."

"Oh? Is she at the gallery?"

"I don't think so. She left a number—it's by the phone."

Hood dialed the number Susan had scrawled on the message pad. It turned out to be the offices of Carran, Klein, Piggot—a Park Avenue law firm. The receptionist put him through right away.

"What's up, Sherri? Was something stolen?"

"No. It'll be in the papers tonight, probably." Her voice was quavering, which was so out of character that Hood was immediately alarmed. "We got some trouble at the shop. Buncha broads are out front picketing—passing round a petition, trying to get people to boycott the show."

"You're kidding."

"I wish! Some asshole named Monica Stahl—that one at the opening—got hold of I-don't-know-how-many different women's groups, and they're marchin' up a storm outside the store."

Hood sat down heavily. "What the hell's their problem?"

"Yeah. That's what *I* said."

"Is it because of 'The Confession'?"

"Bitch got a photo of the thing somehow, and showed it round to these groups. They bought the whole song 'n' dance."

"How many of them are there?"

"At last count, seventy-five."

"Jesus Christ! Will people be able to get in?"

"Oh, yeah—the cops've got barriers up so they can't actually stop traffic. But they're makin' a hell of a racket! I already hired a security guard for inside, and I'm talkin' to Bob Klein right now about what we can do. Unfortunately, what we can do is nothin'; they got a constitutional right."

"How nice."

"I gotta run, Nick. Listen, I'm sorry. Maybe I coulda handled that broad a little better. None a this woulda happened."

"You handled her fine."

"Well. Onward and upward."

The cool October breeze had turned frosty by the time Hood got to the gallery. He was relieved to see that there were now nowhere near seventy-five demonstrators; the cold had sent most of them homeward for supper. A tight circle of perhaps thirty women marched back and forth near the entrance to the Novack. Some carried signs, saying WOMEN AGAINST PORNOGRAPHY, BOYCOTT THE NOVACK, and END VIOLENCE AGAINST WOMEN. Others shouted to passersby, "Art, yes! Obscenity, no!" or "This show degrades women!"

Hood had hoped they would look half-crazed, but unfortunately, aside from their having to shout above the evening traffic, they maintained a strictly rational demeanor. A curly-haired woman in a yellow anorak, who obviously didn't know whom she was addressing, pressed a leaflet into Hood's hand and said quietly, "It's just got to stop somewhere." He read the first two sentences, which pointed out that there are laws in the United States that prevent people from advocating violence against any person or class of persons, then tossed it into a garbage can.

He saw the woman who had made the disturbance at his opening night. She bore a large sign on her shoulder like a cross, but she had probably shouted herself hoarse long ago, for she remained glum-faced and silent. For one brief moment, Hood considered engaging her in an argument, but knew he was too angry to talk rationally. The signs, the leaflets, and most of all the women's air of solemn integrity made him want to attack them with a bullwhip, like Christ driving the money-changers from the temple.

In itself, the picketing was not big news; in New York City, people were always picketing something or other. But two factors combined to turn what should have been a story of only minor interest into a major media event. The moment Sherri realized she could get no help from her lawyer, she turned instead to a high-priced publicist. In two days, the story received major articles in all three daily papers—articles that took no overt stance for or against the demonstration, but that happened to carry flattering pictures of Nicholas Hood. Attendance at the Novack immediately tripled. The second factor was not so pleasant. That Thursday, Hood was on his way out to the studio when he received an urgent phone call from Marcia. She wouldn't tell him what it was about; she just kept repeating in a breathless voice that he had to come down right away.

Hood arrived at the gallery to find it locked up tight. The women outside were not marching now, but stood around in clusters talking quietly to one another. In addition to the usual quota of crowd-control police, there were two uniformed officers standing right in the doorway. They would not let Hood so much as ring the doorbell before he produced his identification. Then the smaller of the two cops gave Hood a sympathetic glance, and pushed the bell for him. Indicating the women with a jerk of his head, he drawled, "Everybody's got rights, huh?"

"Tell me about it," Hood said.

Marcia opened the door and let him in, carefully locking the door behind him.

"What's going on, Marcia?"

She started walking toward the back. "You may as well just follow me. There's no good way to tell you."

Hood went with her to the back gallery, and what he saw there made his heart drop down several inches in his chest. "The Confession" was mutilated. Someone had sliced an arc through the canvas from the bottom of the bed, right up through the murdered woman, and across the killer's face. A semicircular flap of nearly three feet in diameter hung down from the picture. Instead of the girl's legs, the blood-soaked bed, and the mouth of the killer, one saw white gallery wall, wooden struts, and bare wire.

Marcia said, "I'll go get Sherri. She says it can be fixed."

Hood could neither speak nor move; he stood utterly motionless, staring at the terrible wound in his creation. The shock prevented him from feeling any sense of loss or hurt, for the moment. All he could do was gaze in wonder at the exposed struts and wire, the way a man might stare at his exposed plumbing, were his house suddenly hit by a bomb.

"Nick, hon, I'm sorry." Sherri had come into the room and set a plump hand on his shoulder. "Words I don't have—to tell you how sick I am about this."

Hood managed to say, "How did it happen?"

"Why don't you sit down?"

"No. Tell me."

"I was in the office; Marcia was out front. Since Wednesday, we've had a guard on duty all hours. He was standing right at the corner there where he was supposed to—can see front and back from there. Broad number one comes in, looks like a career girl—come on upstairs, I'll show ya."

"Tell me what happened, Sherri!"

"No point tellin' ya when you can see for yourself on tape. Monitor's upstairs."

Hood turned on his heel and strode ahead of Sherri to the

elevator. They went up together in silence, then Sherri opened the shipping room, where a small TV monitor sat on a metal cart, extruding several black cables. She turned it on and slipped a tape into the player. Hood was too unnerved even to be reminded of the last time he had watched a videotape.

The screen was filled with a fuzzy black-and-white image of the front gallery, seen from a high corner angle. "As I was saying," Sherri said. "Broad number one comes in."

A woman dressed in an Armani business suit came into the gallery and walked slowly around, looking at the paintings. She stood thoughtfully for a time in front of the picture of Valerie, laughing on the pier, before moving off toward the back and out of view.

Sherri stopped the tape and took it out. "Fine," she said. "She moves to the back gallery. Passes right by the security guard."

"No one'll ever recognize her from that tape."

"It's the same setup banks use. If they've got a record, the cops'll probably be able to match pictures."

The second tape, again from high, showed the girl wander into the back gallery and approach "The Confession." She walked slowly toward it, peered at Hood's signature, and then moved away again. She took a seat on the padded bench in the middle of the room.

Sherri said, "She look dangerous to you?"

"I don't know."

"Come on, Nick. Would you be nervous about that broad? Tell me the truth."

"Probably not. She looks like an executive."

Sherri slipped in the first tape once more. "Enters broad number two. Catch the wardrobe on this babe." This second woman wore a floppy hat, a long black raincoat, and dark sunglasses. Long hair, possibly a wig, tumbled out from beneath the hat past her shoulders. In contrast to the leisurely pace of the first woman, she strode directly to "The Falling Boy" and stood within three inches of the canvas.

Sherri said, "This point, the guard gets very nervous. He flatfoots into the room." Sure enough, a neatly uniformed black man came discreetly into the room behind the woman. The high camera angle gave Hood a view of the back of his head. The woman threw a nervous glance over her shoulder, then moved swiftly away from the painting toward one of the smaller works on a far wall, reaching into her long dark coat.

"Jesus."

"You better believe it. Guard was shittin' bricks."

Sherri changed tapes. Once again a high view of the back gallery, where the woman "executive" was contemplating the crucified girl. She looked at her watch. Then she stood up and took three quick steps to the painting, pulling something from her purse. She bent over and stuck the blade into the bottom of the painting before drawing it upward over her right shoulder in a wide crescent. The canvas was tough; she had to work at it.

"Arrgh! You fucking bitch!"

Sherri's voice was soft with sympathy. "It's a real crime, Nick. I'm sorry it hadda happen to you."

"Oh, Christ . . ." Hood walked away from the monitor, but he didn't know where to go. He paced back and forth in the room as if it were a padded cell, muttering curses over and over. Finally, he said, "Why would anyone *do* something like that! It's just a painting, for God's sake! If it hung there a thousand years, it'd never hurt *anyone*! Jesus, Sherri—why didn't you have a guard for each room!"

Sherri looked down at the floor, waited a moment before she spoke. Then she looked right at Hood. "I asked myself that question. Possibly, it woulda helped. But think about it. In the end, it's just as easy to distract two guards as one—pretend you're sick; start a fight—if you're that determined . . ."

"I don't know, Sherri."

"Ask around. Check with the museums. Hell, check with a lawyer! Maybe you got grounds to sue me!"

Hood walked over to the window and looked down on the people below, the women in their little groups.

Sherri said, "The good news is, we can fix it."

"Oh, come on! It's practically sliced in half!"

"We can fix it. We can use it. And—as God is my witness, Nick—I'm gonna sell it."

Hood had thought at first he would never recover; but in the event, his recovery took less than twenty-four hours. Sherri had already established that her insurance would cover the cost of restoration, and she had an expert coming that afternoon—an Italian named Egidio, whose cheerful brown eyes contrasted with a lugubrious mustache.

When it had been sufficiently photographed in its torn state, Egidio and Hood took the painting into the shipping room and went over the damage together. Luckily, the assailant had used a very sharp instrument in her attack. "This we can fix," Egidio said. "You don't worry."

"I'm not worried; I'm in mourning."

Egidio raised a nicotine-stained finger. "I understand. But you must help me." He pointed to the gory bedclothes. "You can match these shades exactly?"

"I can try. I don't know about exactly."

"You do it exactly. I know." Egidio clapped a hand on his shoulder. "You got an eye, mister."

The Italian made no comment about the content of the painting. He approached the work with all the gravity he might have brought to a Dutch master, and Hood felt the relief of a parent being assured by a warm, confident surgeon, "Yes, your child will live."

While they worked at restoring the painting, Sherri's publicist went to work on the media. It was on her advice that Sherri made the dramatic gesture of closing the gallery. It gave the newspaper and television reporters an extra "hook" for their stories, and Sherri's Brooklyn accent became a familiar sound on the local newsmagazine shows. Hood's picture was in all the papers, and *The New York Times* carried photographs of "The Confession" as it looked before and after the attack.

Hood's phone was ringing constantly with requests for interviews. Once again following expert advice, Sherri asked him to turn all of these down until the reviews could appear. Her publicist happened to know they were going to be "warm and encouraging." This turned out to be an understatement.

Seven months ago, I reviewed a group show at the Novack Gallery, and chose to pass over in silence the work of Nicholas Hood, who was prominently represented. After seeing his one-man show which opened Monday at the same address, I confess I have no excuse for this lapse. For there were at least two, and possibly three, masterpieces on view at the Novack, until it was closed by an hysterical act of vandalism.

Nicholas Hood is arguably our most important living artist. He turns a pitiless gaze on the world as he finds it, and transmutes his raw material into works that are terrifying and beautiful. He has the power to burst through the boundaries of the art world into the general consciousness of society, affecting the way people think and feel. Yes, it has happened again: Genius has been ignored, and now it is being held up to contempt.

Thorne went on to the describe Hood's beginnings as a follower of Delvaux, influenced by the hyper-realists, and stated his opinion that the paintings now on display (except for the subject matter) might be the work of a different man.

The first painting one sees on entering is a triptych depicting self-immolation: In the first panel, a man is about to set himself on fire; in the second he is alight; and in the third, he rises from the ground in a blaze. (Possibly, this was inspired by a recent suicide in Washington Square, but I suspect it must have been begun before that tragedy, unless Mr. Hood conceptualizes and paints with inhuman speed.)

There is a figure in the three panels which falls to its knees like Peter at the calming of the storm, knowing his world is forever changed, in fact, forever gone. Reflected fire on the face of the witness runs through the flesh tones like liquid gold. This artist has chosen murder as his subject (self-murder being only a subspecie) and no one, with the exceptions of Goya and Delacroix, has handled it with such authority before.

This painting alone ensures Mr. Hood a place in history, but there is another: "The Falling Boy," wherein a youth executes a perfect swan dive, and himself, at a blow. The old obsession with perspective lies hidden under the thick surfaces of acrylic—its edges blurred, smudged, as if the artist couldn't wait to capture this death on the wing. But it is the serenity suffusing the young man's face that makes this a passionate, a great, a moving work of art.

Thorne seemed very touched by what he called Hood's "lyrical" side, as displayed in the five smaller works. He was particularly complimentary about the picture of Susan playing the harpsichord in a ruined temple.

If the subject ultimately is death, it is death at a remove, the inevitable loss of a loved one, mourned in advance. Another small painting, rather like a snapshot, shows a girl laughing on a pier, as pretty and sad as a blossom about to fall. Perverse indeed that the creator of such works should be accused of misogyny.

And then there is the cause of all the trouble, the notorious "Confession." It is supremely ironic that this painting, which more than any other is responsible for Mr. Hood's current celebrity, will be the first to be forgotten. This painting is neither pornographic nor obscene, but it does depict a vicious murder with enough impact to send the fainthearted running from the room. Personally, I find the composition messy and inadequate, and the addition of a halo around the victim's head a little silly.

Nevertheless, in Nicholas Hood we have cause for celebration. A luminous talent has arrived with a vengeance. You may not like his work, but sooner or later, if you have the slightest interest in our culture, you will have to deal with it. And for the record—no, I do not think Mr. Hood is advocating the murder of women.

Nigel Thorne hadn't caused such a sensation since he had called the pop art craze a "vacant obsession" some twenty years before. The review was widely quoted on TV and in print, and became in itself a news event. Thorne was widely interviewed— as was Sherri, and even Leo. Susan declined the honor many times.

Hood spoke only to those magazines that could do his career the most good. Sherri considered *New York* magazine the most important, so Hood found himself taken to lunch by a no-nonsense, good-looking female reporter, who asked him question after question with an almost sexual intensity. He was therefore surprised and a little crestfallen when he read her opening sentence: "Nick Hood is not a man you'd want to spend a lot of time with." Despite this ominous opening, the article actually went on to give a quite flattering portrait of an intense, dedicated, austere, and spooky young man—a portrait quite in keeping with the alarming cover photograph, which made him look like a very hip funeral director.

There were articles in everything from *The Village Voice* (not impressed) to *The Nation* (very impressed), from *People* (highly excited) to *Time* and *Newsweek* (which gave good reviews of his reviews). Hood read them all with interest but didn't bother to save any of them, with one exception. He carefully clipped a photograph from the *Times,* which had been taken at an artists' rally Sherri had organized—during which two hundred exuberant painters and sculptors cheerfully outshouted the much-reduced circle of protesting women. It showed Nicholas Hood under the affectionate arm of a person the paper described as "fellow artist, Peter Laszlo."

In less than a week, the painting was repaired and on the wall, and the show reopened with a much louder noise than could have been imagined before the slashing. As for the picture itself, Hood's close work with Egidio paid off. The damage was completely invisible, except where the murderer's face had been cut. On the left side of his face, a thin scar curved down from cheekbone to lip—but no one who did not know could have guessed this was not part of the artist's original intention. By the end of that week, Hood received an unlisted telephone number and a statement from the bank that put his balance at just over half a million dollars.

There was not a word from Andre Bellisle.

For the next couple of weeks, Hood did practically no work. The distractions of celebrity were amusing for a time; he even found himself worrying about his appearance. He knew it was vain and stupid, but he had no fear of being sucked into the superficial life that beckoned with open arms. The moment he had an idea he would be locked into his studio as surely as the impoverished aspirant he no longer was. At the moment, however, he had no ideas.

One night he was watching a western on the late show when Susan came out of the bedroom in her nightgown. Hood looked up from the couch. "I thought you were asleep."

She leaned against the kitchen door, arms folded. "When did you paint Valerie Vale?"

"I don't know. A few weeks ago—maybe two months."

"You never mentioned it."

Hood watched Walter Brennan explaining life to a young pioneer. "I don't always tell you what I've done. I don't see why you pick on that one."

"Because she's young and good-looking, and I think you're having an affair with her."

"I'm not."

"Don't lie to me. It makes you look stupid."

"You're very sure of yourself, for someone who doesn't know what she's talking about."

"I know you're lying, Nick. And the reason I know is because you never used to do it. I just figured out that that's what it is—that's what's changed you. It isn't the publicity. And it isn't the money, which doesn't really seem to excite you. It's that you don't like me anymore, and so you don't think it's worth telling me the truth."

"I am not screwing Valerie Vale."

"You wouldn't tell me if you were, would you?"

"Maybe not. But the fact is, I'm not."

"Look at me!"

Hood took his eyes off the television, making an effort to hide whatever must show in his face.

Susan said, "It's very simple, really. Either leave or don't leave. But if you're going to stay with me, you're not going to sleep around with every woman that comes across your path. There's going to be a lot more of them now, and I will not put up with that. Understand? I will not be lied to."

"Fine. Go back to bed."

"Well, are you screwing her, or not?"

"Yes, Susan. Every day. When I'm supposed to be working I go over to her place and we fuck our brains out. She's amazingly acrobatic, and quite imaginative, too."

Susan left the room.

She woke him up at ten o'clock the next morning by shaking him roughly. "There's someone here to see you."

Hood tried to wake up. "What? Who's here?"

But she didn't stay to talk. He threw on a pair of jeans and a sweater with a hole in it. He found Detective Lauzon standing by the front doorway, twirling his hat in his hands.

"Morning!" His smile was awfully bright for the early hour. "Had breakfast?"

He walked with Lauzon down West Broadway, on the sunny side of the street. It was surprisingly warm for November, and the people they passed were taking their time going about their morning business. A ragged man lay sleeping in a doorway, his torn trousers revealing filthy legs covered with sores. Lauzon slipped a bill into the man's gaping pocket. "It's easier to give them something when they're sleeping. It's so embarrassing to look them in the eye."

"I never give them money."

"How come—too much of a hurry?"

"Too selfish."

"I doubt it. A truly selfish person wouldn't be aware of it."

"You have an optimistic view of human nature."

Lauzon laughed and pulled open the door of a coffee shop.

"That's the first time I've been accused of that!"

They talked about Hood's recent emergence as a news item, over preliminary cups of coffee. When their food arrived, Lauzon dug into his omelet with enthusiasm. "This is perfect. I love it when it runs all over the plate."

Hood was shaking pepper over his scrambled eggs.

Lauzon gestured with his fork. "To get back to optimism: I think it's just that I've been lucky in life. Number one, I have a terrific wife; and number two, I'm in a line of work I really enjoy. Consequently, I'm free of the two worst frustrations a guy can have, and maybe it comes across as optimism. You're lucky, too. All the celebrity!"

"Yeah. I had to change my phone number."

"Which, by the way, is why I appeared unannounced. I could've gotten the number through police channels, but it didn't seem right. A well-bred person would have dropped off a note, of course."

"I'm glad you showed up. My wife and I are a little . . . at odds."

"Nice lady. She didn't seem upset."

"Yes, well, appearances deceive."

"All the time," Lauzon agreed emphatically. "All the time." He took a long drink of milk. "But I'd say on the whole you're a lucky man."

"You can't be serious." Hood paused with his fork in the air.

"Nice wife, lots of money . . . fame. Doing what you want."

"If you call having twenty-seven dollars in the bank at the age of thirty-five lucky."

"That's all over now."

"It'll be some time before I believe it. It's been a long haul."

"Paid off, though, you have to admit."

"Through effort. Not luck."

"Not both?"

"Luck doesn't enter into it."

Lauzon nodded slowly, as if a philosophical point long obscure to him had suddenly been made clear.

Hood said, "How's your own Life in Art proceeding?"

Lauzon grinned. "It's very kind of you to remember! I just got an A-minus on an essay about the Pre-Raphaelites."

"God. How did you get on to them?"

"One thing led to another. I was writing about inspiration, and from that I got onto models—believe me, you've heard it all before." He finished the last bite of his omelet, washed it down with milk. "In fact, I wanted to ask you about your own sources of inspiration."

Hood snorted. "Another form of luck. I don't have any."

"Oh, come on!"

"It's absolutely true."

"Now, wait. I've been trying to do some painting of my own—just to understand it better—and I haven't come up with one thing, not one thing, that was worth putting down. I haven't got one idea in my whole head." He made a wide circle in the air, as if his head were the size of many football fields.

Hood didn't know how to respond.

"Now, you stuff is chock full of ideas! I mean, who would've thought of 'The Falling Boy,' the way you did it? And 'The Burning Man,' like a holy picture? All of your pictures are so different! You have to tell me where you get your ideas. I know it's a naïve question, but naïveté is the only virtue I have left."

Journalists had been asking him that same question, so Hood slipped into a well-rehearsed answer. "Violence frightens me. It's endemic in our lives, and we don't know what the effects are—so we live with this low-grade fear, like background radiation. What's a safe level? I paint things that occur in the corners of our consciousness, and I guess in the forefront of my own. How could I be short of ideas, living in New York? Just look at television—it's like a porthole on a sea of blood."

Lauzon nodded and chewed, his head bobbing up and down in agreement. Hood wanted to get off the topic of inspiration, when Lauzon, apparently without intention, speared him with the next question: "What about that guy who set himself on fire in Washington Square?"

Hood tried to gauge what was on Lauzon's mind, but his curiosity seemed like that of a barroom philosopher—constant, but easily satisfied. Hood said, "The man set himself on fire. That's the only similarity. They have nothing else in common."

"But that's where you got the idea, right?"

"The most important element of the painting is the man standing beside him—his witness, or disciple. That's where the picture gets its strength."

"Absolutely right. You're right. I don't mean to diminish the painting in any way; it's just that I have this thing right now about inspiration."

"It was a coincidence. They happen all the time."

"Sorry if I hit a sore spot. You have to admit, the setting looks like Washington Square."

"There are buildings in the background, yes."

"Well, there's an arch, too."

"No, there isn't." His denial was instantaneous, but Hood knew, even as it came out, that there *was* an arch in his painting. He put his fork down, his appetite gone.

Lauzon said, "There is an arch, if you check again."

"So what if there is?"

"Am I upsetting you?"

"It's just that I've been asked about that painting a lot recently—as if it were a photograph, or something. You think some guy actually knelt down in front of this man—as if he was a human fireplace?"

Lauzon looked at him for a long time then, and Hood noticed for the first time that his eyes were a very bright green. He looked out the window in self-defense. Lauzon said, "You know a kid dove off a roof not long ago, too?"

"They do it all the time. You know the statistics better than I."

"Jumping, yes. Diving, no. Friend of mine in the Twentieth Precinct called me up after it happened. Well, I mean—you have the hotel in there and everything, so you must've at least *heard* about it. I'm just interested in how the real world takes shape in an artist's mind. I don't mean to criticize."

"All right. Yes. It was based on that incident. What's your point?"

Lauzon looked bewildered. "Point?"

"You seem to be insinuating something in a vague way."

"Oh, hell no! I'm sorry I made you mad—it's the last thing I want to do. Please accept my apologies."

"I'm not a patient guy, all right? If you want to talk, talk plainly. Anything else is a waste of time."

"You're right. You're right." Lauzon explored his teeth thoughtfully with a toothpick. "Let me start over. Forget everything I said, all right?"

"Fine."

"I'm not talking as a cop now—you understand? I'm just fascinated."

"I'm going to leave if you don't get to the point."

"A kid does a swan dive off a roof; you paint a picture. A guy sets himself on fire; you paint a picture. And finally, a girl is cut to shreds in a disorderly house. And you paint a picture."

"The fire was a coincidence. The rest I read about in the papers."

"But there were no pictures in the papers."

"I didn't use the details. The concepts may be based on real events, but everything else is made up. It's out of my head. I certainly didn't need any pictures."

Lauzon looked both ways, then leaned forward like a conspirator. He spoke in little more than a whisper. "Are you psychic? At all?"

Hood nearly laughed out loud with relief. So *that* was it. He tried to look thoughtful, and spoke slowly. "I recognize there are . . . states of consciousness about which we know nothing. I do go into a sort of trance when I paint, but no—I'm not psychic."

"But you say you have these sort-of trances! Maybe you've had these powers all along and you didn't even know! It's possible, isn't it? Don't you think it's possible?"

"Don't go off the deep end, Detective. There's no need for parapsychology to explain anything I've painted."

Lauzon pulled a small envelope from his jacket pocket and opened it. He handed three color snapshots across the table and said, "Not unless you knew these people personally."

Hood recognized them instantly. Sweat sprang out on his forehead; his mouth was full of cotton. The boy's was a high school photograph; the man's looked like it was from a driver's license. The girl had been photographed by a professional—there was a phone number at the bottom. Hood's tongue clicked when he spoke. "My painting couldn't resemble these people in any serious way. I assume they are the . . . the ones you were talking about."

"I got called in on the girl. I've been working on a prostitute killer for three years. Not this guy, as it turns out." He took back the photos and slipped them into the envelope. "When I went to your show, I couldn't help but recognize the murder scene in 'The Confession.'"

Hood slowly lifted his coffee cup, the closest thing to hide behind. The coffee was cold, but eased the dryness in his throat.

"My pictures—it couldn't possibly. It couldn't be the same. I just made it up—out of my head."

The bright green eyes stayed on him, as Lauzon reached into a pocket and pulled out a manila envelope. From this he removed several more photographs, and handed them across. He said, "I'm not keeping you from anything important, am I?"

Hood shook his head.

"We could do this another time . . ."

Hood said quietly, "Jesus Christ," and went through the photographs. "Jesus Christ."

Lauzon said cheerily, "It occurs to me that maybe breakfast was not the best time to . . ."

Hood was staring at a black-and-white picture of the girl—her face with the streak of blood on the forehead, the torn-out abdomen.

Lauzon reached across and tapped the picture with a thick finger. "Notice the cruciform position. Her feet are tied together, not apart. Not spread-eagled like you'd expect."

A cold drop of sweat rolled down Hood's rib cage.

"And this." Lauzon moved his finger. "A telephone. Very unusual in a whorehouse."

"Is it?" Hood said, faintly.

"Oh, yeah. Take my word for it. Doesn't all this just amaze you? I mean, look at the boy!"

Hood shuffled the pictures. The boy had one arm thrust at an unlikely angle on the crumpled roof of the car. Blood, a deep black in this black-and-white picture, formed a plume at the side of his head. A stray tooth lay nearby. Lauzon said, "Look at what he's wearing."

"Jeans. A T-shirt."

"Jeans turned up at the cuff, as in your picture. A striped T-shirt, as in your picture."

"I'd say that's almost a uniform. He was Puerto Rican."

"Look at his neck—can you see it there?"

"I don't see anything."

"He's wearing a cross!"

"Lots of Puerto Ricans do."

"I guess so." Lauzon leaned back in the booth and looked out the window. "Look at what's next to the car."

"Nothing. I can see the sleeve of a cop's uniform."

Lauzon just kept staring out the window. He sighed, as if suddenly fed up with Hood's evasions. "There's a streetlight. Right next to the kid."

Hood threw the picture across the table, as if making a discard in a game of poker. "You're being ridiculous. My painting is a night scene."

"This isn't?"

"In any night scene, you need a source of light. Since my kid is diving off a roof, he's bound to be lit by a streetlight."

"In your picture, he's diving right *into* the light. Just like this kid must've." Lauzon sighed again, and sat forward. He poked at the next glossy photograph. "There's a coat thrown over this man. You can't recognize him, because he's burnt to a crisp. Unrecognizable."

"Well, it's not surprising, is it?"

"The coat was found on the guy, just like that. He obviously didn't lie down under there himself. Someone put it over him—in other words, a missing witness. You said yourself, the important element in your picture is the witness. Well, there *was* a witness. At least one; maybe more."

"There are always people around that place."

"But how does your painting come to look like this man who is not recognizable? You saw the enlargement from his driver's license. It's the guy, the very man in your painting!"

Hood heard the words but could not connect them into any kind of meaning. "I'm sorry," he said. "Could you repeat what you just said?"

"Your picture shows the man who set fire to himself. Not

another man. Not a made-up man, but the man in the license photo. There were no pictures of him in the papers. And he was burned to a crisp. My question is, when did you see his face?"

Hood blustered. "I didn't see his face! I painted what I saw in my head!"

"How did you see his face!"

"I didn't!"

"You must have!"

"I didn't see the boy, or the girl, or any of these damn people! What are you trying to say! That I was there! At all three of these horrible . . . deaths!"

Lauzon let his green eyes wander all over Hood before speaking. Finally he said, "Obviously, you can't have been at all three incidents. How would that be possible?"

"You tell me! You're the one with the pictures."

"But, Nick—*you're* the one with the pictures."

"I don't believe the resemblances are all that strong."

"Really? You think I'm imagining?" Lauzon furrowed his brow, as if this were a real possibility.

"I grant there's enough to make one sit up and take notice. But beyond that, I mean . . ."

"You think I'm off the deep end?"

"Yeah," Hood said. "I do." He stood up and put on his jacket. "I just remembered I have an appointment. Uptown."

"Oh, sure. Don't let me keep you from anything. I'll take care of this."

"What do you mean?" Hood wanted to run; his leg muscles shook.

"The check. I invited you, remember?"

Hood managed a ghastly chuckle. "Right, right. You did."

Lauzon stood up—as if Hood were a woman leaving the table. "I'm sorry. This has obviously upset you."

"No, no, no—you're right to bring it up. It's just—it's just a little—"

"Kind of spooky, isn't it?"

"Yeah. It is."

Lauzon put out his hand. Hood's was soaking with sweat, but he shook hands anyway. He tried to smile, but felt his cheek muscles seize up. "Are you going to charge me with murder?"

Lauzon's mouth formed an instant O. "How could I do that? Two of them were suicides. And the girl's killer confessed in a matter of hours."

"Oh. I just—"

"I understand. Gimme a call, when all this sinks in, Nick. I think you have my card."

Hood nodded, tightly.

"Take care now. Maybe you better go home."

"Yeah, yeah. I think I will."

Lauzon smacked his own forehead. "I forgot! You just told me you have an appointment!"

Hood bared his teeth in a rictus of amusement, then turned and walked to the door. He had trouble with the doorknob, his hand was so wet. Nevertheless, he tried a cheery farewell. "Thanks for the breakfast!"

Lauzon showed him his straight little teeth. "We'll do it again sometime."

TWELVE

OUTSIDE, the sun was as yellow and happy as a child's crayon creation; inside, Hood's soul was a black ruined landscape of misery and fear. It struck him that every person on the street—from the homeless man to the pin-striped youth, from the cabdriver cursing out his window to the woman of forty examining her face reflected in a window full of shoes—all were happier than Hood, no matter what private sorrows and pain their pale, tense faces concealed. And yet, a hard core inside him remained unimpressed with their comparative ease—he was still superior—for even his unhappiness, though he wished it gone, was magnificent, opulent, beyond the reach of the common man. To survive it would be a great thing.

Susan had left a message marked urgent for him to call Sherri. Hood picked up the phone, but didn't dial the gallery. Instead, he dialed information and got the number of *The Village Voice*, then dialed again. "Yes, I want to place an ad."

The girl rattled off various options, and an absurdly complex system of prices.

"Listen. I don't care what it costs. Here's all I want to say: Andre Bellisle, bold letters, call Hood. Put it on the back page."

"There's a minimum charge, sir. You can get more words for—"

"That's all I want to say."

He called Sherri next. After a brief coughing fit, she said, "I got no good way to tell you this. Are you sitting down?"

"What is it?"

"You're not gonna be in the Whitney show." There was a

COLD e y e

pause. He could hear her wheezing. "Are you still there?"

"Yes. It's all right."

"You're crazy! It's a fucking disastah! There ain't gonna be another show like this for two yeahs!"

"I know. I have something else on my mind right now."

"What the hell's wrong with you? Ya sound dead."

"I have to go, Sherri."

"Don't you wanna know who they picked instedda you?" She waited for him to ask, and when he didn't, said, "Sam Weigel."

"Sam Weigel." A sudden memory of Weigel and Bellisle, emerging from a gallery together.

"Yeah, really. I think it's disgusting."

"It's all right."

"What is this 'all right'! What are you, Born Again? It's a fucking tragedy!"

"I'm just not feeling too well, Sherri."

"Well, go to bed and take a couple aspirin." She hung up.

Hood wandered numbly into the bedroom. One disaster seemed to cancel out the other. The prospect of being arrested and thrown in jail far outweighed the loss of a group show, however prestigious. He got undressed and lay down in bed, pulling the covers over his face. He made a sobbing sound to see if it would bring tears, but none came. The pressure in his heart kept building and building, as if a tumor were growing there. He threw off the covers and got dressed again. He was having trouble buttoning his shirt, when someone rang the doorbell. Hood froze—a useless instinct, since whoever rang the bell was five floors below at the front of the building. The bell sounded again.

Hood went to the window and peered out, careful to remain invisible to the street. Below him, Andre Bellisle's blond head flashed in the sun. Hood slid the window open. "Hey, Bellisle!"

Bellisle looked up, shading his eyes.

"Come on up!"

A few moments later he could hear Bellisle's footsteps approaching and opened the door before he knocked. The sight of Bellisle's face made him catch his breath. That face, which had been such a paragon of ugliness, was now beautiful beyond words. The curve of the eyebrows, the rise of the cheekbones and the slight hollow beneath them were so perfect they were like a theory of the face, and no part of flesh and blood. Bellisle looked at Hood with amusement lighting the bright blue eyes, an ironic half-smile lifting one corner of the mouth, the full lower lip. And then came the thrill of his sawtooth voice, sensuous and cold as iron filings on paper. "It's so good to hear from a friend."

When Hood said nothing, Bellisle leaned toward him and said, "You called."

Hood finally blinked, and stepped aside, allowing Bellisle to enter. "Your face," he said. "What happened to your face?"

Bellisle waved the subject away with a languid hand. "You can cancel your proposed ad in the Personals. Unlike yourself, I have no need to see my name in print. It's the thought that counts—I do appreciate the thought."

They remained standing between the doorway and the kitchen. Hood said, "The police are after me."

"Why? What have you done?"

"You damn well know what I've done. You got me into this—now you can get me out."

"I'll be delighted to help. But what must I get you out *of*?"

Hood told him about Detective Lauzon, the photographs of the victims.

Bellisle smiled, showing bright, almost translucent teeth. "The man hasn't charged you with anything. He hasn't arrested you. Indeed, what could he arrest you for? You witnessed two suicides. You watched a videotape of a murder. Legalities don't interest me, but I would guess the most you could be charged with is abetting a suicide."

"I couldn't stop them!"

"The *most* you could be charged with. If someone wanted to see you behind bars, they might stretch a point, but I doubt that any court would get excited about it. As for the other, well—you saw the killer come out of the house, but you didn't know he was a killer then, did you?"

"No."

"There's the videotape, of course. You might be charged with withholding evidence."

"I should've called them."

"Why fret? They have the tape; you've done no harm. The fellow confessed, and they have the tape—there's no shortage of evidence. How could anyone know you were there?"

"Lauzon knows. Believe me, he knows."

"He suggested you might be psychic."

"He doesn't believe that."

"What's the alternative? You were present at three unrelated and violent deaths. Which is harder to believe? Besides, our friendly detective likes you, admires you—he doesn't want you behind bars. You only torment yourself! It's not as if the man is *after* you."

"He *is* after me!" Hood pounded his fist on the door.

Bellisle looked at him with something like tenderness softening the blue of his eyes. "You know your trouble, Nick? You don't have enough fun. You lock yourself up in paint fumes all day. You don't have any friends. You don't have any sport."

"I don't want any sport."

"I know. I would have provided it."

"I want success. That's what you promised. It almost looked like it was going to happen. And now I'm just known as a mad pornographer." He grabbed Bellisle's lapel, crushing black velvet in his sweaty fingers. "Why did you get Weigel into the Whitney show! It should've been mine! It would've put me over the top!

You were supposed to be helping *me*! Weigel is nothing!"

"Calm yourself, dear boy. You shall be in the Whitney show." He removed Hood's hand, it was like the touch of a steel wrench. "I assure you, it has all been looked after. You shall be in the show."

"Oh, yeah. What do I have to do for it?"

"Nothing." Bellisle looked at him, calm as a hill. "The wheel is in motion. You are down at this moment, but on the rise, and soon someone else shall be down. It's merely the way things work—as others brighter than you have realized. Do you have something new to show them?"

"No."

Bellisle put his hand on the doorknob, ready to leave. "How are you fixed for subject matter?"

"I've got lots of ideas. Nothing definite."

Bellisle opened the door. "Fifty-five East Seventy-seventh Street—the Spierborg Institute."

"When?"

"Monday night. Seven o'clock."

Hood's fear of the police wore off. His confidence came back, but still he did no work. He spent his time staring out the window across the Hudson—a dull sight at this time of year, no longer autumn, not yet winter. It was Friday now. He sat there all morning watching a swag-bellied sky refused to rain. He would have sat there the whole day, but his Novack show was closing and he had to discuss with Sherri arrangements for moving the unsold works. Of the smaller works, only the picture of Bellisle as vampire remained, and of the larger, only "The Confession."

On his way to the gallery, the sky let go with a cold, pelting rain, and he had to run the last two blocks.

Marcia looked up briefly as he brushed water from his jacket, then returned her attention to the newspaper spread open on her desk. "I guess you heard about Sam Weigel."

"Yeah. Sherri told me last week."

"Oh, not that." She looked at him over the top of her glasses. "He's dead."

"Weigel?"

"His studio caught fire." She turned the newspaper around and pushed it across the desk. Hood leaned down to read.

There was a picture of a burning warehouse, with firemen training hoses on it. The story underneath was brief, saying only that the fire department had ruled out arson. They believed the cause was careless smoking. There was an obituary on another page, which Hood didn't bother to read. A life and a life's work, up in smoke.

Hood sat down heavily. He remembered Weigel leaning on him in this very room, breathing vodka into his face. "I had a future once," he'd said. As if he had known, Hood thought, and felt a shudder pass through him. Then he recalled Weigel on the Central Park bridge with Bellisle, carrying a bottle in a paper bag. Bellisle had laughed at his fit of jealousy. "We go to *bars* together!"

"I can't believe it," Hood said.

"I know." Marcia folded up the paper. "He was such a nice guy. He tried so hard to stop drinking, but—" She left the desk and hurried toward the ladies' room, sobbing.

He heard Sherri's voice and turned in his seat. Gerald Mallon was with her, nodding, his countenance grave, as Sherri escorted him to the front door. He raised his hand when he saw Hood, and called across the width of the gallery, "How are you?"

"Fine! Thank you!"

"How is Susan!" Mallon shouted, still at the front door.

"She's fine!" Ridiculous, calling across the room like this.

"Tell her I asked after her!"

"I will! Thank you!"

A limousine pulled up in front of the gallery, and Sherri held open the door. Mallon opened his umbrella—not a man to be caught short by circumstance—and made a dash for it.

Sherri crooked a finger, beckoning Hood to follow her into the office. She sat down with a groan and pulled out a pack of cigarettes. "I'm dyin' for a smoke—Mallon claims he's allergic. Ever notice? People don't like somethin', they make up an allergy. You hear about Weigel?"

"Just now. It's quite a shock."

Sherri took a deep drag on her cigarette, so that her words came out clad in smoke. "You probably know what it means for you."

"I'm in the show."

Sherri nodded. "Shoulda been you inna first place. Only reason they asked Weigel was 'cause he's abstract—they didn't want it to be all figurative guys, which it will be now. You're not excited."

"Well. The circumstances—"

"Forget that. You're in. You deserve to be in. The rest ain't up to us." She opened a drawer and pulled out a slip of paper. "Take a look at this."

Hood took the check from her. "My God!"

"Mallon bought 'The Confession' for their permanent collection."

"Jesus."

"They were gonna buy it anyway, so don't worry about Weigel."

Hood stared at the amount: four hundred thousand dollars. "You certainly made them pay through the nose."

"They got a bargain." She hoisted herself up from the chair and crushed out her cigarette. "Listen, kid. It's been a long day, and the Novack Gallery is going home to soak her feet and read a trashy novel."

Hood knew there would be no celebration, no claps on the back. Sherri moved around the desk with an absent, mournful air. "Mallon was wondering if you might have something tucked away nobody's seen."

Hood got up, and they left the office. "Nothing worth showing—it's all old stuff."

"You got eight weeks."

"Forget it, Sherri. Get the buyers to lend all this stuff."

"I'm just tellin' ya what the guy said. Let me worry about the buyers." She looked as if there had been a death in the family.

Hood said, "Were you very close to Sam Weigel? Did you know him well?"

She didn't really answer the question; she stood very still, and said, "Sam Weigel was a real nice fella."

Hood got up very early on Saturday, hoping to beat Leo to the studio. He was writing out a note for Susan when she came out of the bedroom, her hair in an opulent tangle. In a voice breathy with sleep she said, "What time is it?"

"Early." Hood crumpled the note and tossed it into the wastebasket. "I'm going to be locked up in the studio for the next few weeks. I have to get something ready for the Whitney show."

Susan went into the kitchen and opened the fridge door. "I thought you were out of the running!"

"Not anymore. I want to bring them something really big."

"Oh, Jesus." She came out of the kitchen, a carton of milk in her hand. "You've got tons of stuff."

Hood shoved his feet into a pair of boots. "It's nice that you're so pleased for me."

"I would be, if success were making you any happier, but it's quite the reverse. You're miserable all the time—tense, irritable, cold. You couldn't care less whether I'm here or not."

He pulled his coat from the closet and headed for the door.

"Nick, wait!" Susan stepped between him and the door and put her arms around him—a gesture to which he found himself unable to respond. He felt her breath on his neck as she spoke. "Please come back to me. You're not the same anymore. You spend too much time alone and the things you paint—they're all so negative. It has to bother you, thinking about violence, murder all the time. Just *looking* at your last paintings made me sick—I can't imagine what it must be like to live with them day after day, night after night."

"Susan, we've been through this before."

"Well, what's bothering you! If it's not the painting, it's something else!"

"I don't know what you're talking about."

"Neither do I, unless you tell me." She let him go, and stood back a little. "I don't know if you're screwing somebody else or not—and maybe that's not what matters—but you're not even my friend anymore."

Hood reached to open the door. "Things'll be better after the Whitney."

"They were supposed to get better after the last show. They were supposed to get better when we had more money."

"I have to work."

The elevator clattered and groaned through its slow descent. Hood tried to sort out his lack of emotion. How could the unhappiness of someone he was supposed to love be so utterly without interest?

Leo had beat him to the studio. And to make matters worse, Hood found his own half of the premises occupied by Detective Lauzon. He turned from the window, his ring of hair backlit and haloed with daylight. "Your colleague, Mr. Forstadt, was kind enough to let me wait inside."

Hood glanced over at Leo, who only shrugged. Hood said, "I have a lot of work to do."

"Fine. Maybe we could take a little walk."

It was cold on the pier. The damp breeze reached into Hood's small jacket. He looked at Lauzon, whose large down coat made him look inflated. "Let's make it fast."

"This is a totally unofficial visit, Nick—I'm not here as a cop. A detective's job is not really crime prevention." He gestured at the frigid sky. "You should've worn a coat."

"I didn't intend to paint outdoors."

A tugboat sounded its horn and Lauzon swiveled slightly, looking downriver. A dredger spewed silt high into the air. "I've never made a visit like this before. Probably never will again. It's hard to know where to begin."

"Just hurry up! What's the big deal!"

"These paintings of yours." Lauzon directed his gaze back to Hood. His eyes were a pair of green tacks. "You have three paintings. All involving extreme violence. And all of the events really happened. Either you were there, or you weren't."

"I wasn't."

"So you say. On the other hand, there are just too many details in the pictures—details you couldn't have picked up from the newspapers or television."

"Look. We went over that. I can't explain it any better than you."

"Let me ask you a question."

"Ask."

"What does your wife think of your work?"

The question was so unexpected that Hood looked at him blankly for a moment. "She thinks it's fine—why?"

"I can't see her looking at your work and not being a little . . . upset by it."

"That's her problem. Can we get to the point, please—assuming there is one." Hood was shivering all over. Lauzon took his arm as if he were a little old lady and guided him back down the pier.

"The point is, I've been dealing with murderers for fifteen years. And I have to say, Nick, that I never met anyone who looked more like a murderer than you."

Hood pulled his arm away. "Is that supposed to be funny?"

"No, it isn't. Leaving aside the question of whether or not you were physically present at that girl's murder, the fact that you could see it, and paint it, makes my blood run cold."

"I never thought cops were so sensitive."

"I like to think of myself as an exception."

Hood picked up a stone and tossed it into the river. An indignant sea gull flapped skyward.

Lauzon said, "I don't think I could watch someone have their intestines torn out, and not say anything to anybody—let alone paint a picture."

"You're not an artist."

"It means a lot to you, that word, doesn't it?"

"It describes what I do."

"No, sir. Doesn't come close. Watching people kill themselves? Watching a girl get cut up?"

"I wasn't there."

Lauzon took a sudden step toward him, but stopped—apparently checking an aggressive impulse. "You watched that murder—most likely on the TV monitor where we found a very sick videotape. And you didn't do a thing. First, a kid dives off a roof. Then a guy burns himself to death. And then the girl gets chopped up. I mean, what are you going to do for an encore? What comes next? Whatever it is, I'm here to ask you not to do it."

"This is your attempt at crime prevention?"

Lauzon started back toward the studio. "I like you, or I wouldn't have bothered. Somewhere, buried in your work, there's a good man. Also an evil man."

"Thank God you're not a psychiatrist, if you can't do better than Jekyll and Hyde."

"There's nothing subtle about it!" Lauzon turned, so that he was toe to toe with Hood. "I look at you, you know what I see? I see a murder waiting to happen."

"Go fuck yourself."

"This was friends, Mr. Hood. Let's hope next time it isn't cops."

A fresh canvas was propped on his easel, waiting to turn in his hands to a fierce, rectangular world. But it lay there impervious, opaque, and flat. If Lauzon had set out with the sole purpose of thwarting Hood's work, he could not have been more effective. Hood sank inward.

"You are in trouble with the law?" Leo was standing at the edge of the partition, tugging on his mustache.

"No."

"Can I help? Can I do anything at all?"

"There's nothing you can do. There's nothing wrong."

Leo retreated. Hood could not imagine how they had come to share a studio. His old friend was receding on a distant shore; Hood hadn't the energy to wave good-bye.

Having accomplished nothing by the early afternoon, Hood left the studio and walked up Hudson Street to Valerie's place.

The door was opened, and she broke into a grin. Hood covered her mouth with his hand, and her eyes widened. He looked into their twin surprise, shaking his head, until finally she nodded, understanding he wanted complete silence.

They passed three hours in bed together without uttering a word, and parted in silence.

"I thought you were going to work late," Susan said, when he got home. "It's not even five o'clock."

"Should I go back?"

"No! Why don't we go out somewhere, for a change?" Poor

Susan, still trying to pretend they had more in common than a SoHo loft.

Hood hung his jacket on the back of a chair. "I don't feel like going anywhere."

"Would you rather stay in and be miserable?"

He looked at her to see if she were trying to goad him, but her face showed nothing. "It's what I had in mind."

"Okay," she said, brightly.

And so he spent another few hours in the silent company of woman. He pretended to watch television, while Susan read a book. Later she got up to play the harpsichord, and Hood went into the bedroom to get away from the noise.

When she was getting undressed for bed she said, "Are you coming to the recital Monday night?"

"Sure."

"You just have to be at the studio at a quarter to seven."

"Studio?"

"WQXR. It's being broadcast live."

"Oh, yes."

She went out to wash, and got into bed a few minutes later. Hood stared at the page of his book, praying she would fall asleep. It seemed his prayer had been answered, until half an hour later Susan said, "You couldn't care less if I died."

"Susan . . ."

"Sorry. Did I disturb the genius?"

Sunday was no improvement. He had the studio to himself, but on his way up the stairs he had so dreaded the possibility of finding Detective Lauzon there, that his day turned sour anyway. He turned on the space heater, made himself coffee, and sat down in front of his canvas, still wearing his coat.

The canvas was as vast and threatening as Antarctica. Hood had no idea to set down, no wish to paint, no desire. Since the arrival of Bellisle into his life, he had painted his best pictures.

They could not have been conceived without Bellisle. But he had never been blocked in his work before their paths had crossed. It was as if Bellisle were a drug, and diminished the very powers he stimulated. If Hood continued under his wing he would not lack for subject matter, but what would become of his talent? His work no longer came from inside himself—it came from murder, from suicide.

From Bellisle. He summoned that beautiful face, so that it shone in his mind like a hologram. He looked at the eyes, so blue and all-knowing, and at the sensuous mouth, so quick to smile, and was overcome by yearning.

The address announced itself to him: Fifty-five East Seventy-seventh Street. Monday. Seven o'clock. And the trackless white canvas swam back into view. It was getting dark outside—the days were shorter now—and Sunday was gone.

Monday was much the same, except that Leo was in the studio with him. They said nothing all day. Toward evening, Hood felt a stirring in his belly, as if a new life were blooming in there. It was nothing more than an urgent anticipation, but it made his heart begin to pound. Anticipation turned to dread, and dread to outright fear, but before another hour could pass, all this emotion dissolved into one feeling. It was not pain exactly—it was an uneasy stimulus, an electric secret. It was the feeling he'd had before the boy dove, the man burned, the girl was slaughtered. Huddled before his undone work, Hood wondered if this sad, unholy thrill was all that kept him alive.

He left the studio at five-thirty, unable to sit still any longer. He took a cab up Sixth Avenue and over to Madison, his driver wailing curses at the rush hour traffic as if it were killing him. Hood abandoned him at Seventy-fifth and headed uptown on foot, a jaunty spring in his step.

THIRTEEN

IT was half an hour before his appointment with Bellisle, so Hood stopped at a pastry shop on the corner of Madison and Seventy-seventh. His coffee and Danish were absurdly overpriced, his waitress absurdly young. He passed the time by examining a floor plan of the Metropolitan Museum that a previous diner had left at his table. At five to seven, he paid the bill and left the shop.

As he turned the corner onto Seventy-seventh, Hood could see the cane and the blond hair advancing toward him down the brightly lit street. They met in the middle of the block. Once again, the exquisite lines of Bellisle's face put him at a loss for words; the satin, seductive voice. "Good of you to come, I'm sure." He pointed with his cane across the street. "We're over there."

They crossed the street and stood in front of a well-kept brownstone. A brass plaque beside the door announced, THE SPIERBORG INSTITUTE.

Hood said, "Did you kill Sam Weigel?"

Bellisle held a key in his hand; he was wearing white gloves, and smiled his thousand-watt smile. "I wouldn't harm anyone! I'm not capable! Oh, no, no—Weigel killed Weigel." He held open the door and Hood stepped inside. "I want you to know it's been a pleasure doing business with you. We may not see each other again, but truly, it's been most entertaining."

"Oh, yes," Hood said. "Delightful."

"I gave you what you wanted, didn't I?"

"I suppose. And you?"

"Oh, I'm perfectly satisfied. You've been most generous." He closed the door and waved the cane at a small black directory. "It's Beale we want. Third floor."

They crossed the foyer under a glittering chandelier, and started upstairs. Bellisle seemed almost to glide above each stair, as he rose—as if he were lighter than air and only held on to the balustrade so that he wouldn't lift off and bump his head on the ceiling. Hood followed close behind, excited. They stopped in front of a heavy oak door, and Bellisle produced another key.

Hood followed him through a waiting room and into what looked like the study of a very successful author. One wall was solid with books from floor to ceiling. There was a large oak desk in front of the window, and in the corner beside it, masses of fresh flowers exploded from a vase. Only the white leather couch, one end slightly raised, indicated that Madeleine Beale was a psychiatrist.

Adjoining this was an observation room the size of a closet, and it was here that Bellisle and Hood ensconced themselves. They had a perfect view of the doctor's office through a one-way mirror.

"Not a sound now. They won't be able to see us." Bellisle's shape was no more than a blot against darkness, his breathing like that of a distant furnace.

Hood's heart began to pound—there was someone coming. He luxuriated in surrender, as if the opening credits of a movie were rolling up on the screen of the one-way mirror. A woman entered the frame and switched on a floor lamp. She was in her early forties, broad-shouldered, large-breasted, and there was an easy authority in her movements as she adjusted the light, pulled up an armchair, and gestured for her client to sit down. A woman to reckon with, Hood thought.

A tiny man had crept into the room in her shadow, as it were. His hair was slicked sideways over a bald spot, and he wore wire-frame glasses that he kept touching, as if fine-tuning the focus of his life. He hesitated in front of the couch, clearing his throat repeatedly.

Harpsichord music suddenly blasted into the room.

"My goodness!" The doctor turned it down. "Sorry. The cleaning lady must have brushed the volume control. Don't you want to sit down?" She sat in the armchair near the one-way mirror. Hood drew in his breath and held it. He could have stroked her chestnut hair had there been no glass between them. The doctor repeated, "Don't you want to sit down?"

The small man lowered himself onto the couch, where he teetered on the edge like a child.

Dr. Beale smiled at his silence. "Suppose we start by finding out exactly why you needed to see me tonight, instead of our usual Friday morning."

The man lifted one foot into the lamplight, and turned it this way and that, as if inspecting his shoe leather.

"You said it was important, on the phone."

The man let the foot drop.

"You sounded quite agitated."

He remained perfectly still, a silent contradiction.

Hood was startled by a whisper from Bellisle. It was like a roar in the close darkness of the observation room. "You recognize the music?"

"Bach," Hood whispered. "So what."

"Ah, but *whose* Bach?"

Hood peered at him. No emotion showed beneath the placid beauty of Bellisle's face. The music was hardly relevant to the situation, and . . . Susan. He remembered Susan was being broadcast live from the radio station. Those slender hands, the long delicate fingers finding their way over black keys. She was playing a familiar prelude and fugue—very slowly, Hood noticed, perhaps out of nervousness. He should have been with her; it was a milestone in her career. But the little man on the couch was saying something.

"—with a carving knife in my hand. I called you right after."

The doctor nodded. "You've had this sort of experience before, haven't you."

"No! Never!"

"I believe that's why you were hospitalized two years ago."

"Oh, that." He drummed his heels against the couch. "Yeah. I guess."

"Have you been taking your medication?"

"I don't need it anymore."

The doctor shifted in her chair. "You're not taking it?"

"It makes my head all cloudy. I'm telling you, it took a few weeks for it to clear up. I don't need that stuff. It doesn't do anything but make me sleepy and stupid."

"You don't think it helped keep you out of hospital?"

He shrugged, staring at the carpet. The notes of the harpsichord hung in the air like icicles.

"What did you do with the knife?"

He mumbled something.

"Pardon me?"

"I buried it."

"Why did you do that?"

The little man shrugged, then rolled his head around on his shoulders, grimacing.

"Why did you bury the knife?"

It was like a freeze frame in a movie, Hood thought. Doctor and patient were absolutely motionless. She began to jiggle her foot, ever so slightly. Somewhere downtown, Susan continued playing the fugue—the fluency and grace of her performance mocking the ineffective little man. He kept clearing his throat.

Hood turned to Bellisle. "Pretty slow going."

"Shh. It gets better."

"Don't tell me the ending. You'll spoil it."

Bellisle responded with a barely audible chuckle.

The little man eased himself down off the couch and onto his knees. Then, to Hood's amazement, he crawled across the thick carpet toward the doctor. He sat on his heels, his face level with the doctor's knees, and panted like a little puppy. He put a hand on her knee.

"You must not touch me."

He left his hand on her knee.

"John, you're trying to test the boundaries of our relationship but you know very well it does not include the physical."

He put his other hand on her other knee.

"Please go back to the couch."

He didn't move.

"John, if you don't go back to the couch, or at least stop touching me, we will have to conclude this session. You are trying to make physical a relationship that should not be."

He lowered his head to her knees and said something.

"What did you say?"

He raised his head suddenly. "I want to see your breasts."

"No."

He took his hands away, and sat back once more on his heels. "I have to lay my head on your breasts. It will make the voices go away."

"Are you hearing them now?"

"Please."

"Are you hearing the voices now? Or is it just the music."

"Please!" He closed his eyes tightly, screwing up his face.

"Tell me what you hear."

The man was breathing in rapid little gasps, a cornered squirrel.

"Tell me what you hear, John."

He uncoiled from the floor and went straight for her throat.

He hit her with such force that the armchair overturned, tipping them both onto the floor. The little man was quickly back on his knees, clutching the doctor's throat, so that she couldn't make a sound. Hood couldn't see her face, which was hidden by the upended chair. He craned his neck, but all he could see was the wildly thrashing legs, the hands tearing at the little man. Susan's harpsichord continued stitching and unstitching silver threads of contemplation, while the doctor's skirt rode high up her legs, and the feet kicked vainly toward her attacker's face.

Hood glanced toward Bellisle. "I really have to question her judgment on this one."

"Mm. Amazing the value some women place on their breasts."

The heavy thighs lay still. The sweating little man lifted himself from the doctor, and she rolled to one side.

"Have to give her two points for stamina," Hood said.

The doctor was swaying on her knees now, her eyes red and unfocused. She sucked at the air, her throat making sounds like the last of something disappearing down a drain. One hand reached out blindly for support, catching the edge of the desk.

The little man was moving around the room looking for something, probably a knife, and not finding it. He searched the bookshelves, behind paintings, under magazines, hardly glancing at his victim. She made that terrible sucking sound again, and he came back and kicked her in the belly. She doubled over, and curled on the floor like a shrimp. He kicked her a few more times.

"He's a tiger, this guy. Serious business."

Bellisle just grunted.

"Uh-oh. She's going for the phone. This is really gonna piss him off."

The man watched the doctor pull the phone from the desk by the cord, and it clattered onto the floor. He stood still, hands on hips, while she scrabbled to get the receiver out from under the desk. Then he picked up the brass floor lamp, and swung it over his shoulder, making the room suddenly dark, except for a small tensor light on the desk.

He swung the lamp and caught the doctor at the base of the skull, knocking her flat. He raised the lamp again.

"Jesus," Hood said. "Mickey Mantle time."

The lamp went down with a thud, and up. The man rested it on his shoulder a moment, but the doctor didn't stir. He swung the lamp again. When he brought it up to his shoulder, he flung a posy of red blossoms onto the glass before Hood's eyes. He swung again and again, each time raining red on the glass. Then he leaned on his lamp, panting, and blood rolled down the mirror in scarlet strands.

"The slower tempo allows you to feel the spaces between the notes—you find in Bach that the silences are just as important and moving as the melody, and of course there wouldn't be any such thing as melody without silence. It's like space in architecture."

The interviewer asked Susan another question, and the little man flung his lamp to the floor, like a batter who has just struck out. He left the room, and shut the door quietly behind him.

"That's the great thing about Bach—he can be submitted to so many different interpretations. It'd be pointless to play him the same way every time."

Hood sat forward and watched the blood stray down the window in crimson highways.

"Well?" Bellisle said. "What do you think?"

"Quite a show, Mr. Bellisle. Quite a show."

"Will you be able to use it?"

"I think so. Depends on my mood, really—how things strike me when I get into the studio. I might do something entirely unrelated."

"I hope I haven't wasted your time. Would you like to see something else?"

Hood gave a short laugh. "Not just now, thanks."

Neither of them made any move to get up. Hood was slumped down in his chair now, allowing thoughts and impressions to flow over him.

The radio chattered on over the doctor's lifeless body. The interviewer asked Susan about life with her well-known artist-husband. "*We encourage each other to do well*," she said. "*I can't claim to understand his work better than anyone else—he doesn't talk about it much. In fact, we probably discuss art and music a lot less than people who aren't directly involved in them.*"

"I imagine two people of the artistic temperament must have occasional difficulties."

"*We might*," Susan said. "*But we never see each other.*"

Bellisle said, "We'd better leave now—unless you have some compelling reason to stay."

Hood got up and stretched, yawning. He was stiff from the straight-backed chair. Bellisle took his arm, and spoke in a confidential tone. "The next date is a Tuesday. February nineteenth, at four-thirty in the afternoon."

"Whereabouts?"

"You'll know, soon enough."

They walked through the doctor's office. The dead woman lay near the desk, her legs wide apart, the blood on her face turning darker as it dried. Susan was playing an air from one of Bach's cantatas. It was precise and sweet, a rich embroidery of poetry and math, and Hood wondered when Susan had learned it.

"Brilliant," said the blonde in floor-length blue satin.

"Such masterful control of line," said an up-and-coming dealer.

"Easily the best thing in the show. Best thing the Whitney's had in years." Mr. Fisk turned from the painting and called into the crowd. "I say, Mallon! Good show! You've finally discovered Nicholas Hood!"

Hood was more or less hiding behind a round steel sculpture, listening to the responses. He saw Mallon wade through the crowd toward Fisk, balancing a champagne glass in one hand, and adjusting his hair with the other. "You like it?"

"Fucking masterpiece, in my view."

"You know Hood?"

"Oh, Monsieur Le Whitney! You're looking at the owner of his 'Falling Boy'—which, I might add, is now worth three times what I paid for it less than six months ago. Of course, it doesn't have the scope of this thing."

"No. Apparently he painted this in a matter of five weeks—or so his dealer tells me."

"She's having you on, old boy. Look at those faces. Look at his right hand where he grabs her throat—the detail! Just to plan this whole thing out! The composition alone would take—"

"Nevertheless, Sherri says it didn't exist two months ago. She ought to know."

"Four months, minimum."

"You'd think so, wouldn't you?"

"Minimum!" Fisk thrust out an arm and plucked champagne from a passing waiter.

Mallon said, "Frankly, the thing sends a shudder down my spine every time I look at it."

"Mm. Damn violent."

"It's not that. It's those two faces peering out of the one-way mirror. It's not a picture of violence. It's a picture of evil."

"There's a spooky element in all his work. I think that's what's so riveting about it. The element of the forbidden and all that. Have you ever met Mr. Hood?"

"Once or twice," Mallon said. "That was enough."

The crowd around the paintings began to thin out. People headed for the elevators in twos and threes, hoping to enjoy some of the food before it all disappeared. Hood came around the sculpture. "So, gentlemen. What's the verdict? Am I in decline? Have I descended into self-parody? Do I have any future?"

"A great future!" Fisk declared, his face turning pink. "A magnificent future!"

"And what does the Whitney think?"

Mallon looked him up and down. "The Whitney thinks you're fishing for compliments. How is your charming wife?"

"Still perfect, after all these years." Hood turned toward the elevators. Sherri was there, dressed in a bizarre getup of green chiffon. She was laughing her raucous laugh and clutching the pale, smooth arm of Melanie Grace.

Mallon said, "Whatever can Sherri be saying to the Museum of Modern Art?"

"She's saying, 'More!'" Fisk said. "'I want more!'"

It was like walking into a room made of light, an antechamber of the next world. Half of the roof, and one complete wall were made of glass. Had it not at this moment been obscured by low-lying clouds, Hood could have seen the whole length of Central Park. The landlord had gone into the kitchen to demonstrate some rare and valued feature of modern cuisine, but Hood wasn't listening. His footsteps echoed in the enormous room, the sound bouncing off the glass surfaces. He said, "I'll take it."

Despite her success in concert and on radio, Susan had been out of work for some time. As always whenever she felt underemployed, she launched into a thorough cleaning of every corner in the apartment. She was running out of things to clean now, and Hood sat at the breakfast table watching her wash the windows. She was on tiptoe on the fire escape, stretching for the top panes of glass. Her hair was tucked up under her woolen cap.

"I've taken a new studio," Hood said when she came inside.

She was having trouble with the knot on one of her sneakers and sat down on the floor to work at it. "A new studio? With Leo?"

"No. It's just for me."

"You'll miss Leo, you know. Even if you don't like his taste in music." She pulled the wet sneaker from her foot, and stood up. "Whereabouts is it?"

"Central Park South."

She suddenly looked him full in the face, like an animal caught in the headlights. Behind the fear in those wide brown eyes, Hood could see her checking his arithmetic—performing the sad operations of subtraction and division.

He said, "I'm going to live there. Full time."

Every muscle in Susan's face seemed to slowly sag from the bone. She stood there, holding one wet sneaker in her hand, and yanked the woolen cap from her head. Electricity made her hair frizz out across her shoulders. She half turned from him, as if to make herself a smaller target.

He went on, "We've had it with each other. I want to be alone from now on. It's not as if we have a wonderful time together."

She pulled a strand of hair away from her eyes. Her cheeks were pink from the exertions of window washing.

"Why don't you say something?"

"Don't go," she said.

"I need to change my life. Everything's changed, except my life."

She remained standing, almost perfectly still. She could have said, "All those years I fed you, looked after you, and now that you're a success you go away," but she said nothing. With perfect justice, she could have said, "I was faithful, I was kind, when you were worried I stayed cheerful—I wanted so much to make you happy, but you never wanted to be happy." Susan said none of these things; Hood only heard them, watching her remaining utterly still in the window light, a slim young woman with pink cheeks and a wild halo of hair, a shoe in one thin hand, its laces dangling. Hood made a mental note to remember just how she was standing, the curve of her shoulder, the tilt of her head; he would use it one day. Her body was far more eloquent than anything she could have said—so eloquent, it began to annoy him. He felt so little for her now, that the appeal to his emotions seemed a little too much, as if she were a perfect stranger, whining for a loan.

He spent a lot of time lounging on his brand-new bed, watching the clouds chug across the skylight, gray and heavy as freighters. Now that he had the perfect studio, and all the time in the world to paint, the urge to create had left him. He had set his easel up right away, and the canvas had shone in a wash of soft northern light. In no time at all, an outline had appeared—a hill, half-hidden in a shroud of fog, a stand of bare, grieving trees—a winter scene, perhaps in upstate New York.

But then his imagination had seemed to fail, to dim like an electric light when there is a drop in power, because he could not come up with a face for his killer. The figure was fine—set toward the foreground, with a pronounced, almost Neanderthal stoop. To amplify the primitive look, Hood had given him a primitive weapon, a narrow club. But he couldn't come up with a face. He worked around it for a couple of days, sketched in his victim, and finally, lacking any better idea, simply painted his own face on the killer's body.

When he had turned his attention back to the victim, the light of his imagination had flicked and then gone dark altogether. A female form lay broken and bloody, with no identity at all. The work gave no feeling of a person being obliterated; it would have no power. Hood toyed with the idea of painting Susan there. Perhaps this picture was a rendering of his guilt for having left her. But he hated to analyze a painting that way, especially before it was finished. And so he had put his brushes away and covered the canvas on which he had captured everything except a victim.

Having set this failure aside, Hood felt as if some plan had come to fruition, as if some campaign had been concluded; yet he had no sense of triumph. He felt only that he would never paint again.

Sprawling on his bed, he dragged the telephone across the floor by its cord, and dialed Valerie's number. "You sound out of breath," he said.

"Yeah. I was just leaving. I hadda run back upstairs."

"I want you to come over and see my new bed. I want to do terrible things with your body."

"Horny, huh?"

"It's a virgin bed."

"I can't. I'm going up to Connecticut. I wanna see if I can get some new ideas and stuff while my folks are away."

"Come over here first. Then maybe I'll go with you."

"Really? You'd come to Connecticut?"

"Maybe. You have my new address?"

"I'll be there in half an hour."

Hood hung up and went to the window. Central Park was dissolving in a February drizzle. There hadn't been a real rain for weeks but only a constant, cool spray that made one feel always damp and irritable. Hood noticed at noon, when he'd gone out to buy a paper, that the temperature had suddenly risen to somewhere in the fifty-degree area. Maybe that was why the clouds were rolling into the park beneath him. Their moisture would still be cold and heavy. It was eerie how they clung to the trees—like the fog in those movies where raven-haired women awake in the crypt.

The image of Andre Bellisle was suddenly in his mind—not as he had first seen him, small and repulsive, but as he had last seen him—gorgeous and tall and innocently wicked, smiling his millionaire smile. He thought of Bellisle, because he was feeling the old sensation again, the electric anticipation. Yet, they had no agreement to meet, had they? Hood couldn't remember. He hadn't seen him since the previous November, when they'd watched that psychiatrist, whatever her name was, get beaten to death. He hadn't thought of his mentor very often since then.

And yet the old urgency was throbbing in his gut, as if he had a time and place just around the corner, an appointment with murder. It made him shiver, made him nauseous, but it also thrilled him to the marrow. He wished with all his heart that Bellisle would call; he hadn't the slightest interest in Valerie Vale.

The house phone rang, just as he got out of the shower. He told the doorman to send her up and pulled on a pair of jeans.

"My God," she said. "What a place! It's made of light and clouds!" She put her purse down on a chair and walked slowly around the room, exclaiming over this and that, while Hood buttoned up his shirt. When she turned her attention to him finally, she looked suddenly worried. "What's wrong, Nick? You look like you just woke up from a nightmare."

"I don't think I've woken up yet."

"Were you sleeping?"

"No, no. It's nothing. Nothing." His stomach was twisting, pulsing with anxiety. "What is the date, exactly?"

"The date? February nineteenth. Nick, what's wrong? You look sick! I think you better lie down." She started toward him, her face tender.

"Stay back! I mean, don't worry. It's nothing. I've just—I've got an appointment somewhere and I can't remember where. I made it a long time ago and I forgot all about it. It's Tuesday, isn't it?"

"Yes, but I think you better—"

"The trouble is, I can't remember where it's supposed to be. I can't remember where the hell it is!"

"Sounds like it couldn't be too important, then."

"Everything depends on it! My future . . ."

"Well you can't go anywhere like this. You're drenched with sweat." She reached out to touch his forehead, but Hood jerked his head back. He went over to the window.

The street below was becoming indistinct in the fog. Thick clouds of it were rolling into Central Park.

"You look so shook up, Nick—I've never—"

"It's this appointment! I can't remember where it's supposed to happen!" Hood pounded the window with his fist—once, twice, then put his fist right through, and screamed. His arm was sliced open.

Valerie cried out, "You're crazy! You're having a breakdown or something, my God!"

Hood gritted his teeth and extracted his hand, the blood slipping through his fingers to the floor. Valerie ran into the bathroom and came back with a small towel, which she wrapped around his arm. She urged him over to the bed. Hood was beginning to feel faint, and didn't resist. He sat down on the edge of the bed and then lay back.

Valerie said, "All right. Let's get you cleaned up." Hood held his arm up for her. "I don't think it's too deep, really. I don't think you'll need stitches."

"I have to get out of here."

Valerie squeezed his arm with the towel, and said, "You have to get out of New York. That's what you need. Why don'tya come with me to Darien—you said you might, on the phone."

*   *   *

Hood fell asleep for an hour, with Valerie holding his arm. When he woke up, and it seemed certain he would not bleed to death, he agreed to go with her to Connecticut. The thrum of electricity was gone now. In its place there was nothing but a slight, aching hollowness. It stayed with Hood all through the ride on the filthy, crowded train. Their car was full of pinstripes and briefcases, all in a rush to miss the afternoon stampede.

"It's not usually this crowded," Valerie said. "I guess people gotta leave their cars in the city 'cause of the fog 'n' that."

Hood grunted.

"You don't have to talk or nothing. It's just gonna be so nice having you around." She gently touched his cheek. "Having you all to myself."

Hood leaned his head against the window. He couldn't see anything through the dirt and the fog.

An hour later, they were in Darien. Valerie's home wasn't far from the station, so they walked there through the chill damp fog. Hood's arm was stinging again, so he allowed Valerie to carry his overnight bag.

"There's still snow up here," Hood said.

"Yeah. It stays a lot longer. Stays a lot cleaner, too."

"So I see."

"I love the fog, don't you?"

"I think I'd rather see where I'm going. But I know what you mean. It makes a change."

They left their bags in the front hall of the Vale house, but Valerie wasn't ready to stay in just then, so they walked down to the water of Long Island Sound. "God," she said. "Usually you can see the houses on Long Island! I can hardly see the water now!"

"What's up here?" Hood said, pointing northward.

"Well, it's sort of a private beach, but I don't think anyone's gonna get upset this time of year."

"If they could see us."

"Right." She walked on ahead of him along a path of colored paving stones. Somehow the fog made her look smaller than usual. "There's a little kind of park, too."

He followed her with no particular wish to see the water, or the beach, or the park. He followed her because he had no other desire, either. Billows of wet fog brushed against them, like huge, ethereal cows. Hood could see twelve or fifteen feet ahead, no farther. He wondered what exactly Valerie planned to paint in this weather.

The paving stone path was gone now, and they were walking on sand crusted over with trampled snow. Rows of headlights prowled an invisible highway a hundred yards away. The silence was profound.

"Oh, look!" Valerie said. "There's not one footprint!" She was pointing to a perfect rectangle of snow, surrounded by a low fence. "I think it's for lawn bowling or something, in summer." She climbed over the fence and made a trail of ridiculously small footprints into the middle of the rectangle. It was at that moment that Hood caught sight of Bellisle.

At first it was just a dull flash of yellow in the corner of his eye. But when it came again, he was ready, and he saw him duck behind a tree, just as he turned to look. A swirl of fog came between them. Hood started toward the tree. "Bellisle?"

Bellisle was gone. There was no one by the tree and no sign that anyone had been. The snow underfoot was quite trampled here, so even if there had been footprints, they wouldn't have helped. Hood turned to look the other way. Valerie was invisible now. He heard her call his name. "I'll be right back!"

He went a little farther uphill. Again the flash of yellow, and again Bellisle slipped away among the trees. Hood ran a little way, but tripped over the roots of a huge oak. He got up and hurried through the fog, calling Bellisle. The fog was like a gathering blindness, pressing up against his eyes. There was only the dull glow from a streetlight overhead, and the foreshortened beams from the crawling headlights. Bellisle reappeared, off to one side on a rocky ledge.

Hood pushed his way through some bushes. The branches tore at his hair, and he lashed out, cursing. He had entirely forgotten the long cut on his arm. When he reached the ledge, there was no one; everything was gray, wet wool. He heard a footstep on gravel, behind him. He whipped around, stumbled, nearly fell.

Bellisle was standing there, tall and serene, his arms folded under a black cloak. His beauty was quite inhuman now—he was not handsome, or pretty, but something far more than that. He was a field of stars in a deep black sky, or a pebble sinking down through an unfathomable pond. He was an asteroid making an arc around the coldest, most distant star. Hood could see the blue of his eyes, even through the fog, and the sound of his voice—resonant, sensual—nearly brought Hood to his knees. But he fought the rising sense of awe, vowed to remain in control.

Bellisle said, "Together again, after all this time."

"You fucking vampire," Hood could hardly bear to look at him. "I'm going mad. You've driven me mad." An odd sound came from Bellisle—a rasping sound, like a file on a metal bar. Hood lunged toward him, but there was nothing there.

He ran forward. He heard footsteps again, followed them across some rocky ground, and downhill. At the bottom of the incline, a string of cars curved away, their motors throbbing, their lights dull. They nudged each other forward, inch by inch. Hood thought he discerned a shape in the fog, about twenty feet away. But when he stalked it slowly from behind, it turned out to be a statue of a long-dead general.

Bellisle could not be far away; Hood could feel his presence.

Electricity went coursing through his veins as never before. The hair on the back of his neck stood up, and his heart was drumming on the wall of his chest. He felt the predatory thrill, half fear and half desire, that had brought him, trembling, to watch others die. He stumbled downhill, and banged his thigh on a low wooden fence.

Someone was singing, in a high, pure voice, not altogether on key. It was a sweet song—a vaguely Celtic melody that Hood had never heard before. The fog thinned for a moment, and Hood saw that it was Valerie, sitting on the fence across the white rectangle of snow where he had abandoned her. Her head was tilted back, and she sang without a trace of self-consciousness. Her form would fade for a moment, then come clear again with the changing textures of the fog. Hood stood there, transfixed.

Father, dear father, you do me great wrong
You've married me to a boy who is too young
I am twice twelve and he is but fourteen.
He's young, and he's daily growin'.

Daughter, my daughter, I've done you no wrong
I've married you to a rich man's son
He'll make a lord for you to wait upon.
He's young, and he's daily growin'.

She saw him as he climbed over the fence. "Nick!" She stood up and started across the white square. "Did you get lost? I heard you calling!"

She reached out for him, but Hood pulled back. "Where's Bellisle?"

"Who?" She looked at him through a thin veil of fog. "Nick, you look so strange! What's wrong?"

The snow around them hadn't been disturbed all winter; it was still and white as a new canvas.

Hood felt a tingling sensation in his fingertips; the blood was pounding through his veins with terrifying speed. "Stay there," he said, although she was less than three feet away.

"You're being awful weird, Nick. I think maybe you lost a little more blood than you thought."

His breath was coming in tiny, hurried gasps.

"You're still not feelin' too good, are you? I don't know why you can't just admit it." She watched him bend down and thrust his hand through the crust of snow. "Why don't we go back to the house now. I'll make you a cup of tea."

Without taking his eyes off Valerie, Hood stayed down and felt around in the snow. His fingers were aching, as he reached this way and that. Where was it? He knew it was here, somewhere—right beneath his feet. The glazing of ice was sharp against his wrist as he cast about for the thing.

"What are you s'posed to be doing down there?" She shook her head at him, as if he were a mischievous puppy.

Hood's eyes remained fixed on Valerie. She was outlined in the fog against the snowy background like the beginning of a painting. He knew just how the work should look, where the blood should be. Separate details flashed one after the other into his mind—the outstretched arm, the scared blue eyes, the dead-looking trees in the background. A painting from the life.

And then he found it, exactly where he knew it would be. His fingers closed around the object underfoot—a length of pipe, by the feel of it. "But I shouldn't really know it's here," he said aloud.

"Huh?"

He knew it didn't make any sense.

"What are you talking about, Nick?"

He pulled the pipe out of the snow. It was heavy, about eighteen inches long; it was just right. Hood got to his feet, stomach buzzing, heart wild.

Valerie never saw it coming, so he turned out to be wrong

about the fear in her eyes. When he brought the pipe down on the crown of her head, she merely looked astonished. It was almost funny. She remained standing there, perfectly still, though she must have been seeing stars. Then Hood gave her a backhand swipe that blasted the stars forever from those eyes. The blow caught her in the temple; the skull cracked and the pipe broke through, lodging in the brain. Blood sprang from the wound in a fountain, even as she fell. With the pipe stuck in her skull, her weight pulled Hood down to his knees.

The heat of her blood took him by surprise as it ran hot tongues over his fingers, drenching his hands. Steam rose from the snow where it turned from pink to deeper and deeper red. Hood got up, stood back. He knew, if he should ever paint again, he would use only that color. Nothing else compared to this brilliant crimson, cooling on his skin. He stumbled backward a few steps, then turned, climbed over the fence, and ran as fast as he could through the fog.

FOURTEEN

IT was as if he were running through water, not fog. The short distance to the train station seemed to stretch out beneath his feet with every step. He was on the platform, where a large clock indicated that it was 4:36, when he remembered he had left his overnight bag at Valerie's house. He remembered this, and yet he did nothing. He paced back and forth on the platform, and began to know the meaning of infinity, over the nine minutes that tormented him, before the 4:45 train to Manhattan arrived. He got on board the train, and watched the station slide away behind him, knowing that his name was on the overnight bag, and they would be coming for him within an hour of Valerie's body being discovered. It wasn't that he didn't care, or that he was afraid to go to the house; he simply had not yet begun to see himself as a criminal, and so couldn't really conceive of being a suspect, a wanted man.

As the train neared the city, however, his numbness, his vague feeling of immunity, gave way to fear. Fear seeped in around the edges of his soul, until there was nothing there but sheer anguish. He had kept his hands in his pockets until he'd reached the Darien station, where he had gone into the washroom and washed his hands. He examined them now, and could see crescents of deep red under two of his fingernails.

Grand Central was swarming with rush hour traffic. Hood might have welcomed the crowds, except that he was moving against them, and felt he must stand out like an obvious killer. It was safer in the subway car, jammed as it was to bursting with people going home from their harmless occupations. It was such a normal part of city life that Hood was reluctant to leave the discomfort at Columbus Circle, where he got off the train and moved once more against the crowd.

He struggled through the slush on Central Park South toward his new home, Somewhere in the fog nearby, a man called out for a taxi. A horn blew, and then there was the squeal of tearing metal. Shouts pierced the thickening gloom, diminishing as Hood slogged against a human tide bristling with umbrellas and briefcases.

He had to avoid the front lobby. He waited outside his building, until a long black Cadillac turned in and was sliding into the parking garage. Hood walked down into the basement before the overhead door closed, and hurried across to the freight elevator.

Fog was squirting into his apartment through the hole in the window he had made with his fist. He double-locked his door, then left his clothes in a heap on the floor while he took a hot shower. When he had dried himself and put on a fresh pair of corduroys and a sweater, he took several strips of masking tape and made a cross over the hole in the window. Then he curled up on the bed.

Sleep would never come, he knew that, but he stayed on the bed, curled up like a slug and wondered when they would find Valerie's body. It was dark out now, and no one was likely to find the body until morning, if then. But still he had the feeling that everybody knew. The whole world must know. He waited for the banging on the door, or the sound of a megaphone, Lauzon's voice telling him give up, you're surrounded.

The minutes ticked by, and no one came. Hood lay there staring at a little blue box of tampons that must've fallen out of Valerie's purse. It was on the floor, near the window, as if a piece of the sky had fallen there. What did one do with evidence like this? Burn it? And then what—drive back to Connecticut with a shovel and try to bury the body in the frozen earth? He lay there staring at the box of tampons, and at the cross on the window, waiting for something to happen. Hours went by. He lay unmoving, unsleeping, tormented by images of Valerie and Bellisle that flared up before him like tongues of flame.

Unable to stand it any longer, he got up and tore the cover from his abandoned painting. He even went so far as to mix up some paint. But when he turned on the light, he could not even see his canvas; he was blinded by the image of Valerie's face, which blazed in his mind the moment he lifted his brush. She was almost living! He could smell her short dark hair, could see her pale, otherworldly skin, with its tracing of tiny, lilac veins. He could look right into her eyes—her deep blue eyes, so intense with frustration, with questions, with love.

But he could not paint. Hours after hour went by, and he stood motionless before the easel, as if he himself were a figure in a painting—the product of some vile creative force that had captured not only his likeness, but his heart—so that he would never again know any life but this, know any world but this, this fake existence in a cruel interior.

It was still dark out when the telephone rang, jerking him back to reality. For one wild moment, he thought it would be Valerie, calling to tell him she was all right. But it was Susan.

"I'm sorry to call you so early, but I wanted to make sure you were in. Did I wake you up?" She sounded near tears, her voice thin and fragile.

"No. I was awake."

"You sound strange. Are you all right?"

Hood said nothing. He was listening to the universe howling down the telephone wire, burning a hole through his brain.

Susan said, "I wish you'd come home, Nick," and then she broke into sobs. She tried to speak again, but couldn't get her voice under control.

Hood hung up the phone and sat up. Soon, people would be walking to the train station in Darien. Some stockbroker, taking his cocker spaniel for a walk, would come across Valerie's body. It was too bad he'd picked someone he'd known. If he'd killed a stranger, there might be some point in trying to get away with it.

He put on his jacket and left the apartment, taking the stairs, not the elevator, and emerged from the back of the building onto Fifty-eighth Street. He walked over to Seventh Avenue and flagged down a cab. He told the driver, "I want to go to SoHo."

"Where in SoHo?"

"I'll let you know."

He let the driver take him some distance past his destination, then walked back uptown. It was not yet eight o'clock when he stood in front of his old studio, the sea gulls crying at his back. He felt in his pocket for the key and hoped Leo would not be in.

"Nick! What brings you here so early and bright!" Leo was crossing the room, beaming broadly. "Let me take your coat— you are a guest here now. I must become the proper host."

Hood let him take the coat and glanced around the studio— the vacant far corner of the room where almost every significant moment of his life had passed. The pale morning light washed in on his vanished career. He said, "I fucked up, Leo. I'm in trouble."

"Hah! Don't tell me you need money, Nicholas! It's too much!"

"I killed Valerie Vale."

Leo's smile drooped uncertainly. He cocked his head. "What's this you said?"

"I killed Valerie Vale."

"Killed Valerie?" Leo shook his head as if Hood had spoken gibberish. "I don't understand."

Hood sat down on a stool, as a wave of nausea passed through him. "Near her folks' place—in Connecticut."

Leo's voice was very soft, as if audible speech might confer reality upon what was so far, to him, only a horrible idea. "I still don't understand," he said. "Why would you kill Valerie?"

Hood shrugged, and stared at the floor.

"Why would you do such a thing, Nicholas?"

Hood looked up at him and sneered, without really intending to. "I wanted to. All right? It seemed like a good idea at the time. What do you want me to say?" Leo's eyes were as round as two zeroes. Hood spoke louder. "She was there!"

"This is terrible, Nicholas." Leo squinted at him. "Did you have a fight? What happened?"

"Nothing happened. She was standing there. I had an inspiration. And she's dead. That's all there is to it. She didn't provoke me, if that's what you mean."

Leo's voice went cool. "You'll have to go to the police."

"Let me stay here for a while."

"They'll find you here, anyway."

"If they find me, they find me. I don't really know why I came. I suppose I wanted sympathy."

"Valerie was a wonderful person. She has my sympathy."

"Oh, yeah," Hood snorted. "She would've lived to be a great artist!"

"Is that why you killed her? Because she couldn't draw?"

"Look, Leo—murder's not nice, but let's not pretend there's any great loss here. She's just another small-town girl who fucked the wrong guy, all right?"

Leo hit him full in the face, knocking Hood from the stool. Before he could get up, Leo was half-kneeling on his chest pounding at him blindly. Hood twisted away and got up. When Leo came at him again, he punched him in the belly, and the fight was over. Leo leaned against his worktable, gasping for breath, tears streaming down his face. Hood went over to the window, and stood there looking at the river, rubbing his cheek. His jaw really hurt.

After a few moments, Leo started putting on his battered leather coat.

"Where are you going?"

"Out. What does it matter?"

"You're not going to the cops, are you?"

"I'm going out for a walk. Then I'm going to Wilson's Frame. They're going out of business."

Hood was suddenly fearful. "What time will you be back?"

"I don't know. A few hours."

"A few hours? To look at frames?"

"They have a warehouse, too."

Hood swallowed. "Couldn't you come back a little earlier? It's hard to be alone."

"You should try and sleep. You look terrible. I'll come back when I can."

Hood lay down on the filthy couch and listened to Leo's footsteps descending the iron staircase. For the first time since the murder, he wanted to cry. To prevent this, he stood up again and went over to Leo's easel. The work in progress was a portrait of Susan in her green velvet dress, sitting in a chair with a black cat on her lap. Unlike Hood's own efforts, the painting captured her sweetness of temper, the amused skepticism in her eyes. She looked like an intelligent, thoughtful woman whom you might want to know.

He went over to the spot where his own easel had stood for so many paintings, so many years. The rough wood floor was thick with splotches from a thousand different tubes of paint—pale green for the image of a tree, violet for the eyes of a victim, ochre, sienna for a hundred different things, bone white, flesh pink, and black, and red. There was more red than anything else—cherry red, rust red, scarlet and ruby, arterial and veinous—as if someone had been cut apart on this spot, and had bled every shade of crimson visible to man.

There was a footstep on the gravel outside. Hood didn't have to look—he knew right away that Leo had called the police. Was it that he had cared so much for Valerie? Or was it his German respect for authority? Hood didn't even stop to grab his jacket.

He bolted from the studio and ran the length of the second floor. He took the fire stairs at the far end, ran up two flights and emerged into a bitter wind on the roof. He ducked down on hands and knees, scrambled to the edge and peered over. There were two police cars. He could see one man moving quickly along the front of the building. Lauzon would be inside by now, banging on the door.

A gap of about eight feet separated Hood's building from the next. He started from the middle of the roof, took a good run at it, and leapt. He cleared the gap and tumbled forward, scraping his hands and knees. Lauzon called out somewhere behind him, "Don't do it, Nick! You won't get out of this!"

Hood rolled over behind a rusty door that was flapping in the wind. It was dark inside, but the layout was the same as the studio building—he knew there would be an exit at the far end. He tore down the stairs and ran along the second floor, then down another flight of stairs. He pushed open the door and came out the back of the building. He heard Lauzon shouting orders to someone. He crept along a dark alley behind the cast-iron shell of an old warehouse and came out onto the street. There was a shout, then a gunshot. He ran back down the alley and out the other end.

He ran half a block north on Hudson Street. The cop shouted again and fired another shot, which ricocheted wildly off a stop sign. A charter bus full of tourists turned the corner and Hood darted across the street while the bus provided shelter from the bullets. He veered into a side street, and ducked down behind a row of cars. The cop ran past the side street, and Hood took off again.

He crossed West Broadway and dodged left into an alley near Broome Street. He pressed his back against the wall and listened. There were no shouts, no gunshots. He ran along the alley and emerged on Wooster. It was only a half a block to his old building.

He no longer had a key to the front door, so he went around the side and overturned a garbage can. He stood on this and reached up for the bottom rung of the fire escape. The steps unfolded and he climbed up, knowing it was hopeless. What safety was he seeking? Why should he run to his former home? He went up four floors, then stopped halfway up the last flight of steps, halted by a vivid memory—Susan in her woolen cap, washing the window, standing on this fire escape.

He kept well to one side, then peered in the window. The scene was like one of those tableaus arranged behind glass in colonial-village museums—a pioneer woman pulls freshly baked bread from a glowing, but heatless, oven. Two children, dressed in heavy clothes, share dinner at the oak table. Father, wearing a leather jerkin, has just come in from outdoors—he hangs his musket on the wall. He is handsome, God-fearing, not above a wholesome joke.

In this particular display, this historical scene, a young woman played a harpsichord—he could hear the notes tapping at the glass. She looked real! Her hands moved over the keyboard with a very lifelike movement. Encased in glass that way—if he cried out, would she hear him? Could she see him, preserved in her phony eternity? Hood pressed his forehead to the window, touching the pane lightly with his fingertips. Such pretty hair the woman had, such fragile wrists—a man could fall in love.

But that would be like falling in love with a star of the silent screen, an ancient image, a woman long withered. She lifted her hands from the keyboard then, and bowed her head. The music lamp caught the highlights in her hair, as she sat there thinking, doing nothing.

Hood could feel someone coming up the fire escape beneath him, but kept his eyes on Susan. Lauzon's voice startled him then. It came from above. He looked up. Lauzon's round face peered down at him, over the edge of the roof. "Mr. Hood," he said, "I'd say this is the end, wouldn't you?"

Hood looked down. A cop pointed a gun at him.

Lauzon said, "Come up now. No point upsetting your wife any more than necessary."

He went up the stairs carefully, staring at his feet. Lauzon took his elbow, helped him onto the roof. The round face looked sweaty and tired and expressed no hint of victory. The detective said in a quiet voice, "Welcome to Earth."

FIFTEEN

HIS lawyer was a youngish man with sandy hair, a polka-dot bow tie, and a shining new briefcase. His name was Tim Fingal, and he had a voice like Jiminy Cricket. Hood asked him for only two things: a speedy trial, and following this, either immediate freedom or death—the latter being a distinct possibility in the state of Connecticut.

The first day in the Stamford courthouse, Fingal entered a plea of not guilty, and from that point on, gave the case his best. At trial, he hoarded bits of contradictory evidence and plucked them from his sleeve at telling moments. He chipped away at the forensic evidence and found weak spots in the testimony of every witness who appeared for the prosecution. Through his manifest sincerity, his earnest application, Fingal succeeded in getting judge, jury, and even the prosecution to like him. He could not, however, perform the same feat for his client.

Hood had refused to plead insanity, or even a temporary aberration. He passed the test of competence for trial and would agree to no procedure that would delay his hearing, even when it would have been to his advantage. He exasperated Fingal at every turn. Bail had been set at one and a half million dollars—a sum that Hood could not readily meet, but which Fingal could have put together for him through various channels. Hood instructed him to forget about bail.

He lay in his holding cell, reading an endless series of paperback mysteries, and refused to see anyone. He turned away Susan, and Leo, and Sherri again and again, preferring to remain in a kind of suspended animation. During this period he made not one sketch, nor did he so much as request pencil and paper.

The prosecution laid out its case with painstaking precision. They could produce no witness who actually saw Nicholas Hood take the life of Valerie Vale, but several who had seen them together in the weeks preceding her death. His doorman testified that she had gone up to Hood's apartment that afternoon, and of course the Connecticut police produced Hood's overnight bag, which had been retrieved from the Vale household. Lab reports matched blood samples to bloodstains on a shirt found in Hood's apartment; and, although it could not be specifically proved to have been a part of Valerie Vale, a speck of brain matter had been found in Hood's coat pocket.

His paintings were produced one by one and set before the court in the order they had been painted. The jury saw people strangled, shot, stabbed, mutilated, dying, and dead—a steady progression in the degree of violence, and in the detail. A psychiatrist testified that the work showed, not insanity, but a steady growth of obsession—an obsession that had been encouraged because Hood was an artist and could sell it.

An element of the occult was introduced when the prosecution set before the jury the painting Hood had done of Valerie surrounded by fog, with hands reaching out of obscurity for her throat. It was firmly established that the painting had been done at least eight months prior to the killing, so only some macabre form of clairvoyance, or eerie coincidence could account for her actual murder taking place in the fog. A meteorologist had already testified about the weather in Darien that day. Fingal did his best to question the relevance of this, with minimal effect.

But it was the final painting that caused the jury to ripple with an audible intake of breath. It had been shown to Hood in the course of his interrogation, at which time he had slipped slowly from his chair to his knees and stared at the thing, openmouthed. He could not remember finishing it! Yes, he had painted the hills with their shroud of fog, the melancholy trees. Yes, he had painted the killer, stooped with the weight of his club, and yes, he could even remember that his imagination had failed and he had painted his own face onto the killer's body. But who had painted Valerie?

He had lurched forward on his knees to see better. The painted version of her murder was not nearly as brutal as the reality. There was no mistaking Valerie—the plume of blood flowed away from her head and did not obscure her facial features, the texture of her hair, the translucence of her skin. At first Hood had denied that the work was his. He admitted doing something similar, but without using himself or Valerie for the figures. But when they had brought it to him again before the trial, with all the other evidence, he had inspected it closely, and knew the brushwork was his own.

And of course the prosecution had several expert witnesses testify that the work was entirely of Hood's own making. Photographs of the living Valerie removed any doubt as to the identity of the painted victim. Fingal questioned the chain of evidence, the qualifications of the experts, the likeness of the images. But nothing could reduce the impact of this work on the jury.

Detective Lauzon was on the stand for nearly two days. He had been brought into the process of apprehending the defendant when the Connecticut police had found Hood's overnight bag. His precinct had been contacted for assistance, and his captain had remembered some connection between Lauzon and the well-known artist. But what kept him on the witness stand all that time was his relating of various violent deaths, not just Valerie's, to Hood's paintings.

There was the case of the boy's swan dive from the roof. Which Hood had painted. There was the case of the burning man. Again, Lauzon produced pictures of the crime scene and related them to Hood's painting, which blazed in front of the jury in a roar of violent color. Although the defendant had denied being present at the death of a psychiatrist named Madeleine Beale, his fingerprints had been found on the one-way mirror overlooking the room where she had died. In Hood's painting of the woman being strangled, two faces looked on from behind such a mirror. Lauzon went on to describe the murder of the prostitute; and "The Confession" was wheeled into court—a cruel rendering of the girl in that cruciform position that perfectly matched Lauzon's crime scene photographs. A wave of revulsion rolled through the court.

Fingal objected repeatedly to this procedure—after all, his client was not charged with those murders, or deaths. But he was overruled again and again on the grounds that the paintings were relevant to the accused's state of mind prior to the murder before the court.

Hood never took the stand. He sat at the table beside Fingal, looking quite bored with the whole proceeding. From time to time he would look at a witness—he stared at Lauzon with more interest than at the rest—or he would glance over at the jury, or members of the press, but his curiosity seemed mild. A trace of annoyance crossed his brow whenever he would catch sight of the rows of people sketching his face for the various media covering the trial. Hood despised them, but he refused to make a big show of it.

Fingal was elegant in his summing up. He did not seek to prove that Hood had been elsewhere when the murder had been committed, but only that his client was completely without a motive in the case. Indeed, the prosecution had shown that Hood had enjoyed a completely free relationship with the deceased and had no need to brutalize her for any reason. His income was well-known, and the victim had had no money, so where was the motive? A painting is not a motive. It was not his duty, Fingal

stressed, to prove his client innocent, and the prosecution had
not shown him guilty beyond a reasonable doubt.

The jury retired on the seventeenth day of July and, within
four hours, returned with their verdict: Nicholas Hood was guilty
of the murder of Valerie Vale on February nineteenth last.

Hood remained in custody while the judge took three weeks
to ponder the matter of sentencing. They came for him on
August sixth—it was pouring rain, the air was thick—and drove
him back to court. The oak-paneled room had a cosy, rainy-
afternoon atmosphere that reminded Hood of childhood days—
rainy days when he would stay indoors and draw charming little
landscapes of places he had never seen. The influence of Paul
Delvaux had lain far in the future, with the influence of Andre
Bellisle.

The judge was late. Spectators and lawyers and members of
the press all resumed talking in normal tones of voice, until their
conversations rolled and crashed against those oak-paneled walls.
The swell of sound ebbed to nothing, however, when His Honor
Judge Stanley Wallace made his entrance, robes flying.

The judge took his seat, poured himself a glass of water, and
cleared his throat. "I have listened to argument from counsel on
the matter of sentencing Nicholas Hood. Witnesses have been
called for both sides, and various studies and articles have been
entered for my consideration. In coming to my decision, I have
been mindful of three things: the retribution which is the
prerogative, indeed the duty, of the state; the rights of the victim's
family; and the question as to whether the defendant, if rehabil-
itated, might make any contribution to society."

The judge shuffled the papers on his desk, and took another
sip of water. Beads of sweat shone on his forehead.

Hood leaned over to Fingal and whispered, "Death."

Fingal said, "Shh."

Judge Wallace continued. "I am not an art expert—neither

artist nor critic. What is paramount, in my view, is human life. There seems no doubt that Mr. Hood is capable of more work which some find disgusting, and others find brilliant. I make no finding one way or the other, and do not feel called on to do so. Fashions in art change—what is worth a fortune today, may be worthless tomorrow. It is certain, however, that Valerie Vale will never walk the earth again. Were his painting equal to the Sistine Chapel it could not replace his victim, nor assuage the grief of her family and friends.

"On the question of rehabilitation I must say that, except for his having committed murder, there is little in Mr. Hood's behavior that requires it. I mean visible behavior. The psychiatrists differ on his intentions, but the jury believed that he intended to kill, and so do I. I do not know why, any more than I know why he paints pictures of death. Since this murder has been explained neither by the defendant nor by anyone else there is nothing, in my view, to prevent him from killing again. Anyone who has murdered is prima facie a danger to society, and Mr. Fingal, though clearly a good counsel, has not shown otherwise.

"If Mr. Hood were eighteen or twenty-one, I might consider that the length of existence left him would allow great possibilities for change. But he is thirty-five years old, and has given not the slightest indication of remorse. Indeed, for all the anguish he has shown, he might be facing this court on a traffic violation."

The judge mopped his brow and nodded to the court clerk, who stood up and said, "Will the defendant please rise?"

Hood rose.

"Nicholas Hood. By the power vested in me by the state of Connecticut, having duly considered the evidence and arguments in the murder of Valerie Vale, I hereby sentence you to death."

A rustling sound went through the court, as people shifted in their seats. There were gasps, sobbing, and from far in the back a short bark of nervous laughter. Judge Wallace stared at Hood without flinching, but Hood could see a tremor in the judge's lower lip. His own knees shook uncontrollably.

Once more, the court went utterly silent. The judge said, "Mr. Hood. In the state of Connecticut, you have a choice of method. You may choose either to be electrocuted, or to die by lethal injection. You may have some time to think about this matter, or you may choose now."

"No, sir—I've given it some thought, and I think injection would be fine."

"Very well." He turned slightly toward the clerk. "Execution of sentence to be by lethal injection, at four o'clock in the forenoon, September fifteenth, on the grounds of Somers Correctional Institute. The warden of that institution, Mr. J. B. Feathers, is charged with the execution of sentence, and failure to comply with this order shall be considered contempt of court."

The judge took a long drink of water and filled the glass again from an insulated thermos on his desk. "Is there anything you'd like to say?"

Hood swallowed hard, to prevent his voice from quavering. "I have a request, Your Honor."

"Make it."

"I'd appreciate it if we could move the date forward. I'd appreciate it if we could get this done tomorrow."

A murmur passed through the court, while Judge Wallace blinked at him. He said, "Are you trying to make a point of some kind?"

"No, sir."

"Your request is denied. The sentence of death is subject to automatic appeal, so it would be pointless for me to name a date any sooner than September."

"Your Honor, I would also like to get on record my wish to

waive all right of appeal. I do not wish to appeal. Having been sentenced to death, I would like to die as soon as possible, with as little discussion as possible."

"Your wish is duly noted. Your sentence will nevertheless be appealed—nothing can prevent this. It is to ensure that no injustice is done, whether through carelessness of counsel (not a fear in your case, I think) or through misjudgment of the prisoner, who is normally considered to be under considerable stress."

"I have one more question."

"Very well."

"Why did you ask if I had anything to say?"

Despite his bravado at sentencing, Hood found to his unlimited disgust that he desperately wanted to live. The realization came to him slowly, and only became a certainty after his final appeal failed to move the Supreme Court to mercy, and the governor expressed apathy. Thus, it was only when his death became a certainty that Hood ceased to embrace it. For the first time since his incarceration six months previously, he began to think about visitors.

He was transferred to Somers, where death row was a set of eight cells housed in a building completely separate from the rest of the prison. Hood was brought here by four guards, chains around his ankles and wrists. Before being locked into his own cell, he was displayed to the other two tenants of death row. One was a huge black man named Titus Penfield who had taken a hammer to his landlord, and all of his landlord's family. The other was a nearsighted youth who had raped and knifed several women in the course of a week. His name was Alex Fine.

Alex Fine squinted up from a comic book but said nothing. Titus, the black man, shoved out a paw as hard and dry as a board, which Hood shook, rattling chain. "Gladta have ya,"

Titus said. "Little too quiet round heah some tams."

The guards locked him in his cell and clonked away on heavy shoes. Hood examined the sink, which was clean but small, and tested the bed, which was lumpy and hard.

A slippery, whining voice pierced his ear, evidently the voice of Alex Fine. "You going to tell us your story, Mr. Hood?"

Hood was standing with a pillow between his fists. He spoke toward the cell door. "I don't think so."

"What's that! You have to speak loud in here!"

"I don't think so!" It was a terrible effort to release even those paltry words. Hood wanted to curl up and cry himself into unconsciousness, but he knew it wouldn't happen.

Then, basso from Titus Penfield: "Man don't gots to talk, he don't want to. Takes some adjustmin', movin' house'n all."

Alex Fine said, "If you want to talk, you'll find I'm a very good listener. It's a good point of mine, if I do say so myself." There was a pause. "You have a date set for the Big Event?"

"September fifteenth."

"Speak up, Mr. Hood!"

Fine's voice hurt his ears, and Hood considered telling him to stuff it. "September fifteenth!"

"Wow-wee! You don't have one hell of a long time! Myself, I'm scheduled for December eighth, but my attorney's going to have that changed—going to push that way, way back. I have roughly fifty different venues to explore before I'm through with the judicial system. Right now, I'm trying to dig up some witnesses who were out drinking with me on the nights in question. I was nowhere near where those criminal acts were committed. Buncha girls got knifed and porked. Kinda thing wouldn't occur to me, and anyone who knows me will tell you the very same thing."

"Mistah Fine heah's one of the great prevaricatuhs." Titus mimicked an innocent child. "'Who, me? Why yo' Honah! I's not that kind of a puhson!' Jes' tell me one thing, Mistah Hood—you innocent? Or you a bad guy?"

"Guilty!"

"Dat's right! Dat's what I like to heah! I am so tahd of Mistah Fine's bulls'it. He like a drownin' rat, catcha hold of any old pice a shit, keep from sinkin'."

Fine's voice uncoiled like a strand of piano wire. "Just because you have a fucking hammer problem, Penfield, doesn't mean the rest of the world is like you. You think because you're guilty, the whole world is guilty."

"I knows desperation when I heahs it, Alex—no offense 'tended. Me, I'm as guilty as the day is long. Got fed up wiv m' landlo'd one day and bash his head in. Kill his wife, three little ones, too. Hadda attitude, you fuck with Titus Penfield you get yo' ass kick good. No se'se prevaricatin'—I's one guilty pahty. Wish I could undo what I done, but I cain't. Don't see how killin' me's gonna help nobody, though."

"You deserve to die, Penfield. I'm innocent!"

"Bulls'it! Bulls'it!"

"Fuck you!"

"Yo' mama, too!"

There was a pause. Hood took a paperback out of his duffel bag and forced himself to look at the first page, trying to make sense of the words. Strange, how a word as common as "the" or "we" could be utterly without meaning, just black specks on paper.

Alex Fine's voice slithered out once more. "Hey, Hood! You hear a strange noise in the middle of the night, that'll be Penfield. Yes, sir! Titus Penfield the Third—crying like a little baby that just lost his rattle."

"Dat's right, Mistah Fine—I's a human bein'. Not like some I could mention. I feel bad. In my heart. You ain't got no heart! Fact, you missin' a whole lotta organs the rest of us is born wiv!"

The bass voice boomed over to Hood. "Man couldn't get no pussy the normal way—gotta take a knife out. Real Cassanova technique!"

"You're going to lose a few organs yourself, Mr. Penfield."

"Real Cassanova technique!"

By the time the supper cart came clattering along the corridor, the other two killers had long been silent. The food was a tough slice of beef in lukewarm gravy, accompanied by instant mashed potatoes and a few chilly carrots. Hood ate the vegetables, but couldn't finish the meat. He pushed the plate out through the front of the cell, and listened to his colleagues scraping up the last of their meal.

The overhead lights went off at eleven o'clock, which frightened Hood at first, then left him annoyed. He had managed at last to enter the novel he'd been starting at. He didn't want to lie there thinking. The bed was so hard, he felt bruises growing in his shoulders and thighs, where he had lost a lot of weight. And then his body began to feel like a shell, or a hollow globe—a hard, conscious surface wrapped around . . . nothing. There was nothing inside, at all.

He was still awake when a guard clanked through on a bed check, and again an hour later, when a different guard came through. Some time after that, when the building was silent, he heard a strange sound, a barely audible squeaking. He thought there was a mouse in his cell. But then it developed into a squeal, alternating with a cough, and finally it flowered into the full-blown stutter and howl of a grown man crying his eyes out. "Like a little baby that just lost his rattle," Titus Penfield was lamenting his crime and his fate.

Hood was taken outside, startlingly early, to exercise in the cold deserted yard, alone. The condemned men did everything separately and alone. His eyes were scratchy from lack of sleep, and his bones ached from the bed, as he ran around the bleak rectangle to keep warm. No one else was in sight except the guards, dark figures in the gun towers high above. A crow flew overhead and cawed twice, before disappearing beyond the wall.

After that, he was taken to the showers—a huge tiled room big enough to hold a hundred men—where he stood under one of the myrid showerheads, alone. Two guards waited for him, talking to each other, not to him. When they took him back to his cell, he found it occupied by a small, round man. He looked up from Hood's paperback and showed him a reddish face and a small beaked nose. He gave a quick, crinkly smile. "How d'you do, Mr. Hood? I'm Feathers."

SIXTEEN

J. B. Feathers, the warden, turned out to be an enthusiastic, breathless Englishman. He stood up when Hood entered and pumped his hand vigorously. Hood said, "If I'd known you were coming I'd've cleaned the place up."

"A sense of humor! How delightful! One of the things that keeps us human, wouldn't you say?" The warden was one of those people who ask questions without wanting any reply. He launched straight into the reason for his visit. "Bit of a ceremony I like to hold, for those unfortunate enough to be facing the death penalty. I fancy there's no torment so cruel as a man's own imagination, so I've come to give you a palliative dose of reality—a rehearsal, as it were. Save you imagining all sorts of horrors, follow?" He thrust his chin out, almost belligerently. "Anyway, what happens is, round about four A.M. on the morning of your death, a man will appear in a white coat—not a doctor—and administer a sedative in pill form. You must take it."

"I'd rather be fully conscious."

"Have no fear, sir. I speak, at this point, of Valium, a muscle relaxant. Facing death, the human is like any other animal. The heart pumps out absolute masses of adrenalin—bound to put you in an excitable state. You won't notice the Valium, I promise you. Clear so far?"

"Fine."

"Questions? Problems? Thoughts? Notions? . . . No?"

Hood shook his head.

"Good-o." Feathers turned his bulk to the two guards who waited outside. "Gentlemen?" A guard stepped inside, and when

Hood was suitably cuffed and chained, Feathers beckoned him along the corridor. "If you'd be so kind?"

"You're English," Hood said, hoping to break the schoolmasterish flow of information.

"Came over when I was a lad, actually. Fourteen. Can't bear the old place now—too stodgy by half."

They went along the corridor in single file: guard, Feathers, Hood, guard; the warden chattering the whole time. "You will be brought along here about fifteen minutes after the pills. There will be a brief pause while this door is unlocked." It was a complicated lock that required the simultaneous efforts of two guards, one on either side of the door.

They turned left into another steel corridor that took them to another steel door. "They call it the last mile, but it's nothing like a mile, really." Feathers faced him while the guards dealt with the door. "I fancy it will seem about two feet long on the actual day. As you see, another pause."

This time, the door gave way to what looked like a corridor in any modern hospital. The tile floor gleamed, and the series of doors on either side was made of wood, not steel. Hood was taken through the third of these doors, into a room that looked like the nurse's office in a public school. There was a locked sink-and-cabinet unit on one side, on top of which was an array of big jars containing cotton swabs and tongue depressers, bandages, and the like. In the middle of the room was a gurney bed—its thin Leatherette mattress covered by a hygienic sheet of tissue paper. Hood's belly rippled with fear.

"You'll notice the gurney has six straps." Feathers took one in his hands and gave it a pull. "They're quite strong, and there are two extra to hold each arm rigid. You will be strapped into the bed—unresisting, I trust—and a catheter will be inserted into veins on either arm. The left's the one we're after; right's a standby—fail-safe sort of a thing. You know what a catheter is, Mr. Hood?"

"Not exactly." Hood felt as if he had swallowed a lead weight. *I am mortal. I can be killed.*

Feathers went to the cabinet and pulled out a stainless steel tube about ten millimeters wide, which ended in a needle point. "This is a catheter. Uncomfortable, but not painful. Sort of an ache, you follow? That done, you shall be wheeled out here . . ." He disappeared into the hall again, followed by Hood. "And taken in here." The adjacent room was much the same, concrete walls and muted colors. At one end was a large pane of glass, and on each side wall there were smaller windows, beneath which were four small holes.

"This, of course, is the last room you shall see—assuming all goes well. That window is for spectators."

"Where from?"

"Oh, there's no shortage. One or two from the governor's office, various other officials. The ACLU always puts in an appearance so they can describe how barbarous it all is. You're allowed up to ten spectators, yourself, but I shouldn't like to see more than a couple of dozen, all told. Any questions? Comments? Opinions?"

"Keep going."

"The little holes under the small windows—on the actual day, there will be tubes and wires through them. When you've been trundled in here, the man in the white coat will connect you up. He'll tape some electrodes to your forehead and neck and chest—no pain, just tape and a dab of conductive jelly. These are to monitor your vital signs—heartbeat, brain activity, respiration."

"People will be watching this?"

"No one that shouldn't be."

"What will I be wearing?"

"My preference would be trousers and shirtless, but I suppose we can be flexible. You have some preference? Some request?"

"Yes. My own things."

"I think we can accommodate you there." Feathers looked around. "Where was I?"

"Vital signs."

"Right. At this point, the man in the white coat will—"

"Who is he, anyway?"

"A technician, not a doctor. Doctors have problems with their Hippocratic oath."

"Is this what he does for a living?"

"Good Lord, no! It'll be someone from the prison hospital! Very competent and matter-of-fact."

"What's his name?"

"Bill. I won't tell you his last name." Feathers turned to a guard. "It is Bill, isn't it? Short fellow? Lot of hair?"

The guard nodded, solemn as a bishop.

The warden clapped his hands together. "Right, then. You're on the trolley. You've got a catheter in each arm. The technician will now connect a length of rubber tubing to each catheter. He will ask if you are comfortable."

"That's a laugh."

Feathers looked blank. "He won't be referring to your spiritual state." He waved at the door. "Exit, technician. He will step into the first room and cause to flow into the catheter a saline solution—plain old salty water—to ensure that the vein is open, the blood is flowing, and so on. He will watch the level of saline diminish, and so establish that everything is tickety-boo. Technician number two will be behind the window on the other side, ready to perform the same functions, should he be required. It is only at this point that the curtain on the big window will be pulled back and the spectators will be able to see you."

"Will I be able to see them?"

"Yes. And I warn you, there may be some of your victim's relatives in there."

"They want to watch this?"

"They often do. The technician will report to me on the status of the operation, as it were, and at the precise moment specified in the warrant, I shall tell him to proceed. Nothing whatever will change in this room. All that will happen is that he will inject a drug into the saline solution which is already flowing into your arm. You follow me so far?"

Hood nodded.

"So. The first drug is sodium thiopental—"

There was a knock at the door. A scowl darkened the sunny brow of J. B. Feathers. "See to it, Fortier!"

The guard stepped smartly to the door and opened it slightly. There were murmurs, and then the door opened wide enough to admit a handsome young man in jeans and a sweatshirt. "Hello, Warden! Just passing by and I saw you wee going through the rehearsal. Thought I'd stick my head in."

"Very good of you, Father." Feathers gestured like a conductor as he introduced them. "Mr. Hood, this is Father Phelan, our chaplain. This is Nicholas Hood."

"My pleasure, Mr. Hood—"

An odd pleasure, Hood reflected, to meet a murderer, but the priest seemed unaware of the irony. He drove full-tilt into small talk. "—heard a lot about you. Seen your pictures—or at least pictures of your pictures in the magazines. Would've stopped by sooner, but I just got back from Philly—had a seminar. Real boring. How are you making out?"

"Fine."

"I'll be seeing you this week. Tomorrow, if possible."

"I don't need a priest."

"'Course not! Who needs another priest! Please. Just think of me as someone who'd like to know you. Let me give you my card."

Hood smiled as he took the card. It was black with raised

white lettering: JOHN PHELAN, S.J., COUNSELING. There were two phone numbers.

"Really, Father—"

"Call me Johnny." He stuck out his hand to have it shaken again, as if repetition would prove sincerity. "Just a guy, Nick. Just a guy." And with that concession to normality, the priest saluted and left the room.

"Not your usual sort of priest, I'm afraid." Feathers gave a little smile.

"He looks like a casino manager."

"Yes, well—I think I was explaining the drugs. Sodium thiopental is a barbiturate. The dosage will be about two grams, or about five times the amount used for surgical anesthesia."

Again, that wave of fear.

"It will render you unconscious within about two minutes. Then the technician will inject into the tubing a hundred milligrams of Pavulon which will stop respiration, and then, finally, potassium chloride, which stops the heart."

Hood tried to say, "I see," but nothing came out. He had always thought it was only pain he feared, not death. But his stomach was fluttering, his tongue was dry. It was not the pain, it was the end of the self one ultimately feared. And the fear embarrassed him. He felt himself blushing.

"It all sounds gruesome, but in fact death is caused by the barbiturate overdose. The others are merely guarantees. You won't be aware of their effects at all, I promise you. As far as you are concerned, you will simply drop off to sleep."

"And then what?" Hood managed to speak, at last.

Feathers cocked his head to one side, like a bird. "I'm sorry? I don't understand."

"The procedure. What happens next?"

"Oh! A doctor will come in and examine the body. To determine that death has in fact occurred. After that, we have a standard coffin and such, unless you want to make particular—"

"No."

"Why don't you think about it." He gestured to a guard, and the door was held open for them. As Feathers led him out of the room, he said, "You can discuss it with Father Phelan, if you like."

"I'd rather eat dogshit."

"A peculiar thought, Mr. Hood." He waited for the guard to open another door. "Fortier will look after you now." Feathers proffered a pink hand to be shaken. "Do your best to make use of the time left to you."

"I plan to. In fact, I've started writing a novel."

"You'll have to write like a demon, at this—" Feathers stopped himself short, then beamed. "You're pulling my leg! Very good, sir! Very good! Keep that sense of humor up and you'll come to a very good end, indeed!"

The guard was holding the door, stone-faced. Hood stepped through, and turned. "Thanks for the tour, Mr. Feathers."

"Not at all. I enjoyed it." And the door was closed on his shining pink face.

Hood took to reading. He read until his eyes ached, trying desperately to be interested in the treacheries of spies, the melancholy of divorced detectives. On finishing one book, he would immediately pick up the next, smothering under a blanket of words the panic that fluttered to life in his chest. In the terrified gaps between books the memory of the killing room, the lethal tubes and catheters, flooded into his mind.

It was terrible to know the date and the time, to be powerless to alter it. Thanks to the warden's rehearsal he had become to that extent like Andre Bellisle, could see the violence to come in fine detail, but could not prevent it. Bellisle, of course, had had nothing to lose. Hood imagined the straps—somehow the straps were the worst feature, precluding as they did all hope of dignity.

Throughout these long tormented nights, Titus Penfield muttered his sorrows, and Alex Fine snored.

Susan was sitting on the other side of wire-reinforced glass, looking into his eyes with that direct stare that had rendered him, upon their first meeting distant years ago, as weak as a newborn child. He could tell she was asking a question, but the telephone through which they were compelled to communicate only crackled and sputtered in his ear. The visiting room was loud with scraping chairs, and a clanging door. Hood leaned toward the smeared glass. "I can't hear you!"

"What made you change your mind about visits?" Her voice struggled through the squelch and buzz as if she were calling from Budapest.

He told her about the warden's rehearsal. Susan listened with a grim expression on her face, an expression that suited her bone structure not at all. Hood said, "I guess I wanted to think there was at least one person it mattered to."

"Oh, more than one," she said, gently. "Leo is very upset. But he didn't want to cut into our visiting time. He gave me a letter for you. I guess you'll get it from the mailman, or whatever you have here."

"Tell Leo I miss his annoying company."

"All right."

"And that I wish him well. You know. All good things."

"He'll be pleased."

Their eyes roved up and down each other like searchlights. Susan said, "I brought some stuff for you—the clothes you asked for. And extra socks and underwear."

"You seem very distant."

The phone crackled as she answered. Hood smashed his fist on the table and cursed. Then she was saying, "Can you hear me now? I think there's a loose wire—I can hear you if you hold it up a little bit."

"Let's get a different phone." He looked around for the guard.

"It's all right. I can hear you perfectly now."

He turned to her again. "Why are you so cool, for Christ's sake?"

"I had to freeze over a little bit. To prepare myself. You told me not to come if I was going to cry."

"How is Leo in bed?"

"I wouldn't know." Susan looked into his eyes, defying him to find any trace of mistruth.

"I think you're fucking him."

"Well, I'm not."

Hood sneered.

"Leo's been very good to me. He's helped me a lot through all this. But we don't sleep together."

"He's probably waiting for the fourteenth. Four A.M."

"Please don't think like that, Nick. There's nothing."

"You're so fucking beautiful—" Hood covered his eyes, and tears flowed over his fingers, hot as blood. He heard Susan saying that she loved him, that she would stay with him to the end. Hood wiped the tears away on his sleeve. He said, "What for?"

"You've never understood that I've always wanted to be with you. Even when you were horrible. When you treated me badly. I wanted to go through life with you, have good times with you, suffer with you—whatever was in store."

Hood hung his head for a moment. He sniffed and said, "Good thing I made you promise not to cry, right?"

"If tears could get you out of here, you'd have been out long ago."

"I'm a murderer, Susan."

"Yes, I know. Valerie . . . it's terrible that you killed her, but Valerie has a lot of mourners. I've always loved you for better or worse, remember?"

He meant it to be lighthearted, but it came out sounding mean. "How the hell was I supposed to know!"

"I treated you okay." She said it quietly.

A guard stepped up behind Hood and said, "Five minutes."

Hood was staring at her. His eyes didn't even flicker when the guard spoke.

"What are you thinking?"

"The bathroom faucet," Hood said. "Does it still leak?"

"I'm afraid so."

"Tell Leo to fix it." Hood knocked his chair over backward as he stood up. He walked away quickly, not looking back. As one of the guards fumbled with the door, Hood said to the other, "Can you guys lend me a gun? I'd really like to blow my fucking brains out."

The guard said, "Tough shit."

In the afternoon, a cardboard box was brought to him in his cell, and a letter from Leo. He opened the letter first. Leo's written English was not as good as his spoken.

Dear Nicholas,

I hope that Susan shall remember to tell you that I wanted to come and visit. I didn't want to shorten your time with Susan, however, so I stayed back and writing.

You have done a terrible thing. You know this, so I won't say more.

I'm missing you a lot. Your damn Philip Glass and your bitchy moods and your great painting, I wish now I said more how much I estimate your works. They have a profundity I shall never have. I am not a critic, thank God, but they are to me great works. It is strange. But the piece I find most moving is Valerie on the dock, smiling. There was something ominous about that painting—as if you were making warnings I was too stupid to see.

I have suffered a setback recently. A vandal broke into the studio and cut up a lot of my work. Maybe twenty canvases. It still hasn't sunk in yet. You know how slow I work. This is years of work gone to nothing. However, I will go on. It's all I can do. I haven't told anyone else.

Lately, I have read the art magazines more, out of interest for your work (they never mention me, as you know). Your work is continued to be admired. It will survive. Most. Maybe not the last two pieces when I think you were sick with death, maybe growing like a cancer inside you.

I remember Valerie—that sunny day on the dock. Why did you kill this perfect person! I can never know! There can be no reason!

Susan has a lot of grief, of course. She cries easily. She cries a lot, and it's for the best.

I will come and see you, if you want this. I don't know how to behave. I called the police because it was right, and I was frightened, but now I don't know.

I never did talk to you much. I think of myself as the friendliest person, but I am probably an old hermit man. I miss you my friend.

Sherri has been writing to you about your work. She has the rights to sell it, as you know, but she wants to be sure you write out what you want done with your money. "Do not allow lawyers to get it," she says, and why in hell don't you answer her letters.

Write to me, if you want. We used to share Art together. Not a small thing.

Your old friend,
Leo Forstadt

Hood reread the comments about his own work several times, savoring this praise from an artist whose work he had always respected. The vandalism in the studio was an artist's nightmare. Hood couldn't imagine how he would have responded, in Leo's place.

He put the letter aside and opened the box. There were socks and underwear, and the black shirt and jeans he had requested. There were cookies, and some mystery novels. Hood searched the box thoroughly for a note or a letter, opening all the books and shaking them. He felt in the pockets of the clothing, but there was no note from Susan. For some reason, the lack of this note pierced Hood right through. He sat there on the bunk and methodically tore the box apart. He took each piece and tore it into smaller pieces, until he could not tear them any smaller, until the box that had held her gifts was a heap of brown confetti at his feet.

Detective Lauzon came to visit. Hood was shocked to see him sitting in the booth, twisting the telephone cord in his hands. He looked up with a grin when Hood sat down and picked up the phone. "How's it going?"

"Fine," Hood said. "Why are you here?"

"I'm really not sure. Curiosity, I guess." The bright green eyes looked him over. "You've lost some weight."

Hood didn't respond.

"How have you been feeling?"

"About what?"

"You tell me."

"You want to know if I cry myself to sleep at night, is that it?"

"I wouldn't put it like that."

"There is a murderer in my cell block who does that. Every night. I can give you his name if you want."

Lauzon sat back with a little half-smile. "Nicholas Hood is being cold to me."

"Nicholas Hood is leaving," he said, and signaled for the guard.

                                *   *   *

Two days before he was to die, Hood looked up from a spy
novel to see Father Phelan standing outside his cell. Alex Fine
was in the infirmary for an ingrown toenail; Titus Penfield was
out exercising. Phelan said, "Hiya, Nick! All alone today?"

Hood looked at Phelan's shirt—there was a little alligator over
the left breast, and a pair of aviator sunglasses hung from the V
of the open collar. Hood said, "I hope you haven't come to talk."

"Matter of fact, Nick, I brought you some reading material."
He tossed a magazine through the bars, and it splattered open on
the floor. It was an issue of *Artforum*.

"I appreciate the thought, but I don't read them anymore.
Funny how one's interest fades."

"Nothing like a hanging to focus the mind, right?"

"Jesus."

The priest gestured to a guard and, to Hood's disgust, the
guard unlocked his cell door.

"I didn't invite this man in here."

"Too bad." The guard breathed onion fumes into the cell as
he shut Phelan in.

Phelan shrugged, clutching a briefcase before him in both
hands. "I kept hoping you'd give me a call, but . . ."

Hood sat up. "I haven't set foot inside a church for twenty
years. I'm guilty of everything, and I don't regret anything. I'm
not interested in the Church, or its salesmen."

"You'll be dead in two days."

"Kind of you to remind me. I'm not going to succumb to a
sudden fit of religion."

Phelan ran a hand through his thatch of curly hair. "Hey,
Nick. No one knows better than me that religion's not cool. The
pope's like a dinosaur and half the stuff the Church says is dumb.
But you're gonna die, fella, and I've got a duty here."

"That's why you come to my cell, right? So I can't get away

from you." Hood picked up his book. "Leave me alone."

"If I thought for one minute you were at peace I wouldn't come around." He raised a hand to forestall interruption. "Of course, I'm partly here as a student of the human soul."

"You wouldn't know a soul if it bit you on the ass."

"I'd be interested to know why you think that, Nick. That's a pretty heavy indictment." He adopted a casual stance—leaning with one hand on the sink, one hand on his hip. He furrowed his thick brows in what he no doubt imagined to be a good imitation of concern.

"I'm not running a seminary here. I've very little time, and you've no right to any of it."

"You'd rather read a detective novel?"

"Listen, Phelan—what ever made you think you'd be a good priest?"

"One has a calling. You look around at the competition and judge whether you can do any better. I thought I could."

"I find the way you dress completely offensive."

"You have a sharp eye for the trivial stuff."

"You look like something that crawled out of Las Vegas."

Phelan laughed, almost like a man too kind to take offense at the railing of a condemned man. "You'd probably prefer an ascetic little man in a hairshirt and a Vandyke beard. But mortification of the flesh is not for me, I'm afraid. No siree. My strength—assuming I have any—lies in my ability to fit in. I'm a chameleon."

"The last thing a priest should be. You're unbelievable."

"Why did you beat that girl to death?"

"For the fun of it." Hood immediately wished he hadn't said it. Phelan had dragged him into his game of pretend. He was playing the hard-bitten criminal to the other's hip young priest.

"Pretty expensive piece of fun—cost you your life."

"Who cares?"

Phelan grasped his shoulder, and Hood almost cried out with revulsion. "I care, Nick. I care."

Hood jerked away from him. "You're too stupid to live."

"Your speciality, isn't it—judging who's fit to live."

"My specialty is acting on it. Keep pushing."

Phelan put on an Irish brogue. "Sure, we've come to a sorry state when we're threatenin' the loyf of a country priest!" He picked up the magazine, and leafed through it. "There's an article in here about you."

Hood lay down, and turned to the wall. The voice continued, relentlessly banal. "Must be nice having things written about you. Good things." He allowed a polite space for a reply, but Hood was silent. "At one time, I wanted more than anything to be famous. God, I wanted it bad! I thought I'd be a singer along the lines of Bob Dylan, if you can imagine that. I had a guitar, and I had the politics, and it looked like a pretty nice life. Couldn't make it, though."

Hood said, "Tough break."

"Best thing that ever happened to me! Because it really wasn't *celebrity* I wanted. I wanted to have an effect on people—really matter to them. I didn't just want their attention; I wanted their souls. The priesthood seemed like a good bet."

Hood spoke to the wall. "I have news for you: you never left show business."

"There's a little showmanship involved—true. But that's true of anything, really." He sighed. "Anyway, I've helped a few people along the way, and I've learned a lot, and I've served something other than my own ego." He took a step toward the bed. "I can help you, Nick."

"By getting out of here." Hood refused to look at him.

"Even at this moment, you're using me to make yourself feel like a tough guy! Isn't that some help? And our service comes with a guarantee: You make a good confession, and I guarantee you will have an easier time."

"I don't even like you."

"Think about it, babe." Phelan dropped the magazine on the bunk and called out, "Guard!"

Hood waited until he heard the cell block door clang open and shut, then he snatched up the magazine and searched through the table of contents for his name.

SEVENTEEN

HOOD read the article slowly, carefully, as if translating from a foreign language. Leo had lied to him, in his letter—no doubt to cheer him up—telling him his work was still highly valued. When he lay back on the bed, sentences and phrases from the article hung over him like sky writing. *Why did the work elicit any interest in the first place? . . . Anyone so eager to copy, without improving, the work of his forebears has little time to actually look at the world. Perhaps aware of this, Nicholas Hood found it necessary to watch real murders as they happened, and finally had to commit it . . . Profound lack of imagination . . . no real power, but only impact . . . talent in every square inch, but not a trace of insight . . . Guggenheim and Whitney have removed his work . . . half its former price.*

He asked for back issues from the prison library and found that his work had hardly been mentioned for the past six months. The few comments he could find maintained that the work had been overrated—that he was a mediocre talent who had stumbled onto a catchy idea. And Nigel Thorne had been removed from his post as art critic for *The New York Times.*

He telephoned Sherri from a cubicle in the counsel room and asked her to sell everything as soon as possible.

"Honey, I ain't had a lot of offers. Not to be rude, or nothing . . ."

"Sell it for whatever you can get, then."

"We're gettin' nothin'! *Nada!* If I *should* get an offer, I'll probably consider it for like two seconds before accepting it. But like I say . . ."

"I want any money to go to Susan."

"Fine. Put that in writing."

A silence spread like a dark stain between them. Finally, Hood said, "Not easy talking to a killer, is it?"

"You got that right."

He broke the connection without saying good-bye, and dialed his lawyer's office. Tim Fingal answered the call himself.

"What can I do for you, Nick?"

"Last will and testament: everything without exception to my wife, Susan Hood."

"Wait a minute—I can't take a will over the phone."

"I'll write it out for you."

"Get it notarized, and witnessed by two people. You should've done this months ago."

"Anther thing, Tim—I'd like a stay of execution."

There was another silence from the other end.

Hood repeated his wish. "I want a stay of execution. I haven't finished with painting yet. There's a lifetime of work ahead of me, and I could get a lot done in prison."

"Not in thirty-six hours."

"So get me a stay."

"At this point, I couldn't even get *heard*. It's five o'clock now, and the court's going to be closed until ten o'clock tomorrow. Which gives me about eight real hours before D day. Nick, you said you didn't want any delays."

"I feel differently now. I want you to appeal to the governor."

"The governor has made his feelings very clear. I mean, I'll file if you want me to, but he isn't going to change his mind. We waived every venue of appeal known to man. Without something that justifies a new trial, or a review of sentence, there's just no hope of getting a stay."

"You try everything! Hear me? Everything! I do not want to die! Do you understand? I do not want to die!"

"Jesus Christ."

"This is my fucking *life*, remember?"

"I'll get to work right away, Nick."

That night, Hood got one of the guards to bring him a sketchpad. He tried to distract himself with drawing—it was his first effort since the murder—and although he made sketch after sketch of the execution chamber, he kept thinking how things would change, once he got the stay. With a review of sentence, he might get twenty-five years. That might mean parole in ten. At the very least the thing could be put off for a year or two, and there was so much he could do with that time. The paintings! The drawings he could make!

He had twelve different sketches of the killing room, but he himself appeared in none of them. The gurney bed was empty. He feel asleep that night, imagining himself as a model prisoner, as an artist reborn. Titus Penfield cried.

The guard who brought his breakfast had to bang his club on the bars to wake him up. "I'm supposed to ask what you want for supper tonight. You can have anything you want."

"Give me the same as everyone else. There's no reason to treat this as a special day."

The guard looked him up and down. "You got guts, mister. I'd be shittin' my pants."

Later, the two guards who watched him taking a shower were uncharacteristically restless. Hood was whistling as he soaped himself, the sound echoing around the huge tiled room. When he glanced in the mirror, the guards averted their eyes. "Hey, come on—you're making me nervous!"

The younger guard said, "You're making *us* nervous!"

Hood laughed. "Just a guy, fellas. Just a guy . . ."

"You been talking to Phelan."

"Father Phelan! That wonderful man! That fine human being!"

It was ten o'clock by the time he was back in his cell. Fingal should be getting into court. Hood imagined his lawyer pleading the case, while he made another sketch of the killing room. He placed rows of blurred observers behind the glass partition. Before their astonished eyes, Hood was rising from the gurney bed, snapping the straps like rubber bands with his powerful arms. He was tearing the tubes from the wall, his face contemptuous. Those who had hoped to witness death, were witness instead to his victory over death, the ultimate triumph. The style owed something to Superman comics.

"You got a telephone call."

Hood followed the guard to the counsel room. Tim Fingal was on the line.

"Listen, Nick—we got a shortage of judges. Bunch are out sick from some food poisoning thing, so everyone's overbooked."

"Well, deal with it."

"I am, I am! Judge Boucher's going to be done by noon, so I'll see him in chambers after that. But who knows what's going to happen? I really don't think it's going to work."

"Tim, it'll work. You'll be brilliant. Tell them I need time to get my soul in order. Whatever it takes."

"Don't get your hopes up, Nick."

"Of course my hopes are up! This judge is going to be struck dumb by your eloquence! Go get 'em!"

His optimism lasted into the afternoon. He made sketch after sketch, tearing them off and piling them on the bed. Then, as if frayed from rubbing too long against the cliff edge of reality, his optimism snapped, and Hood tumbled headlong into despair. It was three-thirty. Fingal had to have seen the judge by now. A sac of poison seemed to burst inside Hood's chest, and his soul flooded over with sickness. And then his heart, having released its poisons, became as small and dense as a stone, sinking downward into such depths of black that Hood lost all trace of it.

He wanted to cry out, but there was no word to cry. Was there

no term for these feelings? Terror? Fear? There was no word—
not that Hood knew. Did anyone know it? Who on earth would
have use for such a word? Only someone facing certain death
on a certain date. No one else would need such a word.

He screamed. Screamed long and loud until his lungs were
squeezed flat. It was a scream that might be heard in more brutal
prisons, where fingernails are torn out. It was a scream that might
be heard in fiercer times, when pain itself was the object of
execution. It was the word he had been looking for; it brought the
guards running.

Perched on the edge of his bed, gripping the iron frame, he
could not even see the guards' faces as they peered in at him. His
eyes had gone dark, and seemed to emit only a black light. He
found another word. This word was a howl, low in the throat and
far away—he had once heard an animal make that sound, just
before it died. It had been the middle of the night—the thing had
been struck by a car, and dragged itself off the road under some
bushes, where it made the otherworldly sound that Hood was
making now.

He blacked out for a while.

When he woke up, a guard was saying, "You got a telephone
call. And your wife is here." But in the corridor, he could not
remember how to walk. He moved like a man who has just had
major surgery, who is missing large parts of his insides.

The guard stopped him, scrutinized his face. "Are you
serious," he said, "walking like this?"

"I'm having some trouble, uh, moving."

The guard looked at him suspiciously. "I don't know if you're
fucking around, or what." He pushed him forward once more.

Hood took the call in the counsel room. Tim Fingal was on
the line. "Is that you, Nick?"

"Yes."

"Jesus, you sound awful. What took you so long? Were you
outside?"

"No. I wasn't, Tim."

"I'm sorry to tell you this. But Judge Boucher wouldn't buy anything—he wouldn't budge. Then I contacted the governor's office and ended up speaking to him personally. But it didn't help. The game's over, as they say. I'm sorry."

"All right. Thank you."

"You want to hear his reasoning?"

"I have to go now. Susan is here."

"I want you to know I'm really sorry." Fingal's voice was sad. Did he want sympathy? "I guess your confidence in me was misplaced."

Hood said, "The world is misplaced. Good-bye, Tim."

"Good-bye."

Hood was taken to a visiting room he hadn't seen before—an underfurnished waiting room. There was a grubby couch and a few chairs against one wall. The rest of the room was empty, except for a small television set near the ceiling.

Susan was brought in. Her smile faltered when she saw him, but she recovered quickly. Her hair swung over his face as they hugged, and the sweet smell of her nearly split Hood's heart in two. He could feel her ribs under her dress, the tops of her hip bones. He began to feel dizzy and said, "I think I'd better sit down."

They sat together on the couch. Susan looked deep into his eyes, and he was afraid she was going to say something final, something tragic, but she blinked and said, "I had a terrible time getting out here. The train just sat outside Hartford for two hours. I ran out of things to read. How are you?"

"I'm scared, if you want to know the truth." He tried to smile but the muscles in his face refused to move. His hand came out tentatively, trembling, and brushed her hair back. "I can't seem to stop shaking."

She leaned forward and held him, making a small moan of sympathy.

"I think it's adrenaline," he said. "I just have so much adrenaline, I can't control my feelings."

Susan murmured into his shoulder, "My darling . . . my poor darling . . ."

"It's like when a sudden noise wakes you up at night. You're not sure if there's someone in the room—a burglar or something. That's how it feels. My heart keeps pounding and pounding."

They both sat back a little and she held his hand. "Your hands are cold," she said, and bent forward to breathe on them—her breath warm and moist. Then she rubbed his cold fingers between her palms.

He said, "People are going to watch me die. I can't get over it. It's as if I'm bleeding to death, and all these people are standing and pointing. They could stop it if they wanted."

"I have to ask you—" She looked at him, her eyes round and serious. "Do you want me to be there?"

Hood thought a moment. "I don't want to think of you going home on the train, while it's happening to me. I guess I'd like to know you're nearby. But I don't want you to watch."

"I'll stay here, then." She squeezed his hand. "I won't leave you."

Her gentle manner brought a wave of self-pity washing over Hood. He cried for a while, and she held him close, making soothing noises. When he had finished, she handed him a Kleenex and started talking about her music, about her new colleagues, and their plans for the coming season.

"I don't often think of you playing music."

"How do you think of me?"

He shrugged. "Sitting by the window. The rain coming down, blurring your face. Thinking of me." He managed a weak smile. "Like in the movies."

A guard opened the door. "Five minutes."

Susan squeezed him so tight he could hardly breathe. She

was hurting his ribs a little. He kissed her ear and said, "I'd better go."

"Oh, God. Don't go . . ." She rubbed her face against his cheek. He felt her breath, her tears hot on his skin. He had a sudden vision of himself curled up, growing younger by the second, speeding backward through manhood—to youth, backward through adolescence, back through childhood, back through infancy, until he was curled inside this woman—to live forever in the dim heat of her womb, beneath the warm and generous beating of her heart.

When the guard came for him, Susan kissed Hood so hard he tasted a trace of blood. He stumbled toward the door, blinded with tears, deafened by Susan's terrifying shrieks as she fell to the floor behind him.

Supper was waiting for him in his cell. Steam escaped from a hole in the tin cover, and the reek of tinned gravy went straight to his stomach. He threw up before he reached the toilet, and continued retching over the bowl. He remained on the floor for a while, resting his head on the cold cement.

A bell went off somewhere, signaling the end of supper. Distant shouts filtered in from the yard. The other prisoners would be going to various activities, or cursing their way back to their cells. Hood sat on the edge of the bed, gripping the frame. He tilted forward slowly, and held himself at a forty-five-degree angle, then slowly tipped backward again. Then he went through the movements again, a little faster. He gradually assumed the rhythm of a ticking clock, rocking back and forth, his hands on the bedframe, his back straight. Back and forth, eyes closed, feet apart.

The rocking soothed him; it brought memories. He recalled a girl from long ago. She had had a swing, a glider, on her front porch. What teenage excitements they had discovered on that contraption! Their hands slid under a blanket, finding what was male, what female, learning which desires could be satisfied, and which could not.

Memories of paintings drifted through his head, museums he had lingered in. He recalled the feel of a brush, aching in his hand. He remembered a country road, the smell of rain on pine trees, the snowbound winters of childhood. Most of all, he remembered Susan—Susan smiling, crying, making love, angry; he remembered her at the harpsichord, the sweet abstraction on her face. He was rocking when the lights went out at eleven. The guards came and went, came and went, saying nothing. Hood didn't care how foolish he looked.

He dozed for a while, after lights-out. His eyes opened again at three A.M. He started rocking again, but it no longer soothed him. His upper body darted back and down gracelessly—a demonic, inhuman motion.

At four o'clock the lights suddenly blazed overhead. He waited for cries of protest from Titus Penfield and Alex Fine, but then he remembered that they had been moved to another part of the prison for the occasion. A guard materialized at the cell door, and beside him a curly-haired young man wearing a white lab coat. The guard pointed at Hood, who was still rocking back and forth. "He's been doing that for eight hours straight."

The technician came into the cell and stood facing him. Hood stopped moving instantly. "Are you Bill?"

"I'm Bill." The technician held out a paper cup. "I have some medication for you."

Hood took the tiny cup. There were four little pills in it. The technician produced another cup and filled it with water. He handed it to Hood and said, "You'd better take them all."

Hood tossed all four pills into his mouth, and took the cup of water. The pills went down. "Are you going to go through with all this?"

Bill looked at him for the briefest fraction of a second, then looked at a point outside the cell. "Mr. Hood, it is going to happen. Even if I decided I couldn't do it, someone else would take my place right away. They bring extra people in, from outside."

"It's not good for you to do this."

But Bill motioned for the guard to open the cell door, and said, "Don't you worry about me."

In the blink of an eye, they came back for him. Bill, cool and professional, said, "How are you feeling? Pills help at all?"

Hood felt thick and slow, but no less fearful. "You mustn't do this."

The guard had come into the cell this time. He gestured for Hood to stand up. Hood rose heavily to his feet and put out his hands, and the cuffs were clicked around his wrists. The guard bent down, and then he felt the bolts slide home in his ankle cuffs, and the technician said, "Let's go."

J. B. Feathers, the warden, had said, "I fancy it will seem two feet long, on the actual day," referring to the distance from cell to killing room. And it was true. A series of doors swung open as they reached them, and Hood once more found himself in that room that looked like the nurse's office in high school. The gurney bed was waiting, straps hanging open.

"Just lie down, Mr. Hood." Bill said it as if it were just a matter of checking his blood pressure.

Hood sat miserably on the gurney. The tissue paper crackled as he swung his legs up and lay back. A fluorescent light sputtered and fizzed overhead. "You can't do this," he said again. But no one responded.

The guards removed his handcuffs and told him to take off his shirt. Hood had difficulty with the buttons, because his fingers were slippery with sweat. He lay back again, and then the curly-haired Bill tightened the first strap across his arms and chest, restricting his breathing. "It's too tight."

Bill slipped a cool finger between the strap and Hood's chest. "You're all right," he said, then cinched another strap around Hood's shins. The cuffs were removed from his ankles, and two more straps were tightened around him, as if he were in the grip of a giant cobra. He was now paralyzed from head to foot and wished he had not lain down without a fight.

His left arm was squeezed by a smaller strap then, and Bill dismissed the guard with a thank-you. The guard left.

Bill looked down at Hood. "I'm going to put a catheter in each of your arms now. Did the warden explain this to you?"

"Yes. Do you think this is right?"

"I don't have any problem with it, Mr. Hood. You might feel better if you don't talk to me. But suit yourself."

"I suppose everything I say sounds like a scream."

"You're not shouting, if that's what you mean."

Cold alcohol was wiped on his left arm.

When Bill turned to him again, he said, "This will sting a bit." An understatement. Hood cried out, "Jesus!"

"It'll stop hurting in a minute."

"It really hurts!"

Bill took a perfunctory look at his left arm. "Looks all right to me." He swabbed the other arm. Just for backup." There was a stinging sensation, which quickly dimmed to a dull ache.

"The left one hurts too much."

"You want me to pull it out? Stick it in again?"

"It just hurts. That's all I'm saying. Not like the other arm."

"It'll stop hurting soon."

The gurney started to roll, and the ceiling flowed downward across Hood's field of vision. He was wheeled out into the corridor and into the next room. He came to a stop under another bank of fluorescent lights.

"I'm going to put some conducting jelly on your forehead and on your chest. It won't hurt." His hand hovered briefly over Hood's eyes as he annointed him. Hood had his eye on the curtains at the foot of the bed. They were still drawn; no one was watching yet. On his left, tubes were snaking out from the adjoining room, and an electrical cable. Bill said, "These are electrodes. So we can monitor your vital signs." He peeled off a piece of tape from a roll, and taped the small metal button to Hood's chest.

"How can you do this? Aren't you human?"

"I'm human."

"Then how can you do this to me?"

Bill taped two more electrodes to his chest and forehead.

Hood said, "You're worse than I am. You can still save yourself."

Bill smiled for the first time and shook his head. "I'm not like you at all," he said. "Not at all." He pulled back the curtains, and suddenly three rows of faces were peering in at them.

"Christ. Tell them to get the fuck away."

The catheter shifted in his arm as Bill connected a rubber tube to it. Hood cried out, "Jesus. It hurts!" But Bill paid no attention. He simply left the room, closing the door behind him.

Hood raised his head slightly and looked at the window, at the rows of solemn faces. Some he recognized from the trial—Valerie's relatives. Others were from the prison. Detective Lauzon was standing in the front row. He held his hat in front of him and kept his head slightly bowed, as if he were attending a church service. It was an official face, officially sad—Hood would never know what was behind it. He recalled that day on the pier when Lauzon had tried to warn him—a lifetime ago.

The door opened.

"Hello, Mr. Hood. Just here to see you off properly."

Hood looked up at the pink face of J. B. Feathers.

"I trust everything is going smoothly?"

"My left arm hurts."

"It does look a little swollen. Did you tell the technician?"

"He wasn't interested."

"I'm sure it's all right. Is there any last thing I can do for you?"

"Let me out. You can let me out."

"Sorry, old chum. Anything within my power?"

"Let me out. You can do it. It's within your power."

"Sorry. Can't be done."

"Get those people out of here. I don't want anybody watching me."

"Justice must not only be done, Mr. Hood. Justice must be *seen* to be done. Any last words?"

"Rot in hell."

"Cheerio, Mr. Hood."

The door closed. Hood raised his head again, in time to see the pink Mr. Feathers join the other rows of faces. The window was like a painting, hanging at the foot of his bed, each face a painted flower. Hood wondered if this thought were provoked by the drugs that must by now be flowing into his arm.

One face suddenly pressed forward in front of the others. It was a hideous, disfigured face—hardly a face at all, it was so covered with pustules, and small bleeding wounds. The cracked lips were peeled back from jagged teeth; the eyes were yellow and diseased. Ulcerated and revolting, the face leered at the bottom edge of the window. Nothing remained of the elegant gentleman Hood had known as Bellisle—nothing beyond the sneering ruptured countenance.

Hood lay back on the bed and roared, "Get him out of here!"

Feathers came bustling in. "What did you say, Mr. Hood?"

Hood roared again, "Get him out of here!"

Feathers said, "Which person are you talking about?"

"The one at the bottom. The hideous face. The sores. Get him out of here."

Feathers looked at the window, then back at Hood, a quizzical expression on his face. "There is no one of that description in the room."

"I can't breathe!"

"You'll be asleep in a jiffy." Feathers left the room again.

But Hood was not sleepy. His chest was going numb; he was having trouble getting air, but he was not in the least drowsy.

Another man was standing beside Bellisle, outside the window. He was a thin, ambitious-looking man who stood there thoughtfully, playing with his tiepin. What kind of man wears a tiepin these days? Then Hood realized the tiepin was a camera; the man was photographing his death. Hood rolled his head to the side and tried to shout, "He's taking pictures!" But his tongue would not work; the words would not form. He could not take in enough air to shout. The man continued clicking away, and no one paid him any attention.

Hood's lungs malfunctioned. He was supposed to be unconscious before that happened. The tranquilizer was supposed to knock him out before the other drugs took hold. He looked at his left arm bulging against the strap, swollen to three times its normal size, and he saw what had happened. The technician had missed the vein. The drugs were seeping into the muscle and then into his bloodstream, and the order of their injection had become irrelevant. The paralyzing drug was working first.

Terror tore up and down his body. He pumped his stomach up and down rapidly, and this brought a little puff of air into his lungs. He lifted his head, and rolled his eyes wildly.

Bellisle pressed his slimy teeth against the glass. The lips didn't move, but Hood felt the ancient, sensuous voice thrilling his ear. "Nicholas. Nicholas . . . immorality awaits."

Hood wanted to spatter the window with blood, turn those faces to a mass of bitter steaming blood and glass. He bit his tongue hard, slipping in and out of consciousness now, and tried to blow blood all over the faces. It only dribbled down his chin.

His body became his tomb, as he lived on without air, his lungs screaming for air. He pumped his stomach up and down again, but this time no air came.

His heart burst out of his body then. It had clawed its way through the prison wall of flesh and bone. He could see the pitiful, froglike thing, leaping and shrieking on top of his chest, spewing blood all over the world. It was so ugly, he thought, so hopeful in its need. He would paint it one day, if he lived.